Art Attack

by

David L. Gersh

A Jonathan Benjamin Franklin Novel
Volume III

Printed in the United States of America.

For information address:

PRIDES CROSSING PRESS
PO Box 50647
Santa Barbara, CA 93150

Library of Congress Cataloging-in-Publication Data

Gersh, David L.

Art Attack/David L. Gersh

First Edition

10 9 8 7 6 5 4 3 2 1

ISBN: 0692633561
ISBN-13: 978-0692633564

Other Books by David L. Gersh

Art Is Dead

Going, Going, Gone

Desperate Shop Girls

Acknowledgments

To my wonderful wife Anne, who not only puts up with my writing, but actually encourages it. She is priceless, which is a good thing, or I wouldn't be able to afford her. I want to give a special thank you to my late friend, Stan Cornyn. This book wasn't to his taste, but he gave it his all. He really worked to help.

Micalyn Harris has read all my books and her comments are always insightful and useful. Harv Champlin has also read all my books and, God bless him, he keeps coming back for more. His sense of humor is a joy. I'm not so sure about his good sense.

Elaine Kendall is the most literate person I know. She has graced me with her friendship and her comments. Tom Weinberger gave up his valuable time to make his comments. Tom is an investment banker and money manager, so when I talk about his valuable time, I know whereof I speak. Not only does he comment on the story and the writing, but he also gives me wonderful advice on the business subplots.

Finally, I need to thank Patrice Handley. She got the last draft of the manuscript and helped me immeasurably with the final polish.

Chapter 1

The cockroaches were confused. They had been dumped unceremoniously from a big glass jar onto the burnished wood conference table without so much as a "by your leave." But they soon recovered their bearings and started to head for the hills – much to the loudly voiced consternation of the assembled Board of Trustees of the Nauton Museum of Modern and Contemporary Art, who were rapidly disassembling.

The large walnut doors of the boardroom had burst open and a throng of at least a dozen people had crowded in, looking more than anything like a bunch of vagrants after a hard night. One was waving a hand-lettered placard reading "AAAA." A sweet, musky smell invaded the room along with them.

"Capitalist pigs," a tall, scrawny man shouted, the long delicate fingers of his raised fist trembling in suppressed rage. He was promptly jostled aside by a rather neatly dressed woman who said in an almost conversational tone, "We want board representation."

She was drowned out by the loud grating voice of a large woman dressed in a man's striped double-breasted suit with a yellow, gravy-stained silk tie, who was pressing her way forward.

"Art is art," she shouted. "Art isn't beauty. Beauty is shit."

"You can't buy us," someone else yelled at the same moment.

Another man with a wispy mustache, cried out, "We want funding."

"Who the hell are you?" a trustee managed to shout out above the raised voices filling the room.

"We're the Artists for Affirmative Action in the Arts," came back a cry. "No," said someone. "We're Artists in favor of Affirmative Action."

"But that's not 'AAAA'," complained the first.

"It's conceptual," replied the second.

They started shouting at each other, forgetting entirely about the board.

Peter Willson was on his feet yelling for security. Damn it, he thought, they'll blame me for this. Just like they blame me for everything else. "Why me?" he said aloud, shaking his head back and forth. This would probably keep him in therapy for another year.

He noticed one of his trustees, a wispy woman in a prim white suit, on a chair doing a peculiar shuffling dance while beating at her skirt with both hands. God.

In the cacophony of raised voices, he almost didn't hear Samantha Jennings, the very wealthy, very liberal socialite with a 45-year-old face stretched above her 62-year-old body, and his newest board member.

"Isn't it wonderful," she said, sweetly, leaning forward towards one of the artists. "You're the AAAA. I've heard of you." She pushed a small, engraved card into the startled man's hand. "Please have someone call me. I'd like to give you a fundraiser."

That stopped Willson in his tracks. His mouth hung open. An enterprising brown cockroach with twitching long antennae started up his sleeve towards the inviting pink maw.

Chapter 2

"I love him dearly," Nicole DeSant said. She pursed her lips at the thought of Jonathan Benjamin Franklin. It transformed into a rueful smile that made her gray eyes brighten.

Her features were handsome. Perhaps beautiful to some. She was dressed in a plain, well-cut business suit, but with that indefinable flair that French women have so completely mastered.

"Sometimes he reminds me of Rufus." Rufus was the little pug she had adopted several years ago, when Jonathan brought him home at the behest of Simon Aaron's ex-wife. She adored Rufus.

"Unusual description," Simon said.

"He is like a large puppy. Snugly, but with a certain clumsiness, if you understand." Nicole was Jonathan's wife of six months, after a long engagement. "Perhaps it is only because he is impatient. But he does not seem to know where his hands and feet are. He needs to be taken care of." Her tone was protective.

"I never thought of Jonathan that way. Not even in a bad dream."

Simon and Nicole met weekly, when they were both in town, to discuss Witten's, the great auction house Simon controlled. Nicole had been his Chief Executive Officer for three years. Simon didn't trust most people. He was self-made and was known on Wall Street for his sharp elbows. But he had learned to trust Nicole completely.

They were sitting in Simon's apartment on the 24th floor of the Carlyle. He had kept the apartment for business purposes, even after his recent remarriage. The detritus of a continental breakfast lay scattered on the coffee table in front of them. Simon still had a cup of coffee in his hand. He put the cup down and brushed some crumbs off his dark brown bespoke suit. He looked rather like a well-dressed bear with a good haircut.

Simon had innocently asked Nicole how she liked being married. It had been a casual question. A personal prelude to a business discussion. He wasn't at all sure he wanted this much information.

"You know, he has a wonderfully supple mind," she continued.

Simon nodded. He knew Jonathan well. Jonathan had been Simon's attorney for years. In fact, Nicole and Jonathan had met when Jonathan was working for Simon.

"He is extraordinary," she said. "His curiosity is astonishing. He says his mind likes to play with him. I think it has to do with that."

"What 'has to do with that'?"

"His sense of humor. I could sometimes throttle him. He likes to play with words. The pun." Her voice was more endearing than her words.

They were interrupted by the room service waiter who arrived to clear the dishes. Simon didn't like the remnants of a meal on his table. It was an arrangement he had with the hotel.

Nicole continued as the waiter cleared. "He can be silly. He says it is very adult, this play."

Adult play, Simon thought. Where is this going?

"He gets this look into his eyes and a little half smile. I know that he has thought of some stupid humor. And that he is about to share it. Mon Dieu."

Nicole had been raised in New York by a French father and the family only spoke French at home when she was growing up. Her English still had a certain formality and the hint of an accent.

"Give me an example," Simon said. His curiosity clearly was overtaking his good sense.

"Did you know Jonathan was half Jewish?"

Simon shook his head. He poured himself another cup of coffee. Good, it was still hot.

"He knows nothing of the religion, but he believes it gives him the right to tell Jewish jokes without being offensive."

"So?" Simon said, looking over the lip of the cup at Nicole. He managed an interested smile.

"I awoke some days ago to find him staring at me with that smile. It is not fair before I awake. I braced myself. Alors."

"I have a feeling this is a very bad idea, but tell me what he said."

"He asked me if I knew the Jews were the chosen people of the Bible. I nodded. I could not bring myself to speak. He then asked me why, if that were so, their reproductive organs were called Gentiles. I moaned." The morning light played on her face, emphasizing the line of her lips.

"Me too," Simon said.

"I think he likes that. He then apologized for telling me an anti-Semanitic joke. I covered my head with the pillow. It was that or kill him."

"I'm not sure you made the right choice," said Simon. "And tell him not to mention to anyone he's Jewish. We got enough troubles as it is."

"But Simon." Her tone had turned serious. "I am quite concerned about him. Since we have come back from our honeymoon, he has been most anxious. I do not think it was wise of him to take a leave of absence from the law school." Jonathan had quit his law practice five years ago to teach at Harvard.

Nicole sighed and worked her hands together nervously. Her eyes drifted to the ceiling as she considered how to express her concern. Then she refocused.

"He paces, rubbing that little silver box he carries. I do not believe he even knows. He tries so hard to hide his distress, but it is apparent."

"Give him Zoloft."

"I have asked my doctor for such a prescription. But Jonathan is so resistant to taking any drugs."

"Put it in his food. That's what we did with our dog. Worked like a charm."

"Simon!"

"Sorry. Kidding. So is he bored?"

"Yes. I think it is what he fears the most."

"He needs something to do?"

"I believe so."

"Perfect," said Simon clapping his hands. "I have just the project. I was going to broach it to him, but he always gives me such a hard time. I think he likes to do that too."

"You are a wise man, Simon. And a good friend," she said, leaning forward and putting her hand on his arm, her eyes sparkling with relief and gratitude.

Simon grunted his acknowledgment.

5

"But Simon. Do not say I spoke of this. It would upset him."

"What, me? The very soul of discretion." Simon smiled, then his face morphed into a frown. "But don't think I'm doing it for him." After all, he had an image to uphold. "He could make a difference in the deal I have in mind. It'll be fun."

Chapter 3

Jonathan Benjamin Franklin was bored.

Time, that once had been a cascade, had slowed to a torpid stream in the shallows of his life. Jonathan had lived for so many years on the curl of the wave. He was an adrenaline junkie.

For 20 years he had practiced Merger and Securities law at Whiting & Pierce, one of the white-shoe Wall Street firms. Then he quit to teach at Harvard. Even after he gave up his law practice there was so much to learn about teaching and, less fortunately, about the petty politics of academia.

Harvard Law School had been an exciting place those first years. Then, of course, there was the occasional consulting assignment to season the stew and to fatten his pocketbook. All in all it had been a good time. Until the last few months.

Jonathan wandered back and forth in the living room of his two-story, clapboard house. A house that sat back serenely on its seven acres, a serenity he did not share. He unconsciously rubbed the small silver snuffbox in his pocket; the one Ben Franklin had carried. The one his father had given to him as a gift when he went off to college.

He just couldn't seem to sit still. He walked into the kitchen and opened the refrigerator door. Same food as last time. Then he returned to the living room. He paced, then flopped into his favorite chair. He picked up his glass from the side table and took a sip of the wine. He was on his third glass. He was trying to cut back, but it was tough when he opened a bottle before six. He struggled to his feet and started pacing again.

It had gotten darker in the last hour. The shifting tapestry of fall leaves had become just shapes and textures. Their wet smell came to him through french doors as their shapes blurred. He snapped on a light.

Maybe his leave of absence from the law school hadn't been such a good idea. He wanted to spend more time with Nicole. But she had her work at Witten's and she was spending more and more time in New York.

He had met Nicole four years ago, while working to save Witten's for Simon Aaron, his sometimes friend. Vincent Rollins had made a run at the company. Nicole engaged his mind, and the force of her personality amazed him. She held his attention.

Jonathan ran down the checklist of his life. He loved Nicole. He was a full professor at Harvard. And still an admirer of women.

He had been something of a womanizer, much to the consternation of his Harvard colleagues. It was a weakness. One he knew he had to correct. He stopped himself. "No, one that I have corrected," he said aloud.

Jonathan was a nice guy. An unusual trait in the rough and tumble world of Mergers and Acquisitions. A mensch, as his mother used to say. But he had always been worried that his humility and his desire to please stemmed more from an abiding insecurity rather than his good-hearted nature.

Jonathan loved Winston Churchill almost as much as he loved Benjamin Franklin. And Ben was family. Maybe it was because of the wit that infused both of them. He smiled now as he remembered one of Churchill's famous quips. The one about Clement Attlee.

"Mr. Attlee is a very modest man," Churchill said. "He has a great deal to be modest about." If the shoe fits, thought Jonathan.

He was 52 years old and felt like he was starting to fall apart.

God, I think about wine like I used to think about women. He reached up to adjust his glasses. They weren't there. He had gotten contact lenses two weeks ago, but he still felt his glasses like an amputated limb.

It was all starting to catch up with him. His medium-sized frame had always tended towards chunky. Now it was in danger of slipping into fat. He pulled in his stomach.

"And, damn it, I have a low boredom threshold," he said aloud." Nobody paid any attention. Actually, the only person there was Rufus, their pug – well, Nicole's pug – who softly snored on the couch, his brown fur rising and falling in a steady rhythm.

Jonathan had picked up Rufus from their New York apartment when Nicole had to go unexpectedly to London for several weeks. Thank goodness she was back now, although she was still in New York.

Some dogs have a desire to please, exuberant in their ingenuousness. They wag and frolic when you come home. They jump on your lap and lick your face.

Alas, that was not Rufus. Rufus was more the "I'm-the-master" type. Kind, yes, but in a sort of imperious way. At least with Jonathan. Rufus graced him with his presence and even allowed him to rub his belly. He was prepared to make some sacrifice to the relationship. Besides, he liked it.

But when Rufus wanted something, usually food, he could be quite demanding. I need to speak to Nicole about Rufus, Jonathan thought. He nodded to himself. Maybe about putting Rufus on a diet. Jonathan shook his head sharply. No, better not go there.

Jonathan liked the way he looked now, more or less. His hazel eyes still smiled but he was a little worried about the bald spot on the back of his head, the one that looked like a monk's tonsure. It appeared to be struggling to engage his receding hairline.

His thoughts slipped back to the law school.

"God, the politics of it all. I don't know if I can stand it much longer."

He was going to have to make a decision soon. He'd been going through a bad patch. Deprived of his prized class in the joint MBA/JD program, he also felt he was being snubbed by the more academic types who thought there was something faintly smelly about business law.

Funny, since they were all pulling in big bucks from consulting. He let out a belly laugh. Rufus stirred on the yellow sofa that he had claimed as his own. His brown muzzle rested on his outstretched paws. He opened his eyes.

Jonathan looked over. "Well, what do you think?" he said. Rufus closed his eyes again and started to snore.

Jonathan went back to his meditations. I don't want to go back into practice. He was thinking of his law practice. He remembered the stress, and the pressure he felt in his chest was palpable.

The ungrateful clients. Like Simon Aaron. But then, how grateful can someone be to a person to whom he's paying a $1,000 an hour.

Jonathan had loved it for a long time. Whiting & Pierce had been his home. Now teaching at the law school wasn't what he had hoped. Picky, he chided himself. What the hell are you going to do?

He was rich enough to do nothing. Not rich by New York standards, but to most people. That was without even counting Nicole's money, and she was a lot richer than he was.

But he wasn't about to go there. He missed the high he used to get from negotiating a deal. The mental stimulation was a kind of drug.

And he was terrified of being bored. Really terrified.

Chapter 4

"Amen," he concluded. He felt better. Rupert Seeling grabbed the arm of his easy chair and levered himself up, tottering a little as he sought his balance. "Darn knees," he thought, hobbling until the circulation return. He paused and nodded to himself. Good. I didn't curse. That's progress.

He shivered and tugged the sweater tighter around himself. He seemed always to be cold now. "Everything's harder since Evelyn died." The memory of his wife of 58 years started a tear in his eye.

He shook off the thought. I need to call Bishop Wesley today, he reminded himself. He looked forward to it. Bishop Wesley had always been a great comfort. It was his faith now that kept him going.

So many things were wrong in the world. It was disgusting to turn on the television. Crime. Drugs. It made him nauseated. Even his son disgusted him. How could he have propagated such a weakling? What was it, three years now since they had spoken? It was just after his son announced he was gay.

He scanned the room with washed out blue eyes. It was silent and dark. He liked it that way. Nothing really interested him. Even his deal making seemed empty. It used to thrill him, his mind honed to a keen edge. Now it was just rote. Funny how it didn't seem to make a difference.

He didn't feel hungry. He never was, he realized. He looked back on it with bemusement. Wine and food had always been important to him. He shook his head sadly.

The heavily starched collar on his pure white shirt bit into his neck as he fastened it. He welcomed the feeling. As he put on the meticulously pressed suit that his valet had laid out, his thoughts were on what he had to accomplish before he could permit himself the luxury of meeting with Bishop Wesley. He reviewed the list in his mind.

Things were becoming lax in his business operations. He intended to put a stop to that. And Rosenstein, that traitor. But most of all, he needed to deal with Peter Willson. He loved the Nauton Museum. It was the one thing that still gave him some joy. It was his.

Henry Augustus Nauton had been mean. Not cruel. Parsimonious. If Mr. Rockefeller could squeeze a dime until it screamed, Nauton could make a penny do the buck and wing. He came by it naturally. He was an accountant.

Nauton rose by his own wits and hard work from a junior clerk in the back office of a corporation owned by the Standard Oil Trust to the presidency of one of its minor oil transportation subsidiaries. Through shrewd dealing in Florida real estate and Drew's Erie Railroad stock, he had made a minor fortune.

Like the robber barons, as he aged, he longed for social position. But he couldn't afford a yacht or old masters. So he settled for modern art. Surprisingly, he had a good eye.

He filled his house with the strange and colorful pictures by artists like Leger and Duchamp. He even bought a couple of paintings by Matisse. He didn't want a Picasso, but his dealer told him he should have one. He didn't really like it.

As he got even older, and his collection grew in size and reputation, progressive museums in New York and other big cities lusted after Nauton's art. He was courted and praised. It surprised him and he liked it too. But he wasn't easily swayed.

Nauton enjoyed the attention. He made half promises but he never would commit. It drove some museum directors to drink. For others it was a short walk.

Henry Nauton became more concerned, some said paranoid, that no museum would properly honor his collection, and incidentally himself. He was intrigued by the rumor that that scoundrel, Frick, had created his own museum. He was going to have his name on it.

Nauton considered himself far more upstanding. And so the Nauton Museum was born upon his death in 1926, for better or for worse.

Nauton wasn't particularly generous. He never was. He left his collection to form the museum. But the endowment he left to run the place was paltry.

His son and various other relatives made up the board for years, along with his son's business cronies. Old money, at least by New York standards. The ink didn't smear on the banknotes. There were no outsiders. No Jews, no blacks, no women. It was only when they spent themselves into the ground that they had to finally bite the bullet.

Oh lord, it almost killed them to beg for the New Money.

Chapter 5

Rupert Seeling had become chairman of the Nauton when it was in deep financial distress. He whipped it into shape. And he controlled it absolutely. But it was in trouble again. His idiot director, Peter Willson, definitely did not give him joy.

Seeling was a street fighter, feared on Wall Street for his blunt judgments and pitiless execution. Those who garnered his wrath paid a heavy price.

Seeling's car was waiting at the door of his brownstone mansion. The wind blew leaves over his shoes. He shivered. His driver held the door as Seeling stooped to get in the back. He caught the door to steady himself. "Damn knees," he thought before catching himself. He hit his hand against the armrest in disgust at his lapse.

The Seeling building etched a marble facade against the New York skyline, reflecting the wealth and power of its sole tenant, Seeling Brothers, Falk & Co. The guard behind the desk in the lobby smiled and greeted him.

"Good morning, Mr. Seeling. Beautiful day."

Seeling continued on with a curt nod. His secretary stood up as he exited the elevator to his penthouse office. She was all business.

"Good morning, sir. Mr. Rosenstein has been here for 18 minutes. I put him in your reception room and made him comfortable. Shall I bring him in to you?

"No. Not yet. I'll call you when I'm ready." His words were clipped, as usual. She had been with him far too long to be offended. Besides he paid her more than she could expect to get anywhere else.

"Of course, Mr. Seeling."

He settled into his spartan office and thought about Herbert Rosenstein. His lawyer. A man he had handpicked for the Nauton board. The Judas. He lifted his phone and murmured a few words to his secretary.

Herbert Rosenstein didn't like to wait. It wasn't often that he had to. As one of the most powerful lawyers on Wall Street, he commanded enormous respect and attention. Even affection. An ex-president of the Bar of the City of New York, he was often spoken of as short-listed for an appeals court judgeship.

But Rupert Seeling was the firm's most important client. A client of the last 20 years. He wondered what Rupert wanted so early in the morning and why he wanted to see him in person.

Seeling was seated behind his desk when Herbert Rosenstein was shown in. He looked carefully at the pale blue eyes, deep set above the long straight nose, trying to gauge Seeling's mood. He noticed that Seeling was almost rigid, as if trying to restrain himself. The delicate fingers were tapping on the desk. Rupert Seeling was angry.

"Rupert, how are you?" Rosenstein asked, trying to inject a cheery note into his voice. He reached for one of the chairs in front of Seeling's desk to sit down. Seeling raised his hand to cut him off.

"This won't take long," Seeling said. His thin lips were a pale line cut across his face. "I wasn't pleased that you voted against my wishes at the Executive Committee meeting."

Rosenstein was relieved. It was something minor. "I understand, Rupert. I'm sorry. But I believed it was best for the museum to reach an accommodation with the staff. Some of their concerns seemed to have merit."

"I don't care what you think." The words were almost a snarl. "I didn't put you on the Nauton board to vote against my wishes."

"I appreciate what you did in nominating me to the board, Rupert. I've been on the board for three years and this is the first time we've seen things differently. But I feel an obligation to act in what I believe is the best interest of the institution. As much as I like and respect you, I don't believe you nominated me to the board just to echo your views."

Seeling mailed a cold, small smile. "You're wrong. I don't feel I can trust you anymore. I will instruct you where to send the legal files for all the Seeling Brothers' matters you are now handling."

It hit Rosenstein like a slap in the face. "Rupert, this is silly. Surely we can disagree and still be friends."

"I think not. That's all," Seeling said, dismissing Rosenstein with a wave of his hand.

Rosenstein straightened. He wasn't going to let Seeling see how much this would impact his firm. The son-of-a-bitch probably knew anyway. To the dime. "As you wish. I will also resign from the Nauton board."

"Yes."

Peter Willson was sitting in the reception room, waiting to see Rupert Seeling. As Herbert Rosenstein emerged, he got to his feet and extended his hand. "Good morning, Herbert." Rosenstein brushed past him without a word. What was that about, he wondered.

"Not again! Willson, why do these things keep happening?" Rupert Seeling's creased face beneath bushy white eyebrows was flushed and mottled. His fierce eyes were directed at Peter Willson. His displeasure occupied the room like an ominous portent.

Peter Willson stood, shifting from foot to foot on the thick gray carpeting, feeling more like an awkward schoolboy than the director of a major New York museum. Seeling hadn't asked him to sit down. And Willson couldn't remember when Selling hadn't addressed him by his first name.

"I've spent more time on your problems in the last six months than I have on my own business." Seeling paused. "I don't like it. Did you see the quote by Andrew Grahm in the New York Times yesterday?" Andrew Grahm was the chief curator at the Nauton.

Of course he had seen the quote. Rupert Seeling had called him at seven in the morning. What an ungodly hour. Grahm was a man Willson had learned to despise and the feeling was profoundly mutual.

"Are things completely out of control over there?" Seeling asked. "Why am I paying you to be the director?"

What was with the "I"? Seeling was on a real tear.

"I'm sorry, Rupert. We've just had a run of bad luck. The curators are giving us fits, but I didn't think they'd go to the press."

It had been four weeks since the cockroach incident. The press had had a field day with that one, what with artists running amok. That was bad enough. Now this story had hit the front page of the Times.

How Willson was corrupting the essence of the Nauton in order to make a profit. A profit. That was a laugh. He was trying to keep the place afloat.

But no. The story laid out how he had torn the heart out of the museum. It recounted every step he had taken to cut the bloated budget. Every curator who had quit. Every staff cut and downsizing. It was disturbingly accurate.

And worse, it recounted every picture he had sold to raise the money the museum needed to cover critical renovations on the old building. No matter that the pictures had been in storage for 10 years and had never been displayed. No matter that the museum had other, better examples.

But he didn't know what to do. Andrew Grahm wanted his directorship. Grahm had been furious ever since the board passed him over. That wasn't going to happen. Not yet.

Oh, he would go, but on his own terms. He needed a good transition. There had already been nibbles from the headhunters. Some major directorships were going to open up soon. The National Gallery, as well as maybe Chicago. They would be a nice step up. But the only way to get one of those was to have a major directorship already.

Seeling tore into his thoughts.

"The board is grumbling. I've had at least two calls suggesting we think about replacing you."

Willson was startled. Not only because the board was discussing his termination, but how bluntly Rupert Seeling had spoken of it.

"I hope I still have your support," he said. "I've always relied on that." His voice sounded shaky.

"You do," Seeling replied gruffly, to Willson's intense relief. Then Seeling lifted his eyes to Willson's and fixed Willson in his stare. "For now."

An internal shudder ran through Willson.

"But you better get that place under control. And do something about Andrew Grahm."

Chapter 6

The doorbell rang. Jonathan instinctively started towards the front door before he realized he didn't have a doorbell, just a big brass knocker. That's why he'd changed the ring tone on his cell phone. It would be obvious.

He turned back into the den. "Now where in hell did I leave that phone," he said aloud. "Boy, am I ever getting absent-minded." Great, the absent-minded professor, he thought. He followed the sound into the living room. "Come on, ring a little more," he called out to the phone beseechingly.

Over there, the overcoat hanging on the coat rack. He patted it down. Nothing. He lifted it off his sweater and fumbled in the pockets. There. It stuck in the fold. Damn. Finally.

"Hello. Hello."

"Yes, I'll wait," he said to the female voice with less than grace. He walked with the cell phone back into the den and sat down in his leather chair, throwing his leg over the arm. The fire crackled and a big log broke, sending up a shower of sparks. He had been looking forward to a quiet evening so he could suffer in silence.

He listened to a new voice. "Simon, if you want to speak to me, pick up the damned phone and dial. I don't like being called by your secretary."

He had known Simon for close to 15 years now. As a lawyer he had done all of Simon's deals. As a friend, if Simon had any friends, he had saved Witten's for him. Now Simon was worth well north of $1 billion. And was Nicole's employer.

"Stop with the secretary bit, or I'll have my secretary call you, too," Jonathan said. If he had a secretary. "Well, I'll hire one," Jonathan responded to Simon's comment. "What do you want?"

He waited and listened. "Simon, I can't afford another favor from you. Every time you do me a favor it becomes a nightmare." He sounded disgruntled, but he always enjoyed these exchanges with Simon. He felt his spirits rise.

To tell the truth, the last couple of deals he had undertaken for Simon had been fun. At least sometimes. As long as he set the rules. He glanced at his watch and it reminded him. This guy can eat you alive.

Jonathan knew Simon well. Not like you'd know a movie star, where you can't get past the glare. No, not like that. Indeed he knew Simon too well. That was the problem.

It was astonishing. Simon was a control freak. And yet Nicole had made him the non-executive chairman of Witten's, a corporation that he controlled completely. Astonishing woman.

"Okay, okay. I'll come to meet with you if it's that important. You don't have to try and make me feel guilty." How did Nicole keep this guy in line? "I know you've taken care of Rufus when I can't. When Nicole's away."

There had been a lot of "away" lately. Witten's was based in London and Nicole was concerned about employee morale. They had been losing a lot of prestigious collections to Sotheby's and Christie's. But it was hard to be together, given Jonathan's normal teaching schedule in Cambridge.

Actually, the six-month leave of absence Jonathan had taken when he married Nicole had made it harder. At least for him. It hadn't been much of a marriage lately. He got up and started wandering around the room.

Simon was still talking. He finally paused, maybe for breath.

"Yeah, well actually Simon, Rufus is pretty sensitive and I have no idea what the psychiatric bills are going to be after his visits with you." Mine are pretty big, God knows.

Rufus opened one coal black eye. Then he opened the other. His eyes moved following Jonathan's progress. He raised an eyebrow. It wasn't time to eat, so what's with the name calling? Rufus was a tough love kind of dog. Jonathan stuck his tongue out at him. They had a very adult relationship. Rufus yawned and closed his eyes.

Jonathan sighed. "How about next Thursday? Jonathan held the phone away from his ear. "Okay, sooner. Send the plane." Simon had a Gulfstream G-550. "Yeah, I'll be at the airport at 9 a.m. tomorrow morning."

"Simon." Jonathan paused. "This better be important."

Actually, Jonathan was kind of happy.

Chapter 7

Rebecca Grahm could be a bitch. It was something Andrew had never quite grasped. A very attractive, middle-aged bitch, but a bitch nonetheless. She was willowy thin, with blonde hair that wasn't dyed, just touched up.

"Oh, no you won't. I'll cut off your balls first, you bastard." They were at the breakfast table. The quarrel ran up and down the scales in a minor key, the bellicose voices intertwining in contemporary dissonance. A malicious autumn wind, beating on the apartment windows, echoed their voices.

"Rebecca, I don't want to argue. This is undignified." He watched her over the top of his coffee cup. "Can't we be reasonable adults?"

He didn't like doing this. He would as soon keep things the way they were, but Barbara was putting a lot of pressure on him, and after all, Barbara Nadine was the most promising artist of her generation. Immensely talented and in his view, a more proper consort now.

"No, asshole."

"Please stop that. I demand you be civilized."

That brought a paroxysm of laughter from Rebecca that had a tinge of hysteria in it. It made Andrew Graham edgy. He was never at his best at breakfast anyway. And he was edgy without his cigarettes, even with the patch. He sipped at his coffee to divert the discussion and gather his thoughts.

"I've made you a perfectly decent offer," he said warily.

She looked up at him. Her dark green eyes were pinpricks. "$6,000 a month? You think I can live on $6,000 a month."

"Well, really Rebecca. That's 50 percent of my salary."

"We don't live off your salary. We never have. You have a damned trust fund. It pays you $500,000 a year."

"Actually, $498,500. Last year."

"Whatever. We live on Park Avenue."

"Well, of course. But the apartment is mine. Mother left it to me, as you well know. You can't expect me to give it up."

"So let me understand this, you expect me to move out after 22 years, give you a divorce so you can marry one of your young arty girlfriends. And take $6,000 a month, for how long?"

"I was thinking about 10 years," he mumbled.

He was lucky to duck the coffeepot. It shattered against the wall behind him as he beat a retreat out of the dining room, grabbing his jacket along the way. A dark stain spread down the peach colored wall.

His quick movement made his swept back gray hair fall over one eye. He brushed it back with his hand in one graceful gesture, still intently focused on Rebecca. He reached behind him and grasped the doorknob as she looked for something else to throw. He slipped out the door before she found it.

He muttered to himself all the way down the elevator. No. He really didn't understand women.

Rebecca Grahm paced the apartment. She reached down as she passed an antique piece of bric-a-brac that Grahm had always treasured and threw it, shattering, against the far wall.

"What the hell am I going to do now?" she said aloud to the empty room. "I put up with his tom-catting for all the years." It'd been impossible not to hear all the rumors. "Who cares, as long as he left me alone." A tear threaded its way down her cheek. She wiped it away with the back of her hand.

She liked her life. The sunny apartment filled with fine art. The people. One thing you had to say for Andrew, she admitted reluctantly. He had a fine eye for artistic talent. They had, or rather, he had one of the finest contemporary art collections in New York. He always seemed to be adding to it. Major pieces. She didn't know where he got the money. It couldn't be the trust fund. The bastard kept telling her how expensive it was to live. As if she didn't know. She needed to find that out where he got the money. Maybe she could use it.

What was she going to do with $6,000 a month? Certainly not entertain as a doyenne of the art world. And at 43, she had no immediate prospects.

Not hardly, she thought, shaking her head. I would have been out of here in a New York minute if he had proposed.

"He" had been a yearlong affair for which she had once held great hopes. But they never materialized. Men were pigs.

She gave a mirthless laugh as her hand closed around another one of Andrew's antique baubles. It exploded against the tile floor in the entryway, 200-year-old shards gouging the walls.

"Damn. What if Andrew just files for divorce." She didn't think a lawyer was going to do her much good. All the trust money was separate property. And she had signed that awful prenuptial agreement. They had had a terrific fight about it but Andrew had told her that his parents were insistent.

"What an idiot." It was unclear to whom she was referring.

Her mouth tightened. Maybe I'll kill the son-of-a-bitch. She smiled for the first time that morning, at the image floating through her mind. Her feet crunched on the shattered pottery on the floor. She picked up the telephone and dialed a private number. Peter Willson's voice answered. She let a sob come into her voice.

"Peter. I must see you. I'm so upset."

Chapter 8

"Oy! You always say no. I don't understand it. I try to make you money, and you always say no." Simon was at his most charming. You could tell when he sank into the vernacular in that beseeching tone of voice.

"Funny, I don't quite remember it that way, Simon. It seems to me like every time I get involved with you, I always come out short." That wasn't exactly true, but Jonathan wanted to make a point.

Simon had called that morning to set the meeting while Jonathan was out walking Rufus in the Central Park. That was one advantage of flying on a private plane. Rufus had his own seat. The flight attendant coddled him outrageously. Simon even stocked the plane with dog food. Jonathan feared Rufus was getting spoiled.

Simon had suggested a restaurant for lunch of which Jonathan had never heard. It had been an effort for the taxi driver to find it, even with the address in hand. But then, Jonathan wasn't entirely sure the taxi driver spoke English.

Eating with Simon had always been a gustatory adventure for as long as Jonathan could remember. Sometimes a three-star restaurant with the most refined service and exquisite food. Sometimes a hot dog stand that Simon had taken a shine to.

Today they were eating goat tacos in a small Mexican restaurant noted for its authentic food and remarkably enough, its wine list. Simon was drinking a Corona. Jonathan was sticking to Zager Chardonnay. Both he and Simon owned an interest in the winery and he was doing quality control. Or so he told anyone who asked. Actually, he had never developed a taste for beer.

"You remember Vincent Rollins," Simon said. It wasn't a question.

Vincent Rollins was Simon's most virulent adversary in the world of corporate takeovers. They had battled over the original acquisition of Witten's and four years ago Rollins had attempted to wrest Witten's from Simon, an attempt that Simon had thwarted with Jonathan's help. He wasn't easily forgettable, and he wasn't a nice man. You forgot about him at your peril. He was a man who held a grudge, and he didn't forget.

"I think he's vulnerable," continued Simon.

Jonathan paused with the taco halfway to his mouth. "You're kidding me, right? This is the business you want to discuss?"

They were half an hour into the meal and Jonathan had been waiting for the pleasantries to end. Simon Aaron did his best to look abashed. He wasn't very good at it.

"You rousted me out on a Sunday morning because you want to rough-house with Vincent Rollins. I thought you'd be in bed with your new wife."

Simon's wedding, a year ago, had been one of the gala events of the season, attended by the art set, the political set, the wine set and the society set. Set, game and match.

Tae Twerminsky was the widow of Susi Twerminsky. Susi was to rubies as DeBeers was to diamonds. Rubies were just red sapphires, but more precious than the blue ones. He had been a great guy and everyone loved him. Then again, Susi was dead. It tended to lower your social standing.

Tae was Susi's third or fourth wife – one tended to lose count – and a real trophy. Beautiful, literate, interesting and smart. But ambitious. She was also rich. The very rich, like Simon Aaron, found that a separate and beguiling asset. Not for the money. It just answered a nagging question on every rich man's mind.

Nicole had told Jonathan that Tae and Simon had met at the annual cock-tail party given by the Italian Counsel General. According to her, Tae had seen Simon, cut him out of the herd, hog-tied him and applied her brand. She then released him to roam free on her range.

It was obviously an exaggeration. Jonathan hoped so. Tae had just become a director of the Nauton Museum. Simon and Jonathan had gotten sidetracked into a conversation about the Nauton. But now they were back to business.

"Just hear me out," Simon said in a voice suffused with self-pity. "That's all I ask. Then you can say no. Better you should say yes." Under the circumstances, it made Jonathan want to laugh.

In fact, he was pleased to see Simon and he hoped there might be a deal that Simon wanted him involved in. He had no intention of saying 'no' this time. Anything for a little excitement.

He was dying here. It was taking all of his discipline not to say, "yes," even before Simon asked. But best not to telegraph that. He had known Simon a long time.

"Rollins just signed another consent decree with the S.E.C. I hear his banks are skittish. I don't think he can go to the market. The disclosures would kill him."

"I can see that," Jonathan said, his interest piqued. "What are you thinking about?"

"You know the Quintiles Group?"

"Sure. Software. Business management stuff as I remember. Rollins' key company."

"Right, he owns 23 percent of the stock. The stock is depressed because of the earnings and because they're investing a lot in R&D and writing it off. But if you look carefully, they have a lot of good products in the pipeline. Good patents. I've had three people doing a detailed analysis and financial projections."

"How does it look?"

"Cash flow positive last year. No free cash flow, though. Too much capital investment and debt service. But they're well placed for any upturn, and I think the economy is improving. I want to make a play for it."

"Sounds interesting," Jonathan said.

Simon sat silently for a moment, the beer bottle in his hand. "Goodness gracious!" Simon said exaggerating each word. "Did Jonathan Franklin just say 'yes'? This must be my lucky day."

"I hope its mine," Jonathan said with a half smile. "How much?"

"How much what?"

"How much are you going to pay me?"

Simon made a face like a little boy whose balloon had just popped.

"What are you charging these days?" Simon said reluctantly.

A waiter came towards them and Jonathan shooed him away with a shake of his head.

"$1,200 an hour."

"That's ridiculous."

"Yes."

"So, how much really?"

"$1,500 an hour."

"But I'm your friend."

"That's why I'm giving you the friends and family discount."

"Okay, so it's $1,200 an hour."

"Just to be clear, Simon, that's $1,200 for each hour including travel time, plus expenses."

"Good lord, Jonathan, I'm a poor Jewish boy. This hurts me." Simon could pout better than any grown man Jonathan had ever met.

"As I recall, last year you were number 163 on the Forbes money list."

"See. Look at all those guys ahead of me."

"Simon."

"Okay, already. But it's a lot of money."

"Uh huh," said Jonathan. "So where are we?"

"I bought three percent of the stock so far."

"What do you want from me?"

"Strategic advice and I want your hand in this. You front it. Field general. But, I'm not going to pay you."

Jonathan held up his hand, palm forward. But Simon bulled on.

"We're partners. You get 20 percent of the profits. I pay the expenses and arrange the money. I figure we get the company or they buy us out. Either way, we make a lot of money. We kick Rollins in the ass. I don't see a lot of downside."

"Simon, stop. I don't want to be your partner. I'm not sure about this."

Simon smiled. Jonathan had seen that smile before and he had a sinking feeling.

"Nicole thinks it would be a good idea," Simon said.

Jonathan was many things. An idiot was not among them. He held up both hands. "When do we start?"

Simon raised his bottle of beer in a toast. "It's going to be a slam dunk. You'll see!"

Chapter 9

"Are you not happy, Cheri?" Nicole had been in New York for only a few days. The question blindsided him. He and Nicole were dressing for a dinner party at Simon's, and he had been thinking about his issues with the law school.

"Of course I am," he responded. "Marrying you was the smartest thing I ever did." He smiled and turned to take her into his arms, half-buttoned though he was. He loved the way the darker gray specks in her gray eyes seemed to make them change in the shifting light. She was sophisticated with her French accented English. And she had a great body.

It certainly didn't go unnoticed that she was an enthusiastic and inventive lover. Jonathan had feared it would change when they married. To his amazement, it had gotten better.

It had been three months since their wedding on the lawn of his home in Concord. Two since they returned from Santa Barbara. Their four-week honeymoon had been magical, as were the warm nights on the patio of the Plow and Angel, the little tavern on the grounds of the San Ysidro Ranch. They had sat, sipping wine and watching the sun tip over and spill darkness down the mountains, turning them from lavender into black.

He loved to see Nicole relax. She was a dynamo. Her energy could warm a room. But the quiet there had settled over her. He could see it in her eyes. Her face mellowed, emphasizing her strong, nearly beautiful features. She only called Witten's three times in four weeks. Amazing. She usually called four times a day. The life of the CEO, even on vacation.

Nicole was again completely absorbed in running Witten's, all day and sometimes well into the evening. He was the stay-at-home spouse. At home in Concord usually. He only came to New York when Nicole was there. Maybe the leave of absence from the law school hadn't been such a great idea. Ben Cohen had been eager enough to grant it.

Come on, he chided himself. Don't be paranoid. But even paranoids have enemies, he added to himself, remembering Henry Kissinger's famous musing. And the law school had many a large ego that liked looking down its nose from the top of the mountain.

The marriage had only been an excuse for his leave of absence. He had to admit that to himself. During the last six months before the wedding, he found himself sitting at his desk at Harvard, hoping that Simon Aaron would call. God help him.

He put his hand in his pocket and rubbed the small silver snuffbox. He had taken to carrying it in his pocket since his father's death. Rubbing it had become an unconscious gesture.

"I'm just unsettled, Darling. I've never been a kept man, you know." He meant it as a joke, but it had an edge to it. Nicole had one of the best jobs in New York. And she was thriving at it.

"Perhaps you will find Simon's project interesting."

"Maybe," he said, struggling to contain his enthusiasm.

Simon Aaron's apartment was full of fresh flowers, as it always was, winter or summer. The surprising thing was that the rooms also were filled with a wonderful fragrance. These flowers were fresh, not hothouse grown. He wondered where Simon, or more likely Tae, got them.

The view across the park was breathtaking, the great city surrounding the park, setting off its black space. The lights of their own apartment on Central Park West were out there somewhere.

"Come along and let me introduce you to some people, my dears," Tae said gaily, taking one of them on each arm. Tae was wearing a long gray silk dress, slit to the knee. It set off her silver hair perfectly. Ruby earrings and a matching necklace were her only adornment. She was one of the most elegant women Jonathan had ever met.

There were 10 or 15 people milling about uneasily in the large living room, each with a glass in hand, making the usual awkward conversation. It was obvious the party had not yet reached a critical mass.

Tae steered them towards a tall, slightly stooped man of perhaps 65, with sweeping gray hair worn a little long. His straight long nose gave him a somewhat patrician look, belied by keen blue eyes under bushy gray eyebrows. An engaging smile creased his long face as he saw Tae approach.

"Adrian, dear. I want you to meet two delightful people, Jonathan Franklin and his wife, Nicole DeSant. I'm sure you have heard Simon speak of them."

She turned to them. "This is Dr. Sir Adrian Asheton. One of Simon's and my closest friends."

Asheton put his hand out. "Delighted. I've heard Simon sing your praises, Professor Franklin." Jonathan smiled, taking his hand. "We were talking about you just the other day. And yours too, my dear," he said, turning towards Nicole and cradling her hand in both of his. "Although he didn't tell me how lovely you were."

Nicole gave him a dazzling smile.

"Forgive me," said Jonathan. "I don't know what to call you. Should I call you Dr. Asheton or Sir Adrian?"

"No. No." Asheton's eyes twinkled with amusement. "I know what you've done for Simon. He's told me all about you. I feel like we're old friends. Please call me Adrian. Or Sir Adrian, if you'd prefer." He laughed. "I still like to hear it actually. They only knighted me last year, you know. Silly ceremony. But to tell you the truth, I was roundly chuffed."

"What were you knighted for, Sir Adrian?" Jonathan asked, warming to this unpretentious man.

"Making a lot of money. You know, we do that in England." He laughed again at the little story on himself. He clearly didn't take himself all that seriously. It was a charming quality in a man so obviously accomplished.

"May I ask at what?" Jonathan inquired.

"It would be boring, I fear, Professor Franklin."

"Call me Jonathan, please, Sir Adrian. And I assure you I won't be bored."

"Well then, Jonathan." Asheton paused. "I work for a company called HST Heartcare. We make those funny looking little things they call coated stents they insert into arteries in the body. Bloody awful business," he finished, making a practiced joke.

"What do you do for them, Sir Adrian?"

"Not very much I'm afraid. I'm the Managing Director and the Executive Chairman, but my real skill is hiring good chaps to run the business."

"I admire your modesty, Sir Adrian, but I've read about your company. It's growing incredibly. You have quite a following on the Street."

"You are kind. We've been most fortunate, you know. It has been quite a challenge. I started the company six years ago. Still have a good bit of the stock."

"Do you live here?" asked Nicole, redirecting the conversation.

"Well, some part of the time. I have a flat in this building. Tae and I are also great friends, you know. It occurred to Jonathan that Tae and Sir Adrian might have been involved before she married Simon. There was an obvious warmth between them. He wondered.

"I live most of the time in London. Bit of a trek. Can't be helped." He paused. Then he turned to Nicole. "I understand you are in London quite often. I would be delighted to give you dinner. If, of course, your husband would not object."

"I would enjoy that," she said. Jonathan wasn't so sure he would.

"Have you known Simon a long time, Sir Adrian?" Nicole asked.

"Oh yes. For years now. We've done some deals together. I was even involved in the original Witten's matter. A bit on the sidelines really. But Simon confided in me. That awful man Rollins . . ." He shook his head.

Tae interrupted. She had a tall, thin man in tow, bald and birdlike.

"Adrian, Peter Willson just arrived. I knew he so wanted to say hello."

"Good evening, Peter," said Asheton with something of a British reserve, totally unlike his manner, at least with Jonathan and Nicole. It seemed a little odd to Jonathan.

"Jonathan, Nicole," Tae said, turning her smile on them, "may I introduce Peter Willson, the director of the Nauton Museum of Modern and Contemporary Art. Peter, Jonathan Franklin and his wife Nicole DeSant."

Tae looked over Jonathan's shoulder and hurried away to greet a new arrival. "Excuse me," said Asheton, almost immediately. "I need to freshen my drink." He turned and wandered towards the bar.

Something clicked in Jonathan's head. He knew Willson looked familiar. He'd seen his picture in the paper recently.

"Mr. Franklin, how nice to meet you."

"Actually, It's Professor Franklin. I teach law."

"So, Professor Franklin then. Where do you teach?"

"At Harvard."

"How impressive. What subject, if I may ask?"

"Business law. Mergers and Acquisitions, Securities."

"Really, that sounds very interesting," Willson said, without much interest.

Willson turned towards Nicole. "I, of course, know of your wife." He gave a small bow. "One of the most important women in the world of art. How good to finally make your acquaintance. I am an admirer of Witten's."

"Thank you," said Nicole.

"I thought Witten's was based in London?"

"It was, but we have auction facilities in several countries, as you know, and our executive offices now are here in New York."

"Do you also live in New York?" Willson asked, turning to Jonathan, clearly puzzled.

"Well, not really. I've taken a leave of absence. Nicole and I were just married."

"Marvelous. My congratulations to you." He smiled and made a gesture to include Nicole.

"How do you know Tae and Simon," Jonathan asked.

"Ah, Tae has just joined our Board of Directors. She is a great addition. So enthusiastic."

More people were arriving at the party. The murmur of voices had increased. Willson leaned in towards Jonathan and paused before continuing. "Please come by the museum next week, Professor Franklin. At any time. Just give me a little notice. We'll have lunch."

He said it with the professional ease of a dedicated fundraiser. "Besides, my general counsel just took maternity leave, and I'd love to pick your brain. I know Tae would appreciate it."

Boring, Jonathan thought. Which only showed how wrong he could be sometimes.

Chapter 10

Peter Willson was suffering from a hangover. His head hurt. It is far too bright and cheery in here, he thought, looking around his office. He shook his head. There was a bolt of pain. He'd have to remember not to do that again. He wouldn't even have come in if he hadn't made a lunch date with that lawyer fellow, Jonathan Franklin.

He sighed. There were days -– nights more accurately –- when being the director of a major museum just wasn't worth it. There had been more of those days recently, he reflected. And far too many receptions. He would have to exercise more discipline over his drinking. But Lord, sometimes he was so bored. And last night…

His ruminations were jarred aside by the ringing of the telephone. He moaned and reached for it quickly to stop the jangling.

"Mr. Willson. Professor Franklin has arrived for your lunch." Willson struggled to his feet and went to the door of his office. He smiled with some effort as he opened it.

"Jonathan," he said brightly, holding out his hand, "it's good of you to come. I'm pleased we'll get a chance to talk. Let me take your coat and umbrella." He helped Jonathan off with his coat and handed it to his assistant. Water dripped from it onto the carpet. Jonathan handed over his hat and umbrella, then straightened his tweed jacket. The fall rains had begun.

"My pleasure, Peter." They shook.

Willson took Jonathan's elbow, pointing him down the hall with his other hand. "Come along this way. Lunch is in the boardroom."

Good heavens, Willson thought, I hope they got rid of the cockroaches. His mental image took him back to that awful night of the board meeting. Lunch there would never be the same. That was for sure.

"It must be a great job being the director of a major museum," Jonathan said as they walked.

"Sometimes."

"Too much travel?"

"Actually less than you might think. Afraid I'm far too busy here," Willson laughed and shook his head. He'd forgotten. He stifled a moan.

Jonathan thought Peter Willson had looked stork-like when they met at Simon's party. No, he now decided, he looks more like a Sandhill Crane. And age had not been kind to him.

Willson had gangling legs and a stick-thin body below a beaky nose. His eyes were bloodshot. A bald, red scalp, fringed with dark hair topped his long forehead. But this particular bird was well dressed in a tailor-made dark blue suit with red pinstripes. And he had a deep, unexpected voice.

To Jonathan's knowledge, Sandhill Cranes didn't wear designer glasses. Red designer glasses. Matching the pinstripes in the suit. Quite the picture of the avant-garde bird. The image struck him as funny. He suppressed a laugh, but the corners of his mouth twitched.

"You know, I envy you, the peace of a place like this," Jonathan said, to try to pry his mind away from the bird image.

That brought a barking laugh and a muffled groan from Willson. "You have no idea of the tsuris I have." Willson liked dropping Yiddish expressions into his conversations. It made him feel cosmopolitan.

Jonathan understood the expression. He had spent 20 years as a Wall Street lawyer. But it was puzzling here. After all this was a museum, scholarly, quiet and refined. Besides, it sounded strange coming out of Peter Willson's mouth.

"I don't get it," Jonathan said as they entered the double doors of the paneled, stately room. The long table was set with starched white linen, laid at one end with two places for lunch. Small salads and sandwiches with cut crusts were on a silver platter. An antique silver service glistened with a subdued light.

Willson glanced nervously around. Not a cockroach in sight. Thank God. "Sit down there," Willson said pointing to the nearer chair, "I'll enlighten you."

"'Tsusris' is a Jewish expression…" Willson started.

Jonathan interrupted. "No. I meant what kind of problems?"

They talked while they ate. Or rather Willson talked while Jonathan ate and pushed his food around his plate. He didn't appear to have an appetite. He seemed desperate to have someone to talk to.

"The board is driving me insane," Willson said. "They brought me in because the place was about to collapse. They were losing a fortune." He put his fork down.

"Isn't there an endowment?"

"Oh, sure." Willson reached for the Georgian silver coffee pot. "Want some coffee?" Jonathan nodded and Willson poured. "But we can't use the money," Willson said. "It's restricted to capital needs, not operations. And there isn't even much for that."

"So the museum has to operate on a 'pay as you go' basis."

"Right." Willson confirmed. "That was the challenge. I was told to get the place on its feet financially, cut the budget, increase revenues and make it 'relevant'." He paused to put the coffee pot down. "That was their word. 'Relevant'."

"Who are 'they'?" Jonathan had a deep and mellifluous voice that inspired confidence. It was a tool he had honed over many years.

"The Executive Committee. Really Rupert Seeling. So, anyway, that's what I did. I cut the staff where I could. You cannot," he elongated the word, "believe the screams from the curators."

"Peter, I know this is dumb. What's the difference between a director and a curator?"

He gave Jonathan a funny look. "You understand that the word 'curator' is derived from the Latin 'to care for'."

Oh, sure, thought Jonathan. I knew that. Doesn't everyone?

"That's what they do," continued Willson, oblivious. They care for their collections."

"Their collections?"

"Of course. Sculpture. Contemporary or Post -War art. Whatever." He scooted back from the table and crossed his long legs. Jonathan was surprised to see he was wearing bright red, striped socks. A pale band of skin showed between the top of his socks and his dark blue trousers.

"We have eight curators in different areas in paintings alone. They're scholars, or at least they should be. I sometimes wonder." He sounded cynical.

"Anyway, they also arrange — we call it curate — exhibits, recommend acquisitions, coordinate conservation and education. They are our hands-on people as far as the art is concerned. What they're not so good at is handling money."

"That's how the place got into financial difficulty?"

"Exactly. I'm sorry to say they're like bright, spoiled children."

"So you cut the budget?"

"I'm afraid I had to cut quite deeply. But that's only part of it. I wanted to reach out to people. Touch them. Do exhibits ordinary people would come to see. Impressionists. Picasso, Pollack. Those kinds of artists. Even motor-cycles."

"You're kidding."

"That was one of our best. It brought in more money than any of our other shows."

"That's good, right?"

"Ha."

"Ha?"

"The public loved it. They loved us. We had wonderful crowds. The staff didn't. They thought we were selling out."

"I don't get it." This was getting to be a habit.

"Wasn't scholarly. And, God forbid, those exhibits brought in a lot of money. I also started a mail-order catalog. It's been a smash."

"The board was pleased though?"

Willson looked toward the ceiling and pulled on his ear lobe. "Not exactly."

"Really? My God, why?"

"I encouraged dialogue with the artists."

"So?"

"The artists revolted. I guess it was because they thought someone would finally listen to them. It was pretty upsetting to the board." He didn't mention the cockroaches. "Thank God, Tae Simon wasn't on the board yet."

"I don't know. Tae seems pretty resilient. She might have enjoyed it. But I don't understand why the artists would revolt."

"You're a little naive about the art world, Jonathan. Artists aren't very important to it. They feel unappreciated."

Jonathan had to think about closing his mouth. "You're kidding. How can artists possibly not be important?"

"Have you ever wondered why there are no artists on any museum boards? They're like rocks in the river of art. The art world flows around them. And it doesn't stop."

Chapter 11

Willson was clearly distracted from his problems. He almost seemed to grow in his seat. He had morphed from student to teacher.

"We depend upon artists for product, at least as long as they're alive. But once it leaves their hands, they're irrelevant. And that's only contemporary art. Which is just one small facet of the art world."

Jonathan nodded, more from a desire to keep Willson talking than understanding.

"Have you ever tried to talk to one of them? Even the best are barely articulate. They don't care about anything except their ideas. Or maybe sex."

Jonathan put his elbow on the arm of his chair and cupped his chin in his hand. This was more interesting than he had expected.

"Oh, there's the occasional artist," Willson continued. "A temporary poster boy the system embraces and lifts onto its shoulders until it grows weary of him. But he's like a Roman general."

"Okay, I'll bite." Jonathan was actually beginning to enjoy himself.

"When a general won a great battle and was paraded in his chariot through the streets of Rome, there was always a slave standing at his elbow whispering into his ear, 'How fleeting is glory'."

Jonathan almost wanted to clap. But he instead thought about how fleeting is time. His time. It suddenly stuck him that artists weren't the only ones in the world who felt under-appreciated. "You were talking about the board."

Peter Willson placed his hands on the table face down. "The old guard hates the new board members. The remnant of the Nauton family feels violated. Sold out. Some of the older board members think we've sold board seats to the highest bidder. They're probably right."

Tae Simon flashed through Jonathan's mind. He pushed the thought away.

"And the board has gotten a lot of heat in the press. They don't like that either." Willson sighed. "I think they don't like me very much."

"You do have a contract, don't you?" Jonathan asked.

Willson shook his head. "It's not what we do here."

"In a way, Peter, you want to make me laugh."

Willson looked up sharply.

"At myself, I mean," Jonathan added, hastily. "School politics are petty, but nothing like what you're going through here. Can I help?"

"Maybe. You met Sir Adrian Asheton at Tae's the other night."

"Yes."

"Did you notice he was a little cool to me?"

"As a matter of fact, I did. Nicole and I remarked on it."

"Last year, with Tae's help, I got Sir Adrian to donate two, related Ben Nicholsons to us. They're beautiful. We got a lot of publicity. It filled a big hole in our Modern Art collection. The board was pleased. I thought I'd turned the corner. Now I'm worse off than if ever."

"Tell me."

"It's Andrew Grahm, our head curator. The board passed him over as director when they hired me. He's never forgiven them. Or me."

"Why don't you fire him?"

"I can't. He has a lot of support on the board. He's been here for 25 years. The curators love him. He's respected in his field. I can't touch him."

"It reminds me of tenure."

"Almost. I suggested he might be more comfortable at another museum. I've even nominated him for other directorships. He's not interested. It's like living with a cobra in the house. It's not if he'll bite you, but when. I think he just bit me."

"How?"

"The Nicholsons. He says they're forgeries. He wants to take it to the board. Poor Sir Adrian is frantic."

"Why?"

"I'm not quite sure."

"What makes Grahm think they're forgeries, Peter?"

"Two things. First, there's just been a rather dreadful scandal in London. It's the talk of the art world. Awful. A ring is accused of forging Nicholsons. They even got into the records of the Courtauld and faked the provenances."

He stopped and looked up at Jonathan. "You do know what 'provenance' is, don't you?" The inquiry sounded a bit condescending.

"Actually, I do. A painting's history of ownership."

"Precisely." Willson said with a smile, rapping on the table softly with his knuckles. "The trial was a terrible shock to the art world."

"You said there were two reasons."

"His eye."

"His eye?"

"Oh, yes. The trained curatorial eye." The cynical tone Jonathan had heard before was back. "Absolutely, the surest way to tell a fake, according to a curator. Andrew Grahm prides itself on being a fake buster. He may have me. Given the way things are going around here, if we get any more bad publicity, I think I'm finished."

"Why should there be publicity?"

"Jonathan, I really don't think you understand our board. Or Andrew Grahm for that matter. He talks about it to everyone. I think it's only a matter of time until it the press starts making inquiries. Or he calls them. And that would be it for me."

Chapter 12

Jonathan was holding the telephone away from his ear and frowning at Simon Aaron. It was brighter outside than in. The Autumn day fairly sparkled.

"Quit shouting. For Christ sake," he said, drawing the bottom of the instrument nearer to his mouth. "We were extending you the courtesy of telling Quintiles we're sending the letter."

Simon was chuckling in the background. It was Simon who had insisted on calling Vincent Rollins and who had also insisted, Jonathan thought rather maliciously, that he make the call. Jonathan wasn't sure that Simon wasn't more amused at his discomfort than he was at Rollins'. But as Jonathan always said, Vincent Rollins wasn't a nice man. And that's when he was winning. Rollins slammed down the phone in Jonathan's ear.

"He didn't take it well?" Simon asked with a straight face.

"You might say that. He suggested we undertake certain self-actualizing sexual actions. I think that was before he suggested he was going to tear off my pendant appendages. And he questioned your parentage. He suggested you were related to Rufus, although I'm not sure Rufus would be all that pleased." Jonathan thought about that and chuckled.

"Well, that's done," Jonathan continued with a sense of relief. He had never been confrontational. He hadn't found it productive and it made him uneasy. "Let's get the letter in the mail and instruct the lawyers to finalize the tender offer papers. Have you given any thought to a price?"

"Yeah. I'm thinking six, cash."

"Wow. That's a 70-percent premium over Quintiles' closing price. Pretty rich."

"I want to bear hug the bastard." A "bear hug" was tender offer parlance for a price so far above market that it leaves the target paralyzed and discourages any other bidders.

"I'd like to see him explain this to his board and shareholders," Simon continued with some vehemence. "How we undervalued the company." Simon's face was set in his hunting scowl. Jonathan had seen it before.

"No doubt, he'll have his investment bankers show how the company is worth a lot more," Simon continued. "Damn lap dogs. At least we'll make them sweat."

"That's great, but do we really want to overpay?"

"Don't be ridiculous." Simon lifted his head and fixed Jonathan with a glare. "I would never overpay. The company is worth a lot more. But only to us. That's what I've been trying to tell you."

Jonathan loved it, the feeling of being back in the game. This time as a principal. He had spent more hours at Whiting & Pierce, his old law firm, in the last three weeks than he had in years. But it had been fun for a change. He was calling the shots. He was the client.

Harv Champlin, their lead lawyer, was his close friend and former protégé, but there was something tasty in being able to get up and leave, knowing that Harv and his three associates would have to pull an all-nighter to accomplish what the work required. Yes -— tasty in a perverse kind of way. Good God, was he getting to be like Simon? But, dammit, he wasn't bored anymore. His blood was up.

Simon interrupted his thoughts. "I want to go public with the offer."

"Right away?"

"Yeah, I think so. Rollins isn't going to agree to negotiate. His board will turn it down with some wise-ass statement. I want to put some pressure on them. We should start calling the major shareholders. You want to orchestrate that?"

"Sure. I'll cross-reference the Quintiles' 10-K and get the names."

"And once the arbs buy in, they'll be screaming bloody murder," Simon observed. Arbitrageurs bought on the difference between the trading price of the target's stock and the tender offer price, betting the deal will close.

"I've always loved how the arbitrageurs play the game. Once they buy in, they'll do anything to get a deal closed so they can cash out. They don't care whether the deal is good or bad. They just want the money. I guess

Gordon Gekko was right, at least in this case," Jonathan laughed. "Greed is good. For us."

"And with a cash deal, they'll have no one to scream at but Rollins," Simon said. "I love it. That bastard made me sweat when he thought Witten's was in trouble. I'd like to crush the son-of-a-bitch."

"I can tell. I really can't think of anybody who deserves it more."

"When will the lawyers be ready to file?"

"They're ready now. We just have to tell them a price to drop in and when to file. We need to get the shareholders list. You know Rollins will do everything he can to delay us."

"So make the demand."

"I'll get the lawyers on it." He paused. "You really think Quintiles is worth six dollars a share?"

"Once we get it cleaned up and sort out the mess I'm sure Rollins has made, with the new business we can put in from Witten's and Sanford's, even without other sales, it'll be making several million dollars a year." Sanford's was the giant English confections company Simon controlled.

"Will that be enough to cover debt service?" Jonathan asked.

Simon had arranged for a $300 million credit line from Citibank to fund the acquisition, on top of $150 million in capital from Sanford's.

"Our guys say yes," said Simon. "One thing you've got to learn is to go with your gut. It's your money now, or at least it will be. You've been trained all your life to be risk-averse. All you damn lawyers are. Well, now it's just different. It's judging the risk that matters, and then grasping the opportunity quick and tight." He paused. "And being damned lucky," he said, chuckling, to Jonathan's discomfort.

"Swell."

"Hey, it's a great ride. Enjoy it. This is what it's all about. I told you, we can't lose." Simon paused again and looked over towards the chair where Jonathan's coat was hanging. He turned to Jonathan with a look on his face. "Do me a favor," he said gruffly.

"Sure. What?"

"Burn that tweed jacket and go buy a suit. You look like a damn law school professor. Or some out-of-town hick."

Jonathan laughed. "Hey, no way. Call it an eccentricity." He stopped and rolled down his sleeves and pulled up his tie. He reached for his jacket. "No, not an eccentricity. A trademark," he said, pulling on the hand loomed Harris

Tweed. He was smiling broadly as he turned to leave. The skin around his eyes crinkled when he smiled.

Chapter 13

Clarece Winterhaven was at Wong Chu's in Mid-Manhattan, sitting at a table with Rebecca Grahm. It was late for lunch, but it didn't matter to either of them. The restaurant was a maze of carved screens and tables with heavy chairs. Brocaded silk fabric hung from the walls. It was not frequented by the art set and Rebecca had chosen it for that reason. At this hour, it was un-crowded and anonymous.

Clarece was blonde, with a $400 haircut, fashionably attired in a green jersey wool dress with a small but perfect diamond at the neck. The emerald ring she wore on her right hand matched the color of the dress perfectly. She was in her mid-forties and starvingly thin. Her washer-board chest was the envy of her friends.

Rebecca and Clarece had a table towards the back. Clarece was leaning towards Rebecca and listening intently. Their plates with shrimp in lobster sauce sat half eaten and congealing. Neither of them were here for the food and it was a distraction. They had been trained out of it by years of self-im-posed privation. Wine was something else. Both were on their second glass of Sauvignon Blanc.

Clarece was Rebecca's best friend. A patron of the art world and the second wife of a 65 year-old, balding corporate buy-out guy. Rebecca, of course, didn't trust her. But she was desperate to talk to someone. Neither felt comfortable talking at home. They often met in mid-town for a late lunch.

"Oh my," Clarece said, raising the fingers of a well-manicured hand to her mouth, careful not to smear her lipstick.

"The bastard. I don't even know where I'm going to get health insur-ance."

"But he just can't walk out and leave you destitute, can he? Patricia Ray-mond is getting $400,000 a year for life."

"I've been to a lawyer."

"Lawyers are awful."

"They are."

"What did he say about your prenuptial agreement? Were you forced to sign one, too? I was." Clarece had a pout on her pretty face.

"I had Andrew wrapped around my finger." The bitterness was manifest. "But his damn parents. I wasn't good enough. I only wanted his money. They insisted." She paused, a thought occurring to her. "At least I think it was his parents."

"I heard those agreements can be broken. What did the lawyer say?" The self-interest in her voice was obvious.

Rebecca was quiet. It had been worse than she thought. The lawyer hadn't been all that encouraging. Not even when she told him about Andrew's philandering. What she had to put up with all these years.

He had tried to sound upbeat; there were fees involved. If there had only been children.

"Rebecca, yoo hoo." She waved her hand in front of Rebecca.

She returned her attention to Clarece.

"He was interested in all the pressure I was under to sign the prenuptial agreement. I told him I had to sign it." She did. She couldn't stand her lousy job for another minute. And she had been 25. I mean really old. "But he told me how difficult it was to prove undue pressure to a jury. All that nonsense."

"But you've put something away. All your beautiful jewelry." It was pretty clear Clarece had.

"It's Andrew's mother's. Andrew never bought me any jewelry. He was a cheap son-of-a-bitch, except for his beloved art."

"Don't you have any money of your own?"

Rececca laughed hollowly. "My parents drank themselves to death after they spent all our money. I had to get a scholarship and loans to get through college."

Rebecca knew how unwise it was to tell these things to Clarece. She was a total gossip. She just didn't care. How could it be worse?

"What can you do?"

"I could kill the bastard."

"No."

"Of course not." Then Rebecca's face changed. Her eyes narrowed and her lips thinned. "But there is the life insurance and the benefits from the museum. I have to say, it's tempting. Do you think I could get away with it?"

Rebecca enjoyed the terrified look on her friend's face. Clarece drew back and inhaled sharply. Rebecca gave an inward smile. It was satisfying to think about doing something horrible to Andrew.

"Maybe he'll have a heart attack," Rebecca said. She lifted her wine glass. "Here's to heart attacks." Her voice was loud enough to cause the waiter's head to turn.

Clarece just sat there with her mouth open while Rebecca laughed.

Chapter 14

"This is outrageous," exclaimed the red-faced man at the end of the table. "This place leaks like a sieve."

There had been yet another article in the New York Times exploring the financial condition of the Nauton. It had even alluded to the possible financial restructuring of the museum. Whatever that meant. An anonymous source was quoted in the article. A knowledgeable anonymous source, based on the information the paper had.

The board room of the Nauton was charged with tension. There were 12 people seated around the mahogany table. A rather sparse turn-out for a board meeting in September.

"Is there no end to these problems, Rupert?" A small man asked in a tentative voice, fiddling with his wine glass. He didn't make eye contact. "Should we be concerned?"

Peter Willson squirmed in his chair. He was sitting to the right of Rupert Seeling. He could see the muscles in Seeling's jaw working.

Willson was having difficulty maintaining his neutral expression. He turned aside and crossed his long legs. Then he uncrossed them when he realized his foot was twitching.

The dinner dishes were pushed back. There was no plate in front of Seeling. He had refused dinner. The caterers were starting to clear and serve dessert.

Rupert Seeling held up his hand. The two serving people paused. "Give us a moment," he said, gesturing for them to leave. He certainly didn't want to have this discussion in front of the servants.

A vain pulsed at his temple. He was not used to being questioned. Rupert Seeling was never questioned.

The comments had come from two of the newest board members. More of Peter Willson's doing. One was some nouveau riche hedge fund manager, probably Jewish, judging by his big nose. The other man was some kind of Asian. How dare they.

Seeling suspected that the hedge fund manager had an agenda, and he didn't like it. He was quietly furious.

"We are working to solve the problem, Mr. Nu," he said, addressing the Asian man. He ignored the hedge fund manager. "The Executive Committee is quite conscious of the issue. No one enjoys this ugly publicity." Seeling spoke coldly. He turned to look at Willson.

Something had to be done. Seeling suspected that Andrew Grahm was the leak. He was a troublemaker. And Peter Willson was an imbecile. He clearly was incapable of maintaining control.

But he couldn't fire him. Not yet. That would only be throwing oil on the fire. He would have to become more involved. Damn it. He admonished himself for swearing, but this was intolerable.

His thoughts were interrupted.

"Exactly who appoints the Executive Committee?" It was the hedge fund man. He had loosened his tie.

"The President does," Seeling replied. "By long-standing tradition." One he had created 15 years ago.

"Isn't that rather…" the fund manager paused. "How do I say this?" He pursed his lips and again paused momentarily. "Archaic? In this day and age when governance is so crucial. I think, Rupert, the board should reconsider these outmoded rules. Perhaps bring a fresh view to our problems."

Where did this man get the gall to address him by his first name?

"I agree with Mr. Chase," said a thin older woman. She was dressed in a Chanel suit with a string of pearls at her neck. The suit looked to be at least 30 years old. "We should look at these issues."

Seeling thought she had been on the board for four years. He could never remember her name. He ignored her.

"Thank you for your suggestions, Mr. Chase. I will ask the Executive Committee to consider them." His voice had a steely patrician edge. He needed to stop this.

Rupert Seeling had no intention of allowing his leadership to be challenged. He'd given too much. It was his legacy. And Evelyn's. She had loved the museum. The thought of Evelyn brought a catch to his throat. He put a hand to his mouth and coughed.

The hedge fund man started to say something, but Seeling cut him off.

"Perhaps," he said turning to Peter Willson with hard eyes, "Mr. Willson would like to address the issue of the museum's finances and these leaks to the press."

Peter Willson nodded reluctantly and slowly rose to his feet. His shirt was damp at his armpits. He felt a constriction in his chest as he fingered his notes and smiled at the board.

Chapter 15

"It's always good to see you, Tae, but this is a surprise. Twice in just a couple of weeks. When did you get back in town?"

The invitation itself had been unusual. Jonathan liked Tae Simon, but they didn't have a personal friendship.

Jonathan put down his fork. They were at Aureole. The scallops in beuerre blanc sauce were superb.

"By the way, your party was a delight," Jonathan said, without waiting for a response to his question. "I know Nicole is writing you a thank you note. But, I wanted to tell you myself. We couldn't have enjoyed it more. You are a truly gracious hostess."

Tae gave him a big smile.

"Sometimes I think you know everyone." He picked up the crystal wine glass of Zager Chardonnay and tipped it towards her in a salute. Then he took a sip.

"Oh, I do," she said.

"I love your sense of humor." Jonathan laughed. He almost spit out his wine.

Tae raised an eyebrow at him.

"Oops."

Then Tae laughed. Her laugh was full of joy and highly contagious. Jonathan realized how poised and desirable Tae Simon was.

He couldn't help joining in. "Somehow, I don't think you invited me to lunch just for my company." Jonathan said through his laughter. "What's up?"

Tae shifted in her seat. "Do you remember Adrian Asheton? You spoke to him at my party."

"Yes, of course. Both Nicole and I liked him a lot."

"I'd like you to help him."

"Huh?"

"You don't understand."

Jonathan felt as if he'd been hearing that a lot lately.

Adrian Asheton's voice was emphatic and tinged with distress. They were walking through the entryway to Asheton's flat. Asheton had asked him to come up so they could talk in private. "Thank you for agreeing to help, but I don't see quite what you can do."

The early afternoon sun gave Asheton's face an unhealthy pallor. Asheton collapsed down into a chair, his hands hitting the arms.

"I'm not a tax lawyer," Jonathan said, "but maybe if you explain it to me, I can figure out something. Our discussion is privileged." He leaned forward. The gesture was deliberate and practiced. He used it to promote a sense of confidentiality. "I mean, really, we're talking about a rather minor issue. At least in context."

"No. I only wish you were right."

"But you told me the paintings you donated were worth $2 million. At worst, you could lose the deduction, I suppose, if they turn out to be forgeries. Maybe $900,000 in tax you would have to pay back. Assuming you took the deduction last year. It's a lot of money, but I would believe not insurmountable to a man in your position."

"It's the audit. I can't let my returns be audited. Bloody disaster." Asheton's fist came down on the chair arm with a muffled thump.

The gesture stopped Jonathan cold. "You're right," he said. "Apparently, I don't understand." His open hands made a helpless gesture.

Asheton turned towards him as he spoke. He frowned and his blue eyes seemed dull and lifeless. "I entered into a tax of shelter scheme in 1999." He shook his head.

"You mean something illegal?"

"Oh no, quite on the up and up. At least, so I thought."

"But then, what's wrong?"

"Let me try to explain. At that time, I controlled a software company doing work in emerging areas of the telecommunications business. We had some important products coming to market. Really quite revolutionary. Most promising. Then Vincent Rollins suddenly tabled a hostile tender offer for the company."

Rollins again. Jonathan nodded his understanding.

"I fought it, of course," Asheton continued. "Finally, it became apparent that I had to do something dramatic to save my company. I exercised all my stock options. Nearly six percent of the stock. I announced I intended to hold the shares, I was so confident of our future. We beat off Rollins finally."

"What about the taxes?"

"Ah, yes. The taxes." Asheton rubbed his hands together. The corners of his mouth sagged. He rubbed his hands together. "Ordinary taxes of some $25 million from exercising the options. I had boxed myself in. I didn't have that kind of cash. The investment bankers insisted that I hold on to the shares, having made a public promise to the shareholders. The lawyers agreed." Asheton looked up at the ceiling as if reliving that moment in the past. His voice was thin.

"Seems like you were in a pretty deep hole."

"I really didn't think so. The shares were increasing in value. The company was doing well. It didn't seem so terrible to hold on. If I could only find a way to pay the taxes."

"What happened?"

Asheton turned and looked at Jonathan. There was a deep sadness in his mild eyes. "Our accounting firm, one of your very big ones, brought me a tax shelter. They said it would defer any tax due until I sold the shares."

"Tax shelters always make me fidgety."

"I never had been involved in one. But our accountants assured me it was lawful. They showed me a tax opinion from a very top Wall Street law firm saying it was sound."

"So you bought in."

"Yes, I'm afraid so. Unfortunately, my software company went bankrupt in the crash of 2000. The shares were worthless. Worse luck, last year, I learned your Inland Revenue Service declared the tax shelter rotten and disallowed it." He meant the Internal Revenue Service, but Jonathan didn't correct him.

"What did the accountants say?"

Asheton got up, rubbing the side of his face with his hand. He went over to the bar. "Perhaps you can guess," he said. "They pointed out the letter I signed saying that they were making no guarantee. When I asked about the legal opinion, they said they believed the lawyers had used reasonable judgment, even if they were wrong."

He poured three fingers of a single malt Scotch into a short crystal glass. Then he reached into an ice bucket and slipped two cubes of ice into the glass. A big drink for this time of day. He sipped.

"I could sue the lawyers, of course, but the accountants didn't believe I had a case. I spoke to a litigator Simon recommended. He advised against bringing the lawsuit. He pointed out that I would immediately subject myself to an audit. And I probably would not win."

He turned back toward Jonathan. "Where are my manners. I do apologize. May I make you a drink?"

"Too early for me. What's at risk?"

"Sorry."

"The tax shelter."

"Ah. Everything." Definitive and blunt.

Asheton took another sip and crossed the room to sit in his chair. He held the drink on his knee. The corners of his mouth sagged.

"My advisers tell me that with interest and penalties, perhaps $50 million. I don't have that kind of money on hand. Does anyone? I can't get it without selling HST Heartcare stock, and I can't do that." Jonathan let that go for a moment. "The statute of limitations runs out this year. In seven months actually."

"Okay. I see the problem. You don't want the IRS to open an audit based on the value of your donation. The so-called forgery opens up a Pandora's box for you."

"Correct."

"Have you tried to unwind the donation?"

"Well, yes, actually. Peter Willson says that it's impossible given the tax report the museum has made reflecting the donation. Besides my accountant says an amendment to my tax return of that magnitude is likely to result in an audit in any event. I asked Willson if I could buy back the pictures for the appraised value. It seems that must go before the board and everything would come out in that case as well." His voice seemed defeated.

He held the tumbler of Scotch up towards Jonathan. "Cheers. Bloody run of bad luck. Thank you for your concern. Tae thought you could help. But quite frankly, as I said, I don't see how."

"I haven't tried yet."

"I must tell you one thing further." He paused and seemed to collect his thoughts. "This is most confidential."

Jonathan nodded. "Of course."

"I'm negotiating for the sale of HST Heartcare. It is rather a nice transaction for us. When we close, if we close, I shall have the liquidity to deal with my issues, whatever transpires. But I cannot be seen being involved in a tax dispute. There are those, Rupert Seeling among them, who would not want to see the company sold."

"What does he have to do this?"

"Ah, the delightful Mr. Seeling. He has taken a rather large position in the shares of my company. So far we have managed to put him off. But were he to perceive my position, he might hope for a prize. Rupert is always looking for, what you would call, an angle. No word must get out. I just need a few months. I'm desperate, you see."

"I can see that. A few months. But isn't Seeling the President of the Nauton? Could he have a hand in this?"

"Perhaps, if he knew of the sale. But I don't think that he could know."

"If you're so concerned about Seeling, why did you contribute your paintings to the Nauton?"

"Well, Tae desired it, and I was rather hoping to appease Mr. Seeling. He thinks of that the museum as his own, you know."

"I forgot Tae was on the board. But wasn't the donation made before she joined?"

"Ah, you don't see. My donation was to show how important an addition to the board Tae would be.

"Got it."

"Jonathan, there is something I simply cannot understand." He spread his free hand with his palm up. The other held his drink. "If it is not Seeling, why is the museum raising this issue? I have a very careful dealer. The provenance of the pictures is excellent. I still believe they are very good."

"Sir Adrian, this may have nothing to do with you. I'm afraid you may be standing in the way of a bullet meant for someone else. It could really be an internal squabble. Peter Willson thinks Andrew Grahm is pushing this to get at him."

"Ah, more rotten luck, I'm afraid," said the older man, downing the remainder of his drink in a swallow. "It is difficult to imagine how it could be worse."

Chapter 16

Rafael Del Gado was in a buoyant mood as he selected his first Cohilbo Siglo of the day. He rolled the cigar appreciatively between his thumb and forefinger, experiencing its firmness. He reached into the pants pocket of his carefully tailored suit and extracted his gold cigar cutter.

Del Gado was a large man, but not tall. He had put on a few pounds with so much fine food over the last years. His well featured face was almost symmetrical with dark brown eyes and a head of curly black hair showing just a touch of gray at the temples. Quite different from most Brazilians. Yet his skin was the color they called cafe con leche. It was the coloring so attractive in Brazilian women. On Del Gado, it looked like a deep tan.

His handsome looks had served him well over the years. That and a natural talent for mimicry, together with a quick intelligence.

He snipped off the end of the cigar and took a cedar strip from his humidor, lit it with a gold lighter and applied it to his cigar, turning the cigar in the flame. He puffed in the fragrant smoke appreciatively and blew it out towards the ceiling. He smiled as the smoke drifted up towards the ceiling.

The rubbed and burnished cherry wood paneling in his large office pleased him, as did the thick wool carpet. The decorator had been expensive, but the custom made furniture set the right tone for a successful business man. He was smart. He had listened and he had learned.

English had been devilishly hard for him, but now he spoke it with little accent. He had come a long way from the favellas. He enjoyed the life he had earned. Del Gado rang for coffee.

The coffee was dark and rich and he sipped it pensively. This was an important moment. His trucking company was expanding and throwing off cash nicely. And the parking lot business was approaching break even.

The shift to credit cards created an issue, but one with which he was not overly concerned. The acquisition of Farmington Electric would close after the end of the year. He still didn't understand all the papers the lawyers wanted him to sign. There certainly were enough of them. He did understand the lawyers' charges. Unbelievable.

But the acquisition would be what these American businessmen called accretive. Immediately profitable. Mr. Morales would be pleased. It was necessary that Mr. Morales be pleased. He was an exacting man. Del Gado was interrupted by a tapping on his door.

"Yes."

His secretary, a petite blonde, opened the door halfway and said, "Your tailor is here, Mr. Del Gado."

He stood as the tailor measured him and made tiny notes in a fine, spidery hand on his chart. Occasionally the tailor would cluck gently. Del Gado didn't like tape measures, and he didn't like people judging him.

"Mr. Del Gado," the tailor said, "I brought some books of new fabrics. I think you will like the Loro Piana 160's. They've just arrived. You've always enjoyed a fabric with a good hand, and these are exceptional."

Dei Gado grunted absently and tapped the ash of his cigar onto the edge of the heavy ash tray. He continued his train of thought as he rubbed individual cloth swatches between his thumb and finger, folding one occasionally into the small rectangular book of samples.

Things were going well. Yes. He put down his cigar. The only real problem was these infernal taxes. He ran a hand through his thick hair. His expensive haircut fell neatly back into place.

It had to be done. He just didn't know how. Mr. Morales didn't care about taxes. "Just pay them," he had said when Del Gado had tried to tell him.

But Rafael Del Gado cared about the taxes. Here was an opportunity. Mr. Morales was a long way away and the United States was a truly foreign country. He liked this New York. He was sure there was a way. Businessmen, he knew, didn't pay taxes.

This country was just not rational. To think, people actually expected to pay taxes. Ridiculous.

Perhaps he could speak to a friend. Obliquely, of course. It was so difficult when you were new to a country to know who to trust.

But such a great country it was. So many opportunities. What was that American phrase. Ah yes, an 'entrepreneur'. He would be an entrepreneur of the taxes. And he would make the profits. It was the American way, no? And Mr. Morales would get all of his money, less of course the taxes he would have paid anyway.

His tailor spoke, bringing him back to the moment. "It will be three weeks for us to do the basic structuring of your suits. If it is in your schedule, we can have the first fitting then. Will that be satisfactory?"

"Yes, of course," Del Gado waived him out absently. "See my secretary for the deposit." He pressed a button on his desk.

"Sir," said the petite blond.

"Have my car brought around," he said in his slightly accented English.

He had been in the city for 28 months. It amazed him how quickly charities had sought him out. New York was like a little Brazilian village when it came to money. Everyone seemed to know where it was and wanted it.

And he wanted to be generous. There were many benefits for a man who wanted friends. Money lubricated the way.

It was one of those remarkable autumn mornings in the city. The light was tinged with pink and the pond in Central Park sparkled. It was warm for late October and the trees were just starting to make their bed of leaves, preparing for a winter's sleep. It was a day that made you want to live here. In other words, it wouldn't last.

Del Gado had been asked to lunch by an art dealer. A Derek Lissome. They had met at a party at a gallery. He was told that Lissome was an important dealer. This Derek Lissome was most friendly. Perhaps he knew about taxes. He had expressed his own feelings after Del Gado had made a remark in passing. Del Gado hoped he did, but he must be most careful.

Perhaps he could start collecting art. Would Mr. Morales mind? Probably not. Pictures were real assets. And they could be bought with cash. But perhaps it was better he should not know. He would not understand art. No.

The black Mercedes 550 stopped in front of a building on Madison, in Mid Manhattan. The driver, a tall, well-built Latino in a dark suit, exited the front and came around to open the rear door for Del Gado. A long scar marred his lip.

"Thank you, Alejando," Del Gado said. "I will call you when I am ready to leave."

Chapter 17

He was sitting in the library of his brownstone mansion off Central Park. The light flooded through the high windows, shadowed by the branches of the elm tree that he and Evelyn had planted so many years ago. A drifting rain softened the light.

The reds and greens in the Jackson Pollack over the fireplace seemed to dance in the flickering firelight. The smell of burning wood filled the room. It was a comfortable room but Rupert Seeling was unaware of it. He was deeply upset.

The teacup trembled in his hand. It wasn't like him. Tea spilled into the saucer and onto the priceless oriental rug on the dark parquet floor. He didn't notice or care.

The house seemed too big since Evelyn died last year. It was unnerving. Evelyn had always been there. She filled the house.

He felt a tear on his cheek and he reacted angrily. He didn't like it. He wasn't in control. He had always been in control. His mind was running wild.

There was a tap on the door.

"Come."

"Mr. Seeling," the butler said, "His Excellency has arrived." His Excellency was his old friend, Bishop Gerald F. K. Welsly.

"Show him in."

Seeling rose.

A small, thin man wearing a clerical collar came in. His florid cheeks were set off by large ears and full lips. His smile revealed yellowed teeth. A few tiny drops of rain were in his gray eyebrows.

Seeling bowed to the priest. He was always formal in front of the servants.

"Would you like a cup of coffee, Your Excellency," he asked.

"Yes, thank you."

Seeling nodded at the butler. "Please, Williams." The butler backed out and closed the door softly.

"Gerald, thank you for coming."

"As always, it is good to see you, Rupert. But you sounded upset."

Seeling motioned to one of the armchairs facing the fire and they sat down. Seeling shook his head.

"Gerald, I've never felt so unsure. I feel I've lost my way. But, please, I wanted to speak to you about my gift to the church, not my problems."

"Now Rupert, you have always been generous to the church. There was a hint of a Boston accent in his voice, which had been disciplined, but not completely tamed. "However, it is more important to me that we talk about you. As a friend."

There were not many people Rupert Seeling spoke to as friends. There were very few people he trusted.

"I'm lonely," Seeling said to his own surprise. It just came out.

"Of course you are, Rupert. Evelyn was a fine woman." It was trite, but somehow comforting.

"But it all seems so empty. Useless."

"Yes, but you must believe in God. He will be your balm. You have always believed."

"I can't seem to focus. My mind wanders when I try to pray."

"Can you think of why?"

There was a quiet tap and the butler entered carrying a tray with a silver coffee service and two thin china cups made with the crest of Seeling Brothers delicately on their side. He set it down on the table. "May I pour, sir?" Seeling nodded. The butler lifted the silver pot and poured the coffee. Then he gave a small bow, turned and left. The door softly snicked shut.

"You were telling me why you are having trouble concentrating," said the Bishop.

"It just seems so many things are going wrong. So many people are betraying me."

"Betrayal is a sad thing. Particularly for a good Christian, like you. How are you being betrayed? Is this betrayal personal?"

"I feel it is. It involves the museum that I head."

"Of course, the Nauton."

"I intend to give a wing to honor Evelyn. And I intend to leave my art to them. It's important to me."

"Of course it is, Rupert, but how are you being betrayed?"

"I believe they are seeking to destroy the museum."

"My goodness, who?"

"All of them. There is a campaign of leaks to the newspapers. The director is incompetent. And now the board is questioning me. It's one thing after another."

Seeling appeared agitated. His fingers trembled on the arm of his chair. The bishop leaned forward to put a hand on his arm.

"Tell me," he said in a soothing voice.

"First there were overwhelming financial problems."

"Yes, I recall your speaking of that."

"These art people are like children. They want so many things. They give no thought to where the money is to come from. Of course, I put my foot down."

"Of course."

"And now, I think they are doing everything to bring the museum to its knees. I can't let that happen. I must do something."

"But you seem so unsettled."

"Don't you see? I think they're trying to get rid of me. The board has started questioning my authority." The bishop sensed Seeling's emotions. He seemed so tightly wound. "People who don't understand what I've done. What it has cost me."

The bishop was becoming worried. All this seemed to be exaggerated. But how could he tell this powerful man, his friend, that he should to speak a professional who could guide him, as he could not.

"Rupert, have you spoken to anyone about your feelings. A person who might help you find your way?"

"No one can help me. No one."

"I'm sorry, Rupert." The bishop felt he had to change the subject. He needed to lessen the stress he heard in Seeling's voice. He would have to ask his secretary for advice as to what to do for his friend. And he would pray.

"Perhaps, Rupert, you would like to discuss your gift to the church. Evelyn would be pleased."

Chapter 18

The Sotheby's auction room was unusually still. As if the room itself were holding its breath. The evening fall sale of Impressionist and Modern art had started an hour and a half earlier.

The sale is a New York ritual of glamour and excess, where power and avarice meet over champagne. A day when the rich genuflect to art; not artists, art. The business of art was not lost on the more insightful among them, nor the similarity to Wall Street. But here, they were the punters, not the masters of the universe.

The stout man in the second row with the broad Slavic face had just bid $100 million for the Klimt, surpassing the high estimate of $95 million. Nothing induced awe like the presence of real money.

Gordon Watley, the auctioneer, turned slightly to his right to look at his assistant at the side of the room holding a telephone to her ear. He raised an eyebrow. Her face was impassive. She was still for a moment, then almost imperceptibly, nodded at Watley.

"I have $105 million," he said. There was a muffled gasp somewhere in the tuxedo-clad room.

The marketing of the Klimt had been a business of hard selling, even by the standards of Sotheby's. The picture had never been offered at auction. Nor had it ever been sold in recent history. The head of Sotheby's had developed a nervous facial tic as a result of giving the financial guarantees required. More than Witten's would offer. They had guaranteed the seller $90 million.

They had sent the picture for exhibition to Sotheby's offices in six cities. And they had produced a beautiful bound monograph on Klimt and his place in art history. Their public relations group had placed articles in every major art publication. The sales effort had cost in excess of $1 million.

But there was a tide of global cash washing around a very few identifiable masterpieces. Their experts had fingered this piece as the prize. The center of the fall sale.

They had been right. But everyone at Sotheby's had been holding their breath. Those who listened carefully might have heard an audible sigh from a chorus of Sotheby throats.

Watley looked towards the Slav. "It is against you, sir," he said. Watley never spoke in much above a whisper, but his voice seemed to boom.

It was so quiet in the room it seemed silence was the only truth. One second. Two. An eternity. A woman in a long red dress leaned forward in her seat to look at the Slav. His scowl sent her back sharply.

Then, in a breach of decorum, the Slav said loudly, in heavily accented English, "$115 million."

Watley frowned at this indiscretion and looked again at his assistant. Her lips moved in silent conversation. She listened. Then she shook her head.

"Fair warning," Watley said. He hesitated with the timing of a great actor, just an instant longer than was bearable. Finally he banged his gravel down. "It is Mr. Zhadanov, then. Congratulations, sir, and thank you."

The applause was sustained and enthusiastic.

Vadim Semyonovich Zhadanov was an oligarch. In the great privatization of the Russian Federation carried out by Boris Yeltsin, clever, well-connected men profited. Some immensely.

In oil and gas Vadim had made the Teapot Dome scandal seem like a petty social squabble. He bought up vouchers that had been distributed to peasants who could scarcely read or write and who had no understanding of share ownership. Where money did not suffice, other means were employed.

There were rumors of KGB connections, of Mafia relationships, of payoffs, but nothing was ever confirmed. During those years, Russia was a teeming economic wilderness. And outside of it, everyone was cheering the emergence of America as the only true superpower. So long as the Russians didn't threaten anyone, they could do what they wanted to each other. And Zhadanov did.

Now he had gathered vast amounts of money and power. The parties at his Belgravia flat were legendary. He owned one of the largest yachts in the world, designed by Philippe Starck. He had come late to art but he was a man of strong tastes and a heavy step.

His name first came to the lips of the art world two years ago when he had won a fierce bidding war with a Chinese gentleman over a fairly good Leger. He bid twice the low estimate. The art world had opened its arms to him like an ill-bred lady, as it had to so many others. Gustav Klimt probably was whirling in his grave fast enough to create a magnetic disturbance.

Zhadanov fascinated the international press. It interviewed him and rhapsodized about his liberal views. There was speculation he might run against the President of Russia. Of course he denied it, but the thought pleased him. And there was the small secret smile that some journalists noticed. Sometimes one slips when one is too pleased with oneself. Sometimes one regrets it.

It was very dark in the forests surrounding his dacha. Only the full moon reflected on the river below. The knock came in the late evening. That was most unexpected.

He had arrived just that afternoon on his Boeing 767 and helicoptered directly to the house. No one knew he had returned to Russia. It must be Sarminian, his head of security. His bodyguards, all ex-KGB, would let no one else near the house. They were ruthless men, very well paid.

It had been a long and tiring trip. Zhadanov was annoyed by the interruption. He opened the door with an angry curse on his lips. His hands froze on the belt he was knotting on his silk robe. They started to tremble.

There were two men in long leather coats. Their broad faces were blank. The older one stepped forward.

"You are to come with us. You are under arrest for money laundering and crimes against our motherland." His hand rested on the Marakov pistol at his side.

It would be dark for a very long time.

Chapter 19

"You've got to meet me right away." The young man sounded excited. It was unusual. But with these types, it was better not to appear too interested.

"Why?" Alex Kinsky said in a dead tone.

A layer of dust covered three brown steel filing cabinets in the one room office in an old building off 30th Street. There was a scared oak desk. Two wooden chairs without arms and a Naugahyde desk chair made up the balance of the furniture.

"I've got some real hot information you might like a lot."

"Oh, really. The last time you had hot information it cost me $100,000 dollars." Not him, but his client. So what.

Kinsky was a small man, narrow faced, with a receding chin. His overbite made him look feral, only accentuated by the two day old stubble on his cheeks.

"Look," the young man said anxiously, "the deal fell through at the last minute. I couldn't call. I couldn't get out of the meeting. I didn't even know 'til after it happened."

That was the problem when you were dealing with a paralegal. They were usually the last to know. But lawyers, you had to be careful with them, even the associates. Approach the wrong guy, and they might blow the whistle. In those big law firms, they paid them too much. Shit, it was ruining his business.

"But this is solid. The deal's going to happen real soon. My friend was just asked to work on the contracts. He'll have to work all night. He was bitching about it to me. I've seen the files."

"So what do you want for this…" he paused, "information?" He let his voice sound skeptical. He figured if he could reduce the price, there might be something in it for him."

"I was thinking about $50,000. This is real hot, and I'm taking a risk, you know."

He let out a snort. "Are you smoking something? That's not even worth discussing." It was, of course. If the kid was asking that much, it must be worth a lot of money. And his client would pay in cash, always a handy commodity. But there was something the kid said that bothered him.

"What kind of risk? Can this be traced you?" He let the edge sound in his voice. He didn't want to end up in jail for dealing in inside information. Not that his client would give a damn. But he had his own ass to cover. There wasn't enough money in this, at least for him. Not to take another hit.

"No way." The kid's voice was emphatic. Maybe a little too emphatic. "No one saw me looking at the files. It was late at night. Everyone on our floor had gone home. I have a key to this lawyer's office who is working on the deal. I have to get stuff sometimes. She's lazy. She doesn't want to be bothered. And I was careful to put everything back after I made copies. Nobody's raised an eyebrow."

He let himself be mollified, at least for the time being. "Yeah. Yeah. Well, $50,000 is still a lot of money. I doubt the man will go anywhere near that."

"Look, you've got to come meet me. If your client doesn't like it, he doesn't have to pay."

Now that was unique. This guy had never offered anything like that before. William Atkins would pay a lot more than $50,000 for the right information. He had in the past.

"If you don't want to meet me, I'll go to someone else. They'll pay me." The kid sounded petulant.

"Don't threaten me." Kinsky's voice was hard and clipped. "That's not a good idea." He made the threat in his voice clear. "I pay you good money to keep your ears open for me. You better make sure they stay that way."

"I'm not threatening you. I wouldn't do that." The kid was almost whimpering. It didn't take much to pierce his tough guy pose. That's one of the things he liked about dealing with these lawyer pussies.

"I'll give you 10 minutes. Make it good. And I want the copies. There's a coffee shop on East 47th at seventh. Be there at 4 p.m."

"But I don't know if I can get away. They're pretty tight around here," the kid pleaded.

"Look, I don't care how you do it. That's your problem. Be there." He hung up the phone and smiled. Something told them this was going to be a good one.

His client picked up the phone on the fourth ring. "Mr. Atkins," Kinsky said. That was the name Alex Kinsky knew. Victor Rollins would never use his real name with someone like Kinsky. Nor had he ever met Kinsky. The phone was a cell phone in the name of William Atkins. It was prepaid a year in advance with a cashier's check purchased with cash.

Rollins grunted at the information the paralegal had provided and hung up. He looked like an old jock who'd given up his gym membership long ago and resented it. His tailor was excellent, but he could still feel the pressure on his waistband when he sat. It irritated him.

Kinsky didn't hear from him again until two days later. The message he left was terse. "Okay, do it. But I have some problems too. You can clean them up."

He had learned to take Atkins literally. He just wasn't aware how literally in this case. When he finally reached him, Atkins took his time explaining exactly what he needed and how to do it.

Chapter 20

Andrew Grahm arrived at his office on the second floor of the Nauton. He was still shaken by Rebecca's unreasonable position. He had been living at the Carlyle. His clothing had to be stolen from his own apartment. Thank God she hadn't changed the locks. It was all very inconvenient.

"Good morning, Mr. Grahm," his secretary said. She was far too sunny. "Mr. Lissome called." She handed him a slip of paper.

Grahm muttered something indecipherable and entered his office, closing the door behind him. Perhaps Lissome will be amusing, he thought, as he dialed the number. I certainly need it. Damn Rebecca.

Derek Lissome was the director and majority owner of the Sifford Gallery. It was one of the few branded galleries in the world, like Pace or Saachi. A branded gallery confers value. It increases the price of any artist it selects to represent. The Sifford had attracted many of the hottest young artists. The up and comers.

Lissome understood promotion. More importantly, he understood that museums had evolved from recognizing greatness to anointing it. He and Andrew Grahm had known each other for years. Those years had been beneficial.

"Derek."

"Ah, good of you to call back so promptly, Andrew. Can we lunch today? I want to deliver your new DeRuk. A lovely one, I might add."

"That would be very nice." The DeRuk would be a wonderful addition to his art collection. He had wanted one for some time. Although heaven knows where he would keep it. "I appreciate you bringing it."

"No, Andrew. Thank you for choosing to include DeRuk in your retrospective."

"It was well deserved." Grahm's tone was flat. Good lord, Lissome could be infuriating. DeRuk did deserve to be in the retrospective. Lissome made it sound like it was some kind of deal.

"I may have something new that will interest you. Very much, I think."

Derek Lissome hung up the phone and fell back in his elegant leather chair. He dabbed at his narrow forehead with a white silk square. The pressure was getting to him. The damned financial crises. Since the banks had cut him off, financing the gallery had been increasingly difficult. His inventory alone was worth $10 million, although he only needed to finance a fraction of that. Most of it was on consignment from the artists. Yes, a large fraction, but still. He'd borrowed from some unfortunate people. They were insistent. Now they were threatening. He was coming to realize they could be dangerous.

They just didn't understand the quixotic nature of the gallery business. He needed to do something and now he had it. Andrew Grahm was the key. Everything else was in place. It was brilliant.

They would usually do Daniel's, but they didn't want to be interrupted. They sat at a back corner table at Tandele's, once a top restaurant, now long past any interest to the wine and food set.

Judging by the Dover sole, it should be long past interest to anyone. The room was quiet.

Lissome laid a bubble-wrapped package on the table. His hands were oddly small. The package was about 20 x 24 in. He tapped it with a manicured fingertip.

"One of his best, Andrew. It will be a grand addition to your collection."

"Thank you," Grahm said. He leaned it against the wall beside him. He didn't smile. After all, he had paid Lissome $20,000 for the DeRuk. A fair price in his estimation. Perhaps a bit on the low side.

Derek Lissome did smile. Broadly. The retrospective had added a million dollars to the value of the DeRuks he had in his inventory. He never liked the one he gave Grahm anyway. Even though he practically gave it away.

"You said there was something else?" Grahm said.

There was almost ennui in his voice. It was annoying.

"This could be quite a feather in your cap," Lissome said.

"Oh?" Mild interest.

"Yes, I think you will be quite pleased."

"Derek, don't patronize me. I don't like it."

"Of course not, Grahm." What an ass, he thought.

Grahm set down his coffee cup with a frown. It was awful.

And Lissome was not being amusing at all.

"Derek, just tell me what you have in mind. You're beginning to bore me."

Lissome's face hardened, and his lips went white. But he needed this arrogant son-of-a-bitch. He carefully modulated his voice.

"I've arranged for one of my clients to contribute a major Purland oil to the Nauton. Through you, of course."

"Interesting." Grahm pursed his lips and thought about Purland. He was important. Maybe Lissome wasn't as boring as he imagined. "I like Purland, although I have to say, he's not one my favorites. It's more in Ailene Brown's area." Ailene Brown was one of his curators.

Grahm gave Lissome a penetrating look. "What else?"

"I don't understand, Andrew?"

"Why are you doing this?"

"Isn't it enough that I like you?"

"I told you once, Derek. Don't patronize me. You never do anything that isn't in your own best interest."

Derek Lissome felt wrong footed. His voice was a little wobbly.

"Well, of course. Doesn't everyone?"

"What's in it for you?"

Lissome didn't like the way this was going.

"I'm selling the Purland to my client, your donor." He hadn't anticipated this. Grahm was so unpredictable.

"That's nonsense," Grahm said. He spoke emphatically. "He'll only get a deduction for the purchase price. He could just give us the money."

"That's not what he wants. He's new to the city. He wants to be accepted."

"Have him give us the money. We'll name something after him."

"He wants to be thought of as an art lover, a man of taste. Not some rich guy."

"And how will you achieve that?" Grahm asked.

Grahm really had his teeth into this. It was getting difficult. Couldn't the man just accept a gift?

"The fact that I sold it to him won't come out. As far as anyone will know, he bought the piece many years ago because it appealed to his eye." God lord, they hadn't even gotten to the difficult part.

"Oh, all right," Grahm said, making a sweeping gesture with the back of his hand.

Lissome paused. "There is one thing, Andrew."

Grahm raised an eyebrow. "Really?"

"My client doesn't want any publicity."

"I thought he wanted to be accepted as an art lover."

"I can do that for him once the donation is made. A word to the right people. Your agreement."

"Yes, I can see that."

"But it would be best if the picture were not shown for a year or so."

"You cause me concern, Derek. Why?" Now Grahm sounded suspicious. "The museum will not be involved in any impropriety. I certainly will not. You do know that we will not value the painting for tax purposes."

"Good God, no, Andrew. It's a divorce or something. I don't know. Unfortunately, the wife saw the Purland. If his name is connected with the picture, she might become inquisitive. Start asking questions about the disposal of his estate."

Graham thought of Rebecca. "I can understand that."

Lissome was surprised. "Good."

"There are no other restrictions, I trust."

"No, none."

"Well, it shouldn't be too difficult. I'll send the picture out for restoration and reframing. Besides, no one has kept track of our archives since the computer system crashed. That idiot, Willson, keeps putting off updating it," said Graham.

"I'm grateful for your understanding."

Grahm nodded.

"If this goes well, I can probably arrange several more such gifts," Lissome continued.

Grahm's eyes fell to the wrapped package leaning against the wall beside him. This could work out well.

Derek Lissome was in a cab on the way back to his gallery. He was pleased with himself. He reached into the inner pocket of his jacket and extracted his cell phone. He dialed.

"Mr. Del Gado, your gift has been arranged satisfactorily. Can we meet next Thursday at the gallery?"

"No, of course. I wouldn't mind coming to your office. Will you be able to arrange the $8 million cashier's check on such short notice?"

"Yes. I'll complete the transaction in accordance with our discussions."

"Thank you, Mr. Del Gado." Lissome ended the call. A smile spread on his face. Now he would have some breathing room. A great deal of breathing room if this went as he planned. After he gave Del Gado back $6 million, he would have a $1 million worth of breathing room. Plus his profit on the sale of the Purland. Perhaps, even more. He needed to think it through.

Chapter 21

It was two in the morning. Simon Aaron's office was quiet. They had finished cleaning this floor of offices. The man looked carefully to make sure everyone on the crew had already left before he let himself back into the office with a small set of metal tools he removed from his pocket.

He took a moment to stand still. He listened for the stillness. It wouldn't be good to be interrupted. When he was satisfied he was alone, he made his way to the office of Lauren Lucier, the Director of Administration. He had been given her name. He let himself in. The door was locked, but it was no more trouble than the front door.

He closed the door softly behind him. He didn't switch on the lights, relying upon the moonlight flooding in through the floor to ceiling windows. It was adequate to boot up the computer.

He input a simple password he got from the slip of paper he had removed from his pocket. He didn't need to get into any of the files. Just the e-mail program. He took another larger slip of paper out of his pocket and typed in an e-mail address in the Cayman Islands. He surveyed the website and found the pull-down menu.

He opened the application form he was looking for. Slowly, he filled it out. He used two fingers. Typing was never his strong suit. It wasn't what he got paid for. "Shit," he muttered as he had to erase several lines he had muddled up.

Then he hit a button that erased the entire application. He had to start again. "This'll take all night," he muttered.

He made sure to check the spelling of the name on the application. He was unfamiliar with it and the spelling was peculiar. Nine letters in the last name. It sounded foreign.

After what seemed like an eternity, he hit the send key. He waited for the automatic confirmation to appear and deleted it. He then instructed that the new account be acknowledged to a g-mail account that he immediately set about establishing using an abbreviation of the name on the application form. One good thing about weird names. No one had used them.

He finally checked to make sure there were no traces of his work on the computer, then closed the program and shut it down. So far, so good.

He carefully surveyed the office to be certain he hadn't dropped anything or moved something. Then he set the desk chair back as he had found it and made his way out of the office, locking each door behind him. He took the steps, not the elevators. At the security desk he told the guard he was on a break and needed a smoke.

He was out of the building in a minute more. He walked for eight or 10 blocks, making random turns, until finally he was on Avenue of the Americas.

Getting a taxi at three in the morning was tough even if you were dressed well. And he was wearing a set of coveralls. Finally a desperate cabbie picked him up. The cabbie made him show the money for the fare.

He gave the cabbie an address that was three blocks from where he wanted to go. He made it a point to keep his face in the shadows of the cab. His ill-tempered grunts soon discouraged the cabbie from trying to make conversation.

The next morning he made his way to a Mail Boxes R Us store three blocks from Simon Aaron's office. He looked inside. The lone clerk looked young and pleasant. He settled in to a coffee shop across the street and watched, sipping a cup of coffee, until the store got busy. Then, he went in and waited in line. It was finally his turn.

"I'm sorry you had to wait, sir. We usually have two people, but we got caught shorthanded today. Can I help you?" the stressed young man asked.

"I'd like to open two post office boxes," he said, keeping the conversation to a minimum and as simple as possible.

The clerk passed across two forms. "If you'll fill these out, we'll be happy to assist you. Come right to the front of the line."

He filled out the forms, one in the same name as he had put on the application that he had completed last night, the other in a different name, as he had been instructed to do. He returned the forms to the clerk.

"Would you like to give us a credit card, sir? Or we can bill you monthly."

"No. I'd prefer to pay in advance."

He prepaid in cash for both boxes for a full year. He didn't plan to come back.

Chapter 22

Derek Lissome bustled into Andrew Grahm's office. His cheeks were flushed from the cold. He was carrying a package under his arm wrapped in brown paper. It appeared to be a little more than three feet square and it was clearly awkward for him. Lissome was breathing hard from the exertion.

Andrew Grahm rose from behind his desk. He seemed to be tired, and there was an irritable twitch at the corner of his mouth.

"Derek," he said by way of greeting. He was not pleased by this interruption.

Lissome had set the package on the floor, leaning it against his leg. He was hastily unbuttoning his gray cashmere overcoat. Grahm's office was unpleasantly warm.

"Andrew, it's good of you to see me." He brushed at the raindrops clinging to the lapel of his coat as he spoke. His voice broke as he struggled to control his breathing. "I wanted to . . . bring the Purland to you myself. Rafael del Gado insisted."

Grahm doubted that Rafael del Gado had any idea that Lissome was delivering the painting. He wants me to thank him, he thought. I'll be damned if I will.

"You needn't have bothered, Derek. I could have sent someone for it."

"Oh, goodness, no." Lissome slipped out of his overcoat. Grahm took it from him and hung it on a hanger behind his office door. "I absolutely wanted to present it in person. I'm so pleased to have been able to do this for the Nauton." He meant Grahm, and Grahm knew it. It disgusted him.

Lissome picked up the package and propped it on a chair in front of Grahm's desk. "Here," he said, tearing off the brown wrapping paper.

He went behind Grahm's desk. Grahm moved slightly aside. "Lissome extended his hand with the palm up. "What a beautiful example of Purland's work." He clapped his hands together.

"Sometimes, I think that contemporary art has gone beyond even me," said Grahm. He was feeling venomous. "Oh, I understand the intellectual content, but I feel no emotion. There must be emotion, mustn't there, Derek?" He turned his head and fixed Lissome with a brief stare before continuing. "They seem like a bunch of squiggles. I don't care for squiggles."

God, this man is a pompous ass, thought Lissome.

"I'm sorry you aren't moved by the painting, Andrew. I, for one, find it very affecting. Purland is so acclaimed." This was outrageous.

"Yes, you do raise another issue, Derek. I'm growing more concerned about the line between art and the horrible conduct of some these artists. It seems to me, in some cases, the more outrageous the artist, the more he is fawned over by certain critics." Grahm clearly was alluding to Whitman Purland, who had made a point of his fright wigs and obscene language.

Lissome owned seven Purlands. He was desperate to change the topic. His eyes caught on two Ben Nicholson paintings leaning against the wall opposite Grahm's desk.

"What beautiful examples of Nicholson's work," Lissome said.

It brought a snort from Grahm that startled him.

"My God, man, you have no eye. Those are forgeries."

Lissome bit his lip. He couldn't afford to alienate this man. Sometimes you had to have a thick skin to be a successful art dealer. He walked over to the pictures and lifted one, turning it to the light. He spent a full two minutes studying it intently.

"Derek, I must go to another appointment." Grahm was getting bored. He really didn't care what Lissome had to say.

Lissome put down the Nicholson and turned back to Grahm.

"Andrew, of course I don't have your eye."

Grahm nodded.

Lissome spoke hesitantly. "But, I've handled many Nicholsons over the last 25 years."

"And?"

Grahm was surprised when Lissome continued.

"Have you sent the paintings out for technical analysis?"

"There isn't a need."

"Andrew, are you sure? Your reputation."

Now Grahm was getting angry. "They are forgeries. I would stake my life on it. And I intend to expose them."

"Expose them?" Lissome repeated.

They were interrupted by the ringing of the telephone. Grahm picked it up.

"Yes, of course I can speak to Mr. Seeling." He made no attempt to apologize to Lissome.

"It is very important, Mr. Seeling. I would not take your time otherwise." He paused and listened. "I would prefer to discuss the matter in person. It is quite sensitive." Again he paused. "Yes, November 14 at four." He opened his calendar, flipped a page and made a note. "Thank you."

He looked over at Lissome with an expression that hung somewhere between gloating and determination. "I intend to tell Mr. Seeling that these retched forgeries," he waved his hand towards the Nicholsons, "must be dealt with now. Otherwise I will not be responsible." Grahm's lips were ridged. There was a suppressed threat in his voice. "I'm sick and tired of this museum being run by incompetents who have no regard for art. This must end."

He said it with a finality that caused Lissome deep concern about Andrew Grahm.

Chapter 23

Derek Lissome sat in Simon Aaron's office. It had been two days since he delivered the Purland to the Nauton.

Lissome's legs were crossed, but somehow it didn't affect the razor sharp crease in his expensive gray slacks. He wore a blue cashmere blazer with a subtly contrasting Hermes tie. The pocket-handkerchief picked up the dominant color in the tie without matching the pattern.

The man was small and thin. He had unnaturally dark hair, probably dyed, Simon thought, and rather small, but well cared for hands. Lissome looked too slick. Simon didn't trust art dealers.

Lissome said, "$70 million."

It was late in the day and the lights were on. The sky brooded as the clouds convened to announce more rain. The first large drops spattered on the immense windows.

Lissome kept glancing over Simon's shoulder, appraising the Picasso oil on the wall. He guessed it was worth $90 million dollars.

Simon sat behind his desk. He was leaning his elbow on the arm of his desk chair with two fingers on his cheek, the knuckle of his ring finger pressed to the corner of his lip, clearly interested in what Lissome was saying. He only wished the fellow would not keep glancing up. It was annoying.

The cigar Simon was smoking was making Lissome nauseous, but he couldn't object. This was too important. He would have to conclude his business quickly. His last comment had startled Simon, as Lissome intended.

"It is the greatest opportunity I have seen in my 30 years in the art world," Lissome added.

"Why do you think it's available?"

"As we both know, the Klimt was sold to the Russian oligarch, Zhadanov I think his name was, last month at Sotheby's."

"Unfortunately, I do. Witten's wanted that picture badly, but Sotheby's outbid us."

"My sources tell me that Zhadanov has disappeared inside Russia. The painting was confiscated along with all of his other properties and possessions."

"But the Klimt is a masterpiece. How can it possibly be available?"

"Yes, you would think that. But it is. There is no appreciation of art among those low level Russian thugs. And no one knew of the purchase. It was too soon. Nor that the painting was in Russia. I am told it is now in storage in a small village outside of Moscow with all Zhadanov's rugs and furniture."

"I can see the possibility. But I sincerely doubt it."

"I have excellent sources in Russia. You can believe me."

"Okay, so say I believe you. Then what?"

"Then, Mr. Aaron, what you can do is buy a great Gustav Klimt work at a vastly discounted price."

"If it's such a good deal why don't you buy it?"

"Ah, would that I could," Lissome said. "But frankly, the amount of money involved is quite beyond my means."

"Can't you get it?"

"There isn't time."

"But why me?"

"Mr. Aaron, you because I knew you'd have the money and would recognize the value. Am I wasting my time?"

Simon ignored the question. "That is a huge discount? The painting would sell for much, much more at auction."

"Of course, but Zhadanov needs cash. Quickly. You could say his life depends on it. You understand."

Simon didn't, but then he didn't really care.

"What about title?" he asked.

"I can assure you, you will be absolutely satisfied. My sources have access to both Zhadanov and to the necessary Russian officials."

Lissome uncrossed his legs and adjusted himself in his seat. He leaned forward to make another point. A mistake. He started coughing from the cigar smoke.

Lissome waved his hand in a gesture Simon thought was meant to allay his concerns. Actually, Lissome was frantically waving away the smoke residue.

"Can I get you a glass of water?"

Lissome croaked "yes" through his coughing fit.

A secretary brought a crystal glass filled with water. Lissome drank greedily and his coughing slowed. He sat back with a sigh and wiped his eyes with a pocket-handkerchief and patted his lips.

"Sorry," he said. "Allergies."

Simon nodded and tapped the ash of his cigar in the heavy, circular ashtray. "We were talking about title."

"Yes, of course, title. I would propose that you establish an escrow, perhaps with your bank. You will have to deposit at least $5 million, as good faith money."

"No one will have access to the money."

"Of course. I would not expect you to be at risk."

"In an interest-bearing account ," inserted Simon. "I get the interest."

"Yes, yes, of course." Lissome brushed the comment away. A small annoyance. He took another swallow of water. "The painting, and all of the title documents will be delivered into the escrow. You will have, say, 20 days to have your lawyers and experts examine everything."

"I' ll need 45 days." Simon was emphatic.

"I'm afraid that's too long. The most I can offer is four weeks. It is quite urgent, as I explained."

"Okay."

"If you are not satisfied in any way, you will instruct the bank to return your money and release the picture."

"No other approval can be required. My signature alone. I don't want my money tied up." Simon had been here before.

"As I said before, you will not be at risk."

"That sounds reasonable. What's in it for you?"

"Ah, Mr. Simon, I was wondering when you might ask. A modest commission. Say one percent of the purchase price plus three percent of the excess of the appraised value over what you will pay."

Simon Aaron gave a slight smile. "That's a lot of money."

"Yes it is." Lissome said it dryly, without expression.

"So, you want $700,000, assuming the price is $70 million. Plus another $900,000 if the picture is worth $100 million.

"I am your only source, Mr. Aaron. But I am prepared to listen to what you may think is fair."

"I'll give you $1 million if the price costs $70 million and 10 percent of everything less than that."

Lissome nodded and seemed to consider what Simon Aaron had proposed. Then he nodded again. "You are very shrewd, Mr. Aaron. That is acceptable."

"Good. I'll have my lawyers draw up the papers."

"There is one more thing."

"Oh?"

"I will need an advance of $250,000 against my expenses."

"That's a lot of money. Why don't you front it yourself if you're so sure of your sources."

"Mr. Simon, you understand as well as I do that these have not been good times in the art market. I cannot. And yet it seems little risk for so great a prize. I could explain my costs, but you may not want to be burdened with the details."

Simon Aaron grunted and took a long pull on his cigar. Lissome winced. Simon turned his head and blew out the smoke. He definitely did not want to know the details.

"Deductible from your fee," he said.

"Mr. Aaron, that is not right." Lissome voice rose slightly. "You, as the buyer should pay the expenses."

"No."

Derek Lissome sighed. The was resignation in his eyes.

"But the expenses will be added to the purchase price in determining your fee," Simon said.

"Then we have an understanding," Lissome concluded and rose, extending his hand.

"My director of administration will give you a check."

Simon Aaron leaned forward to shake the offered hand. He smiled as Lissome turned away. It was a better deal than he had hoped. He was pleased. He liked to win.

Chapter 24

It had been a long night with little sleep. The lawyers needed his input to respond to the S.E.C. Comment Letter on the tender offer papers.

Jonathan was cranky. This wasn't how it was supposed to be. His only consolation was that the lawyers were still hard at it when he left at 1:30 a.m. But then, he couldn't get to sleep. His foot hurt. It wasn't fair.

He was tired and two cups of coffee hadn't helped. Traffic in the city was normal, that is to say, dreadful and the cab ride had been a slow slog.

He would have preferred to walk across the Park but there was no time. Besides, he had sprained his ankle slipping on a pizza box someone had left on the floor at the lawyer's office. That's why his foot hurt.

He limped into Simon's office with the wonderful Picasso oil on the wall. He loved that painting. It felt special somehow, being in a private place with a museum-quality piece of art. Simon was working a cigar and looking cheerful.

"Jonathan, my lad," he said. "Sit down. You look like you lost a fight with a polecat. And why are you limping?"

"Softer," Jonathan moaned. "I'm exhausted. I was up all night with the lawyers. I fell. It's a war wound." Jonathan had no intention of describing his graceless rendition of a balletic split or the round of applause from the young lawyers.

"My, my. I never knew tender offers were so dangerous."

"Spare me, Simon. And why, may I ask, are you so pleased with yourself? It's not becoming, you know. Not this early." Jonathan shaded his eyes to try to block out the sunshine streaming into Simon's office. Small clouds had appeared. Scouts for the rain that would surely follow.

"Tsk, tsk," Simon ticked. "We are in a foul mood."

Jonathan just groaned.

"I am about to achieve a triumph for Witten's. One that, no doubt, will be the envy of the auction world and bring deserved luster to my name." Simon was sometimes a little over the top, but playful when it suited him. He was smiling his Cheshire Cat smile.

"Okay, get it over with," Jonathan said. He was always a little on edge when Simon smiled that smile.

"Ah, we can concentrate."

"Don't be an ass, Simon. I'm under the weather."

"It appears you need some port in this particular storm."

Jonathan moaned softly. "Please," he said plaintively.

"You do remember the sale of the Klimt to that Russian oligarch. He paid more than $120 million for it when you add in the hammer price." The hammer price is the buyer's premium.

"I recall reading about it. A record, wasn't it?"

"Oh, yes."

"Is it available?

"'Available' is a slippery term in this case. Our Russian friend seems to have gotten himself on the wrong side of the President of Russia. Not so attractive a place to be."

"No."

"He seems to have disappeared into the bowels of the Russian justice system." Simon paused. "And if you say 'No shit,' I will definitely think less of you."

"Simon, I would never do that."

"No shit," Simon guffawed.

"So how does this help the renowned and soon-to-be-exalted Simon Aaron?"

"Do you know Derek Lissome? He owns the Sifford Gallery."

"I've heard his name. I never met him."

"He came to see me yesterday. Apparently, the Klimt is available at a bargain price."

"How so?"

"The Russian oligarch needs the money. And not in Russia."

"Is the picture in Russia?"

"It is."

"Doesn't that create a bit of a problem?"

"Yes, a tad."

"What's the price?"

"Lissome says around $70 million. Cash."

"But can you get title?"

"Lissome has a signed authorization to sell the picture. He showed it to me."

"Do you trust the guy? How can you be sure the authorization is authentic?"

"Derek Lissome is a respected dealer. I mean to the extent any of them warrant any respect. He's not going to forge something like that. The Klimt is a major work. If he's not authorized, the media will crucify him."

"So, then buy it."

"Well, there's a little problem."

"Ah."

"The picture was confiscated by the local authorities."

"Then how can you buy it?"

"Lissome says there are ways. The Russians don't know what they have."

"But that's one of the most famous paintings in the world. The Russians will be all over it."

"If they knew. But it was taken to Russia secretly. No one knows it's in the country."

"And the local authorities aren't art connoisseurs."

"Exactly." Simon's broke into a smile so broad it almost split his face. "Can you imagine the publicity Witten's will get in acquiring such a masterpiece?" Simon paused dramatically. "Not to mention the profit when we resell it."

"But won't the Kremlin claim the picture?"

"I don't know how. It belongs to the Oligarch. I mean it's not even by a Russian painter."

"That hasn't stopped them before. $70 million is a lot of money. How can you make sure you will get the painting and good title before you part with the money?"

"Jonathan, I'm not an idiot. I wouldn't trust God with that kind of money, much less Derek Lissome. The money goes into an interest-bearing escrow account at Chase. I'm the only signatory. Actually, Lissome suggested it. The money's not released until the picture is delivered with title and after Witten's has had time to examine it."

"Okay, but how is Lissome going to get the picture out of Russia?"

"I really don't know. And frankly, I don't want to. He only wanted his expenses for shipping and the like. It's a bargain. He has the contacts in Russia."

"What's in it for him?"

"A finder's fee. A million dollars. I believe that's incentive enough."

Jonathan whistled. "Wow, that's more than three hours of billing at my rate."

Simon groaned.

Jonathan felt better.

Chapter 25

The bottle of port was the difficult part. It was a rare wine, a 1933 Croft, and therefore it was dangerous. It might be traced. The solution proved to be surprisingly simple. A collector was advertising the sale of his cellar of wines online. The ad said the port had a low pour to just below the shoulder of the bottle. That was perfect.

Cash, and a delivery service in a distant city. The delivery service sent the port to an empty office with instructions that it be left at the front door. There had been a concern that weather would delay the shipment. That had proved to be wrong. Now the bottle of port was on the table. That had taken less than a week.

A friend had provided the idea. Unintentionally, of course. It had required careful thought and some research. Thank goodness for the World Wide Web. The idea was quite amusing, given the circumstances.

You could purchase 99-percent-pure poison on a dozen websites. No questions asked. Rather unbelievable. But quite on the up and up. A false name was used, of course, to be on the safe side. And the address of a nearby dry cleaners was given, with a note to hold for a customer. The name given was a friend's.

The package was picked up on the day it arrived by a delivery boy he sent to the cleaners with the customer's name. If the friend had asked, there was an answer. The friend never asked. Probably never had known.

The bright lamp made the work easier. Three small plastic bottles were spread on the table next to a hypodermic syringe. It had required some work to find the right size needle, but it was done.

The syringe had been purchased at a large chain drug store in Queens. Just another shopper. But, it had been a long day. Now care was required.

Latex gloves, of course. The contents of the three plastic bottles were poured into a small shot glass. Then the needle was used to draw it up.

With great care, the needle was pushed into the wax seal on top of the port and through the cork. It required continuous pressure and several attempts had been made on other bottles to get it right. The color of the port didn't change. The level of the port rose a bit up the neck. A perfect pour.

The bottle was carefully placed on its side with the neck just over the edge. A match was struck and the sulfur was allowed to burn off. Then it was held slightly away from the wax seal. After a moment the tiny hole in the seal disappeared. The resealing had been well rehearsed and there was no noticeable blemish on the wax. The gloves, the empty bottles and the syringe, were gathered into a brown bag and thrown into a succession of trash bins blocks away.

The next morning, after the bottle was wiped with a damp cloth, it was hand delivered by a hired man to a messenger service with instructions that it be delivered to a leading chocolateer in the city. A cashier's check was included. The typed instructions to the chocolateer were to wrap the port with a box of its finest chocolates and deliver them to Andrew Grahm at the Nauton Museum, immediately. There was no note.

Enjoy, Andrew!

Chapter 26

Andrew Grahm let out a sigh as he eased himself into one of the deep armchairs in his office. He could finally relax. It had been a hard day. So trying.

The staff was squabbling again over the latest cuts. As if he could just snap his fingers and make them go away. Or better yet, make Peter Willson go away.

And that frightful exhibit they were expected to mount. Christ, could they sink any lower? At least he had put Willson in his place. A grin touched his lips. The Nicholson forgeries might well be the nail in Willson's coffin. Willson certainly was nervous. They were so obvious to the trained eye. He needed to think about the timing. Soon. Seeling had just dithered this afternoon. He was an old man.

Grahm settled down. His office was finally quiet. He certainly couldn't go home. His hotel room was so small. It wasn't fair. He had to think of a way to get Rebecca out of his apartment.

He thought of Barbara. No, she was out with some of her artist friends. He wondered what Ailene Brown was doing, but then shook his head. It wasn't worth the effort.

At least he could have a decent glass of port. The '33 Croft he adored. Thank god someone had sent it over. No card. Probably lost. New York delivery people.

He thought about who might have sent the port. Perhaps it was some gallery owner, trying to suck up. Maybe even Derek Lissome. He hadn't heard from him in a week. That pandering twit. Imagine, trying to tell him what to do.

As Grahm went through the ritual of opening the bottle, he mused on the port. Maybe it was Ailene Brown. She knew what kind of pressure he was under. After all, she felt the same way he did. Maybe he should call her after all. He shook his head a second time. No, now was not a good time. He might have to fire her.

Using his penknife he gently pried the wax off the bottle around the cork. Then he carefully worked the blades of an ah-so cork screw down the edges of the cork. These old corks tended to fall apart. He twisted gently, drawing the cork out. It came out whole. That pleased him.

He yearned for a cigarette. His patch didn't seem to be working even though he had applied a second one, what with all the stress.

Autumn was showing its teeth. The walls danced with patterns of muted light. God, I've tried, he thought. I've reached for pure art. How I've sacrificed. But no one cares.

It was so difficult to make his way. No one supported him. They all wanted something.

His office was like an old bachelor's apartment. Heavy, good furniture, much of it antique. A very few, but very good, paintings on the wall. Subdued lighting that gave it a restful feel.

There was a working fireplace, rarely used, but now with a pleasant fire. Alas, gas, but what could one do with all these regulations. So very few people understood what it meant to be a gentleman.

He carefully poured the port into a decanter being watchful of the sediment at the bottom of the bottle. People did not drink really good port these days. Heathens. It would keep for months. There were many pleasures in his future.

There was certainly no one on the board that understood. They thought money was important. And not that imbecile Willson.

Grahm looked across at the two Nicholsons that Adrian Asheton had donated. He kept them in his office. Such hideous forgeries. He had told Seeling about the press nibbling around the scandal. He hoped it would scare him into doing something. Lord, anything.

It brought his thoughts back to Derek Lissome. What a peculiar conversation that had been. He had been properly incensed with Lissome for trying to stop him from disclosing the forgeries that had been foisted on his museum. What business was it of his? The feeling of being right suffused him. He was always right.

And what an absolute splash these forgeries would make in the newspapers. He savored the thought. He was tempted to call the New York Times immediately.

"No, not yet," he said aloud to himself. It had to be the right moment. He liked this feeling of discipline. Mastering himself.

He rose and opened an antique armoire. He selected a Riedel Vinum port glass, held it up to the light to make sure it wasn't dusty, and sat down again.

He enjoyed the feel and the heft of the heavy decanter and the way the port caught the light from the fireplace. He poured a generous glass and held it up to admire the rich ruby color. Then he swirled it and thrust his nose deep into the glass. Ah, truly a heaven that so few knew to visit. He held it up to the light to watch the tears of port trace their pattern down the sides of the glass.

He took a small sip. Superb. Then he took a larger drink and settled back against the leather cushions, savoring the subtle, rich wine and the underlying, almost spectral, sweetness. He stared at the fire, lost in thought.

It finally started to rain. Grahm closed in on himself, enveloped by a feeling of well-being. He loved the rain. Maybe everything was going to work out.

He rose and walked to his private bathroom. The room was small but elegant and he liked that. He picked up the bar of special soap and washed his hands. He sprayed on some of the cologne he favored. Then he walked back across his office to his chair and picked up his glass again.

He was thinking about Rebecca and how unreasonable she had been. The thought made him tense and he took another deep drink of port. He wished he'd never married her.

How could he get her to be sensible. He so hated the thought of disagreeable lawyers and the utter waste of money. But he certainly wasn't going to give her the apartment or part of his trust fund. Perhaps he could offer her $75,000 a year. That would be generous.

He took out his handkerchief and dabbed at his forehead. It was getting frightfully warm in here. He rose to turn down the fire but a severe pain gripped his chest. My God, I'm having another heart attack.

He stumbled and knocked into the small table beside him. The decanter tumbled onto the rug without a sound and the stopper fell free. Grahm went down on one knee, but he crawled towards the telephone. He was having difficulty breathing.

He didn't make it.

Chapter 27

"Is that a dog?" Willson sounded incredulous. He was standing with his mouth open, his extended hand forgotten.

Jonathan tried hard to catalog the variety of responses that ran through his mind. Finally, he said, "Excellent guess, Peter."

Jonathan opened a palm down in introduction. "Meet Rufus. Rufus, this is Peter." Rufus didn't seem impressed.

Rufus was a brown pug with a little black face so ugly he was beautiful. Unfortunately, he knew it. Rufus was Nicole's second love. At least, Jonathan fervently hoped he was her second love.

"He didn't want to stay home alone," Jonathan said.

The truth was that Rufus ran a tight ship and pretty well got whatever he wanted. Jonathan wondered sometimes who was training him, Nicole or Rufus? He was sure of one thing. He was being trained. He sort of liked it. It wasn't easy learning to live full time with a woman and a dog when you were used to wandering around a big house, alone most of the time.

"But this is a museum!" Willson stated.

"Look, Peter. You insisted I come over."

Rufus walked calmly over to Willson and started sniffing his leg, causing Jonathan a moment's anxiety.

"I couldn't leave Rufus. So what would you rather have? No me. Or me and Rufus. He's not going to pee on your paintings, you know."

Jonathan wasn't entirely sure about that. Rufus had a mischievous streak. Jonathan was really basing his opinion on the fact that he didn't think Rufus could aim that high.

"Okay, okay. Forget it. You're here now," Willson answered in an aggrieved tone, reaching down to pet Rufus gingerly on head. He withdrew his hand smartly as Rufus muttered a low growl.

"He's not crazy about men." Jonathan said. "He's Nicole's dog. He tolerates me because I feed him."

They were standing in a large, nicely furnished office with thick, gray carpeting. There was a hush about it, almost like a library. Willson pursed his lips, and retreated around his desk and sat down. Jonathan thought he heard him mutter "Animal!" A particularly appropriate epithet, he thought.

"It sounds like you've got trouble," Jonathan observed. "Who found Andrew Grahm?"

"An assistant curator, Ailene Brown. She discovered Andrew in his office this morning."

"Where is she now?"

"I sent her home. Understandably, she was upset."

"Did she say anything to you?"

"No, as I said, she was very upset."

"What about the police?"

"I personally didn't want to get them involved. It was obviously a heart attack. But the paramedics called them when they concluded Grahm was dead." The phone rang. Willson picked it up. "Excuse me," he said. Then he listened and murmured a response into the receiver. He looked back up at Jonathan as he replaced the receiver in its cradle.

"Did the police come?"

"Oh yes," Willson said. "They came and went before you got here. I called you when I found out the police were coming, but I guess that wasn't necessary. I'm sorry to have bothered you."

"What did the police say?"

"They just looked around and asked me a few questions. They were only here for 15 or 20 minutes."

Jonathan spread the fingers of his hand in a palm up gesture for Willson to continue.

"They just asked me what I thought happened. I told them I believed Andrew had a heart attack. I think they thought so too."

"Peter, you do know they'll do an autopsy on the body. They do in all cases of death where there is no doctor's certification. Did you try to get a doctor to certify the death?"

"I tried. The police asked. I called Rebecca and she spoke to Andrew's doctor. I explained about the autopsy."

"So?" Jonathan was getting annoyed at having to drag this out of Willson.

"She called back and said the doctor hadn't seen Andrew in several months and he was uncomfortable certifying to his death."

"Could Rebecca think of anyone else to call? An autopsy is ugly."

"I asked. The thought of their cutting up Andrew. It was gruesome. Funny."

"What's funny?"

"Rebecca seemed to be rather pleased."

"Yikes."

"Do you think the press will find out about the autopsy?" Willson was fidgeting. Moving things on his desk without seeming aware of it.

"Probably not, but who knows?"

"My God, I don't want there to be any publicity." A red streak rose on his neck.

"I don't think there will be."

"But what if there is?"

"I don't see how that can be helped."

"But. . ."

Jonathan had never seen an upset Sandhill Crane. The sight almost made him laugh. He stifled the impulse behind a cough and cleared his throat.

"I understand, Peter. We'll just have to deal with that as it develops. You don't think there was any question about Grahm's death, do you?"

"Of course not."

"The police may want to talk to the curator who found Grahm. What did you say her name was?"

"Ailene Brown." Willson seemed to deflate. "She'll bad mouth me." The desk phone rang again. This time Willson ignored it.

"Why?"

"She was one of the worst of the rabble-rousers. And she was very close to Grahm."

"What does that mean?" This was going to be bad.

Willson hesitated. He shook his head.

"Come on, Peter. This is all confidential. I'm on your side."

"There was a rumor they were having an affair," he said reluctantly.

"Good Lord, Peter. Have you ever heard of sexual harassment? He was her supervisor. Where was your H.R. person?"

"We don't have one right now. She quit, and I didn't replace her. I outsourced it. I thought I could save some money." He looked down at his clasped hands that were resting on his desk.

"I don't think that was a very good idea."

Willson looked hunted. "I can see that."

"Swell. Is there a chance she'll go to the press?"

The question startled Willson. "Why?"

"She might claim that all the pressure caused Grahm's heart attack."

"I don't know." Willson gave a helpless shrug. He looked like he wanted to wring his hands. "Everything is going wrong."

"We need to consider that she might."

Willson hesitated again. "Do you think you could see her." He was almost pleading. "Make her feel like I'm on her side?"

Jonathan paused to consider how deeply he wanted to be involved in Willson's troubles. He decided that since Tae Aaron wanted him to help, he could go a little further. "I can try. I don't know how receptive she'll be."

"I'll have to call some of the board members," Willson said. "Just to prepare them if anything gets in the press."

Almost as an afterthought, Jonathan said, "Is Grahm's body still in his office."

"Goodness, no. We had an ambulance take him away as soon the police left."

"Can I look?"

"At his office? Why would you want to do that?" Willson clearly didn't like the idea.

"Curiosity more than anything else. And it might prove helpful."

"Won't the police object?"

"It's not a crime scene," Jonathan said. "I don't see a problem." Jonathan was always a curious kind of guy. He really had no other purpose than seeing how a big time curator lived. Or in this case died.

"Oh, all right," Willson said with a grudging tone. "I'll take you."

"Can Rufus stay here?"

Willson stared at Rufus, who stared back.

"Absolutely not."

Chapter 28

Jonathan looked over the splendidly appointed office. The rain had stopped early that morning. The air was fresh. The clouds were white and streaked as if someone had taken a rake to the sky. Light spilled in on the rich red carpeting, gleaming off the polished wood.

"This is really grand," Jonathan said. "It's even bigger than yours." Jonathan, who had seen his office shrink as he rose through the partnership ranks at Whiting & Pierce, was astonished at the extravagance in the not-for-profit world. They weren't as concerned about costs. Anyway, they owned the building.

Peter Willson raised an open hand. "The office was his before I was hired. I didn't want to make a fuss. Besides, I'm not insecure."

Oh, right, thought Jonathan.

"A lot of the things in here are his," Willson continued. "Andrew liked to show off."

Rufus attracted Jonathan's attention. "Rufus, sit," he instructed.

Rufus ignored him, as usual, and continued to snuffle at a dark spot in the carpet. Rufus liked to explore new places. Jonathan continued to inventory the contents of the office in his mind.

He walked to Andrew Grahm's desk and started looking over the items and mementos. A noise caught his attention. Rufus had begun to lick at the carpet.

"What do you have there, boy?" Jonathan said. He moved to Rufus, then knelt down and touched the rug. It was wet. He smelled his finger tips. Jonathan knew that smell. Port. Then he saw the empty port bottle sitting on the side table.

"Where's the glass?" Jonathan asked.

Peter Willson shrugged. "Someone probably picked it up. I must get them to be more thorough," he said, looking at the bottle with distaste.

"But where is it?"

"I have no idea. I suppose they washed it and put it away."

Rufus continued to lick at the carpet. Jonathan pulled him away by the collar. "We can't have a drunk dog, Rufus. I don't want to have to send you to A.A." He shook his finger at the dog. Rufus licked it. He was quite proud of his tongue action.

Jonathan turned back to Willson, wiping his finger on his tweed jacket. As soon as he let go of Rufus's collar, Rufus returned to the port. He had a mind of his own. Besides the stuff tasted good and he had never had it before.

Two hours later, Jonathan returned to their apartment on Central Park West. Rufus had joined him. Jonathan was sitting at the small desk, focused on balancing his checkbook, which was an absolute mess. Rufus lay on the floor making desperate sounds. Jonathan looked down.

"It serves you right," he said severely.

Rufus was still lying on the floor crying an hour later when Nicole came home.

She immediately got to her knees and rubbed his fur. Rufus looked up at her weakly.

"What is wrong with Rufus?" she asked.

"He's drunk."

"He is drunk?" she said. Her voice was incredulous with a hint of concern and perhaps blame. Jonathan paid more attention.

"Yes," he said. "He licked up a carpet full of port at the Nauton."

"Cheri, he does not look good."

"What about me?"

"No, really, I think we should take him immediately to the veterinarian."

"Come on, he's just drunk."

"I do not care. I cannot see him suffer so."

"But what about dinner?"

Nicole gave Jonathan a look any husband understands.

"Right," he said. "Let's go." A good response.

Three hours after they arrived, the vet emerged from his examining room wiping his hands on a towel.

"You're very lucky."

Nicole sat up very straight with a distressed smile battling concern at the edges.

"We almost lost him."

"Lost him!" Jonathan said more loudly than he had intended, bolting forward. This wasn't good. Not on his watch. Fortunately, Nicole was ignoring him. She had her hand to her mouth and was staring at the vet.

"Please," was all she could say.

"He was poisoned. I had to pump his stomach."

"What?" Jonathan said.

"How?" Her voice was trembling.

"I don't know," said the vet. "But it was powerful. The little guy almost gave in."

"Will he be all right?" Nicole asked.

"He'll be fine now."

"Can I see him?"

"Of course. He's asleep. He's had a hard day."

"But did you save anything?" Jonathan interrupted.

The vet looked at him sharply.

"I mean we need something to test."

"No. Of course not." The vet's voice had an edge to it. "But, as I said," he replied assertively, "Rufus will be okay."

At that moment, Jonathan wasn't thinking about Rufus. He was thinking about the port bottle or getting a sample from the carpet in Grahm's office to send to Frankee Perone. Frankee was the private security specialist and ex-FBI Agent Simon and he had employed many times over the years.

He needed to know what was going on. Something was very wrong.

Chapter 29

He made the call to Peter Willson a week later.

"Peter, it's Jonathan Franklin."

"Hello, Jonathan. I'm running. Is it something important?" A lunch was one thing, but Jonathan Franklin didn't have enough money to become a nuisance. Besides he felt he had said too much to Jonathan and he didn't want to compound the problem. The lawyer had even insisted on taking samples of the rug in Grahm's office. It was ridiculous.

"I just had a crazy thought," Jonathan said. "It just came to me."

How nice, thought Willson. Grand of you to call me and share. "Oh," Willson said in a neutral tone.

"It's about the Nicholson paintings Sir Adrian gave to the museum."

Willson became marginally more interested. "What about them?"

"You sent them out to have them authenticated."

"Of course. After Andrew's death it was the first thing that we did. I have the initial results. Everything about them is consistent with the pictures being genuine."

"But you still have concerns?"

"I don't, but Andrew was very vocal about his conclusions among the curatorial staff. And the analysis doesn't prove the negative, of course. I can't just declare them authentic. It would raise more questions than it would resolve." Where was Franklin going with all this?

"Peter, have you thought about doing a forensic analysis on the pictures?"

"What are you talking about?"

"I mean a forensic analysis like the police do at a crime scene. Fingerprints, fabric, dust analysis, microscopic examination."

Willson went quiet. This guy was really off the wall. He had never heard of anything like this in the art world. And he had no desire to be the laughing stock of the curatorial staff. That would be the end. Maybe Franklin had been drinking. He didn't know much about him.

"Jonathan, no crime had been committed. I don't follow you."

"That's what I mean about the idea being crazy. Nicholson was a modern painter, right?"

"Well, I guess that depends on what you mean by modern. Nicholson died in the late '80s. He was an old man."

"Perfect." Jonathan sounded excited. "There's a lot of his stuff around, isn't there. I mean, he was famous."

"He's quite famous and he painted a lot of pictures."

"No, I mean property he handled. Places where he lived. They save those sorts things from famous people."

"I suppose so."

"Look, Peter. Forensic science has made incredible leaps over the last decade. They can do things and make links they never could before. Maybe Nicholson cut his finger and we can get DNA. Who knows. Paint is sticky. There could be hairs or fabric stuck to it. And there will be a lot of comparison samples if he was famous. It may be stupid, but I think it's worth a try. Sir Adrian had a lot riding on this."

"Oh, what?"

Jonathan had over-stepped. He didn't want to go into it. He couldn't. He improvised. "He wants to do the right thing."

Willson now was interested. He might score here. Be a hero to the Board. An innovative Director. Maybe it was worth the chance.

"Who would do such an analysis? We don't want the police involved. We've had enough of that." Willson's voice was quiet, but assertive.

"I don't know, but I know who can find out and get it done for you. We use a security firm that's first rate."

"That sounds expensive. Will it cost a lot of money?"

"Maybe. But you know, I believe that Sir Adrian would be willing to put up the money."

"He's quite angry with us."

"Let me talk to him."

"We must have no publicity." If this turned out to be foolish, he could bury it.

"Of course not."

Willson made a decision. He was proud of himself.

"If Sir Adrian will put up the money, I see no reason why we shouldn't go forward. No reason at all."

Chapter 30

The money was a problem. A very real one. Not that he didn't have it. He did. All $250,000 in cash Atkins had had delivered to him. $200,000 for the deposits and $50,000 for the paralegal.

But he wasn't a fool. You could get caught taking it out of the country. With all the drug trafficking, customs was all over it and the Feds put you away for money laundering. That's why Alex Kinsky was putting the arm on the kid.

"Look, it's a free vacation. Take your girlfriend." He was telling, not asking. He paused and listened.

"No one's going to go through your luggage looking for an envelope. Put it in your briefcase, with some other papers. Hell, let your girlfriend carry it." He was becoming annoyed with the little twerp. Damn paralegals. This one sounded like a lawyer.

"You want the $40,000 or not?" Kinsky listened to the whining voice. The edge of his lip curled up. "I don't give a shit what you think." The kid didn't need to know the man had given him $50,000.

"If this money doesn't get to the Caymans, there's no deal." He paused. "Screw you," he said with a snarl.

There was a silence for a moment on the other end of the phone. He could wait. The kid wasn't going anyplace. Or more precisely, he was.

"That's better," he said more calmly, in response to the reply. "We'll meet in an hour at the same place. You get $20,000 now. The rest when you come back with the receipt."

He stopped again. "Oh, by the way, if the thought occurs to you to keep going with my money, that wouldn't be a good idea. For you, I mean." He said it almost conversationally, which made it sound all the more menacing.

The kid's response was fervent and sincere.

"Okay. Just so you know."

Four days later, he called the man he knew as William Atkins. "The money's in the account. No fingerprints on it at all."

Victor Rollins spoke for a moment. His instructions were precise. Kinsky scratched notes on a pad of waste paper. This didn't make sense. He started to question the instructions. Rollins cut him off. "Do it," Rollins said and abruptly hung up.

Kinsky got on his jacket and locked up the office. He hailed a cab in the street and took it across town to a small Internet café three blocks from Simon Aaron's office. He found a computer towards the back where there were no people hanging around. The place was pretty quiet at this time of day.

The computer booted up quickly, and he typed in the Cayman Islands broker's e-mail address. He placed an order in the name on the account he had opened. He purchased 2,000 calls expiring in 30 days, allowing him to purchase 200,000 shares of HST Heartcare at today's market price. The calls cost almost exactly $200,000. Kinsky authorized the transfer from the Cayman's bank account to cover the purchase.

The trade would be confirmed to the G-mail account he had set up from Simon's office. He shut down the computer and paid in cash at the register. As he walked down the street, he called the man he knew as Atkins on his cell phone.

"It's done," was all he said, before disconnecting.

Victor Rollins smiled to himself. That was the hard part. He picked up the phone and called a reporter at the Wall Street Journal who had been accommodating in the past. He liked reporters with ambition. They were always useful.

"HST Heartcare is in negotiations to be acquired," he said. "At least, that's what I hear." He listened. "The final stages of negotiation." He stopped again. "You can't use my name, but I thought you'd want the scoop."

Rollins knew that even if anyone asked, which was unlikely, the reporter would protect his source. Probably even if they threaten to put him in jail. Even if the reporter cracked, he hadn't done anything wrong. He'd just passed on a rumor.

Now, for just one more call. He dialed his broker in London. It took a moment for him to come to the phone, but just a moment. Vincent Rollins was not a nice man but he was an important person in the world of finance. There were many men like him.

"I want you to buy six-month puts at market for one million shares of Witten's common stock." He listened to the response. "That's right, one million shares. Spread it around. I don't want my name on it."

He listened to what the broker had to say, and then he spoke more firmly. "I know the word in the City is Witten's is doing well. I think the City's wrong. But let me make it clear. I want the right to sell one million shares, at today's market price. Just do what I tell you." He hung up. Why did everyone have a question?

Now all he had to do was wait. He felt better than he had in a long time. It was a pleasant feeling.

Chapter 31

Ailene Brown wasn't quite what she seemed. One of her classmates at Princeton, an English girl, had summed it up succinctly.

"She's no better than she should be," she had said, with an unladylike snort.

Ailene Brown knew what they were saying about her, and she didn't care. At least not that much. She had just snagged the prized MOMA internship with a strong recommendation from her art professor. It was rumored she was sleeping with him.

She looked like such a nice girl, with her big, brown innocent eyes. But her figure made heads snap. She worked hard to keep it that way. Men had pursued her all her life.

She was smart. It ran in the family. Her father had been a leading anesthesiologist at a large Memphis hospital. The best black hospital in the State. Her mother had taught Women's Studies at Rhodes College.

Her father was respected in Memphis, but he was a lousy investor and his losses had led to arguments between her parents late at night. They thought she was asleep. But she lay on her bed and listened to her mother's angry voice and her father's excuses. It terrified her.

She didn't find out until much later about his gambling habit. He had taken an overdose of narcotics from his cart when she was eight.

Her mother had always been high strung. She went into a downward spiral after the suicide. All of the financial problems overwhelmed her. They lost the house. Her mother committed suicide three years after her father's death. But she did do one thing right.

The lawyer her mother hired to sue the hospital where her father had been on staff settled the lawsuit the same month her mother died. They paid $1 million. The lawyer had taken $400,000 and another $50,000 he had said was for expenses. The court had placed the rest of it in a trust fund for her.

She never told anyone about the money. She remembered the foreclosure six months after her father death. Walking down the driveway of her home for the last time, her little suitcase clutched in her small hand. It had been a hot and muggy day. She held her doll against her chest in the other hand. Her mother was crying.

"It's okay," she had murmured to the doll. "We're going to be okay. Don't cry. I'm here for you." She never felt like she had a home after that. They moved from apartment to apartment. She never had time to make friends.

There always seemed to be so little. After her mother's suicide, she went to live with her mother's sister in New York City. She had just turned 17. And she did well in high school. But her aunt resented her and it was roundly reciprocated.

On her application to Princeton, she had emphasized her minority status. The bleak financial situation set forth on her application had demanded a scholarship.

Ailene Brown went into art because she thought it was the surest way to meet the kind of people she wanted to know. She went into theater because she liked it.

As with most women of her generation, she discovered sex in high school. She enjoyed it well enough, but what fascinated her was the power it seemed to give her over men. It made her feel stronger.

She was very choosy about the men she dated. She was very good at being bad. But there was always that lurking fear she could never extinguish.

She put down the telephone and laughed aloud. She had been expecting the call. Her green silk lounging suit had been a gift to herself when she had gotten the job at the Nauton. It was very flattering. She liked to reward herself.

The man had said his name was Jonathan Franklin. Peter Willson had asked him to call. Yes, she would see him, but she needed a week to steady herself after the awful shock of finding Andrew's body.

When Andrew Grahm had come around to MOMA, he had been obvious. It had been an exceptional offer. And Andrew was an attractive and intelligent man. She had needed a mentor.

But there had been a change in Andrew lately. She was attuned to his moods. She had sensed his intangible distancing from her. It was too bad he had to die. Yet he had really exhausted everything he could teach her.

And he was alienating everyone. Good Lord, he was on the verge of doing irreparable harm to the Nauton. Then where would the curatorial staff be?

So she had to think about this meeting with Peter Willson's man. Was this a turning point? Willson could certainly be useful. He had a lot of connections. But she needed to understand his motivation.

She sighed as she settled down and poured herself a glass of white wine. She always enjoyed the falling snow. The first snow. It made her feel content. Sometimes it was nice to be alone. She raised her glass.

"Happy holidays."

Chapter 32

"What you got for me?" Lt. Julian Wayne was in an unusually bad mood. Even for him. His stomach was acting up again. It was eight days after Andrew Grahm's death.

He popped another Tums into his mouth, washing it down with cold coffee. He stared past Detective Robert Tritter at the pale green wall at the back of his small office. The paint was peeling at the corner. The office smelled of stale coffee and cigarette smoke.

"I think I'm gettin' an ulcer," he said sourly. His gravy-spotted tie was pulled down and his jacket was thrown over the only other chair in the room.

That was okay. Bobby Tritter had no desire to sit down. He felt as if he were walking through a minefield. You couldn't side step as fast if you were sitting.

There was no way to please this guy. Smart maybe, but he had the disposition of an old rhino with a sore tooth. One with no desire to have it plucked out.

That was on a good day. This one wasn't. Six open homicides, and the Superintendent was beating the bejezzus out of them. What with the cold, New Yorkers seemed to have undertaken a determined campaign to hold down the population.

Tritter steeled himself and started. "Andrew Grahm. You know, the curator at the Nauton Museum."

"Yeah, I remember. I saw the report. Dropped dead of a heart attack."

Tritter hesitated. Wayne wasn't going to like this. "Uh. . ." he spoke hesitantly, "they just forwarded the autopsy report."

"Shit," Wayne said, looking up with a snarl.

"Yeah, he had a big dose of nicotine in him."

"What the fuck? Was he eating cigarettes?"

"The Medical Examiner said he had enough nicotine in him to cause his death, but he died of a heart attack first."

"Yeah. Okay. I got it already. So?"

Tritter was sweating. He never liked to answer the simple questions Wayne posed to him. It usually ended up with Wayne ripping him a new orifice. But he couldn't see a way out. He paused as long as he could, hoping Wayne might go on.

All he got was a stare that seemed to grow. He sighed to himself and cast his soul on the waters. "I think he may have been murdered."

"You're a fuckin' detective, Tritter. At least, that's what the great city of New York believes. You don't guess. You specially don't think. What the hell's wrong with you? Are you some kind of idiot?"

Tritter just nodded. It was safer. Then he screwed himself up to continue. "But, you see, nicotine is a deadly poison, Lieutenant. One of the deadliest. At least that's what the M.E. said."

"So, I'm poisoning myself smoking? Am I going to die of it before I get cancer? No, I don't think so." Wayne was on a roll.

"It's not the same. I mean you are poisoning yourself, but you aren't." Tritter always stumbled on his thoughts when he was under a lot of stress. Like right now.

Wayne was starting to redden. Never a good sign in Tritter's experience. "What the fuck are you talking about? I never heard such crap."

Tritter stepped back a pace. "I mean, it's not nicotine poisoning. There's not enough of it in a cigarette."

"Oh great. Just what I need. Some pissant smokes himself to death and fucks up my life." Wayne looked directly at Tritter. He pointed an accusatory finger. "No, you are fucking up my life, Tritter. Are you trying to ruin my Thanksgiving, or is it just stupidity?"

Tritter took a gulp. He had a feeling about this and somehow he couldn't let it go. "The M.E. says the guy was wearing a patch, actually a couple of them, to, you know, help him stop smoking. But it wouldn't be enough to kill him."

"So maybe he smoked a couple of cigarettes."

"I looked through the reports, sir. There were no cigarettes or ash found in his office."

"He might have flushed them down the toilet."

"Maybe, Lieutenant." Tritter sounded doubtful. He wasn't sure exactly why.

Wayne continued. "And do you realize, Tritter, assuming you're right, if you should happen to find the alleged person who wanted this guy dead, you have to prove, I mean prove, he was the guy who slipped this Grahm the mickey. You know," he expanded unpleasantly, "got the poison, had the chance to get it in this joker's food, drink, whatever, and send him on his way with a little pat on the ass."

Tritter nodded again.

"And this occurred how long ago?"

"A week, more or less." Tritter said it softly.

Wayne's response was not. "So, we got a real cold trail. No crime scene with, like, physical evidence. You know, fingerprints, fiber samples, photos. The stuff we use to detect." He said it as if it was Tritter's fault. "And, you're aware, what with your college training and all, that if a murder isn't solved within the first 48 hours, the chances go to zip."

Tritter nodded again. He seemed to have lost his voice in this storm of sarcastic reason.

"Have you ever heard of a murder trial for death by fucking nicotine?"

"No," ventured Tritter rather sheepishly.

"You know how many cases I got on my desk and how much overtime I'm puttin' in trying to keep the shit from rising up over my nose here."

Tritter, just stood there. He didn't know whether to nod or not. Best to stay still.

"And you have any idea what the D.A.'d say to me, assumin' he ever stopped laughin', if I brought him a case based on circumstantial evidence in a fuckin' matter as ludicrous as this?"

Tritter hadn't even known that Wayne knew the word 'ludicrous.'

"And you want me to deal with those museum assholes walking up on my tiptoes. I ain't good at tiptoes, Tritter."

An image flashed in Tritter's mind and he turned his head away quickly.

"Now let me tell you what I want."

Tritter leaned a little forward.

"I want you to stick that file up your goddamned ass and get the hell out of my office." Wayne slammed his fist down on his desk almost simultaneously with the slam of the door, as Tritter made a hasty exit. Cold coffee spilled all over the file he was reading. "Shit," shouted Wayne to the empty room as the coffee seeped into the pages.

The only thing was, Bobby Tritter had an itch about this one. He just didn't like it. He couldn't let go. No matter what Wayne thought.

It was a problem with a capital "P."

Chapter 33

"You must think I'm foolish." Ailene Brown was in a state somewhere between anxiety and defiance, fighting a border skirmish for her dignity and not doing so well. "I'm embarrassed."

Jonathan, who had known Ailene Brown for 15 minutes, was a little taken aback. What did she care what he thought. Was she emotionally exhausted, or maybe some kind of drama queen?

They were sitting in the living room of Ailene Brown's apartment. Jonathan found it overheated. He was uncomfortable.

"I made an idiot of myself in front of Peter Willson," she said. "Like some silly girl." She stopped and seemed to be reliving the scene in her mind. "The shock. I literally waltzed into Andrew's office. I had been away for two weeks in Europe. I got back over the weekend. And he was lying there, dead. I was going to tell him all about it."

"It had to be traumatic. I mean to find the body of a colleague." Jonathan was surprised she agreed to see him so readily. He found Ailene Brown quite attractive, which her inner struggle only accentuated.

She looked about 27, with milk chocolate skin and slender hands that she couldn't seem to keep still. Her brown eyes were round and intense. Her mouth was wide, showing even white teeth. There was a small gap in her front teeth that gave her a childlike air of innocence. Jonathan found it very fetching.

"I admired Andrew. He cared about art and the museum. He was a scholar, not some showman." Jonathan surmised she was referring to Peter Willson. She clearly didn't think much of Peter Willson. He would have to tread carefully. Willson was right.

"I had that impression."

"I don't know what we're going to do without him," she said and started to tear up.

Jonathan reached into his pocket and handed her a handkerchief. She dabbed at her eyes and sniffled. "Thank you," she said, returning the cotton square.

"Let me assure you that the museum will do everything it possibly can to spare you further pain. You've been through a lot." Jonathan was feeling a bit of the cad. He was manipulating an upset woman. But part of him felt as if he was helping her.

Ailene Brown was wearing a simple dress that emphasized her slim figure, and its cut showed a pair of shapely legs. She crossed them, pushing up the hemline of her dress. It was starting to distract him. He struggled to concentrate on the task at hand. She seemed oblivious to his problem.

"Do you want to come back to work at the museum? You can. Peter really wants you to. He said you were invaluable." It was a lie, but it was well intentioned.

"I don't think I could face the people. Certainly not Peter Willson. I'll have to find another position."

He liked that. She was being realistic.

"Peter suspected you might feel that way. He asked me to assure you that he'll be supportive. He thought you did a fine job. Of course, the museum will continue to pay your salary while you look."

"Mr. Franklin. . ."

"Jonathan, please," he interrupted.

She continued. "Is this all because the museum is afraid I'll sue them? I mean, you are a lawyer, aren't you?"

Now it was Jonathan's turn to feel embarrassed. He hoped his face hadn't flushed. Only his training let him manage a prompt response.

"Well, the answer to that question is yes and no. Let me tell you a joke."

And he told her the joke about the client who was looking for a one-armed lawyer so he couldn't say "On the one hand this, and on the other hand that."

She laughed at the old lawyer joke.

"You see," Jonathan said, "I am a lawyer, but I teach law, I don't practice."

"Where do you teach?"

"Harvard."

She seemed impressed.

"But to get back to your question, the answer is 'Perhaps.'" Jonathan was playing on the lawyer joke.

He smiled and hoped it was a good answer. It must have been because she smiled back. Then she sobered.

"I'm not the kind of a person who would take advantage. Isn't that a funny thing to say? But it's true. I've never wanted to take advantage of anyone. I never even listed my race on my college applications. And I got my job at the museum on the merits. It was damned hard."

"I'm sure." He liked her spunk.

"Look," he said, "Of course, the museum doesn't want you to sue them. The publicity would be bad. But Peter realizes how awful it would be for you too. He just wants to help," Jonathan prevaricated with a lawyerly grace. "This was before he and I ever discussed the possibility of a lawsuit. What he'd like to do, if it's okay with you, of course, is to make some inquiries around to see if there's a good position available. He has a lot of friends out there."

"I'd appreciate that. It's not easy getting a museum position today, with all the budget cuts." She sighed. "It's not like it used to be."

Was she really just 27?

"Are you willing to move someplace else?"

"At the moment, gladly." She emphasized the word "gladly." "I only came to New York to work for the Museum of Modern Art. I don't really like it here all that much."

"Great. I'll tell Peter to go all out on his search. Now, I think we should get you out of here."

She looked up with a startled expression on her face. "What?"

Her apartment was a dozen blocks from the museum. It was a small one-bedroom in a nondescript post-World War II building on Lexington near 62nd that was somewhat worse for wear. But she had decorated it with taste and a decorative flair, the white furniture offset by the colorful modern oil paintings on the walls. Sculpture stood strategically placed on the hardwood floors. Throw pillows and woven rugs gave the room a lived in feel that Jonathan liked.

"Do you have plans for Thanksgiving?"

Her head bobbed from side to side. There was a puzzled expression on her face. But she responded.

"What little family I have is in Memphis. We aren't close. I can't bring myself to travel anyway. I feel exhausted."

"I have a thought."

"Oh?"

"You're too smart for me to try to fool you, so here's why Peter and I think you should get out of here," continued Jonathan. "This whole thing may leak to the press. It probably will. And as you know, they can be merciless. We don't think it would be a good idea for you to be hounded by them. Asking you a lot of questions, or photographing you."

"I don't think I could stand it."

"There is one thing."

"What?" There now was suspicion in here voice as well as anxiety.

"It is possible that the police will want to interview you."

"My goodness. Why? Andrew died of a heart attack."

"Of course. It just would be to make sure they have all the facts. Maybe they won't have to talk to you. I just wanted to alert you to the possibility. And suggest you might want to have me there if they do."

"I'd be so nervous. Please."

"Here's what I suggest. The museum is willing to put you on paid leave until you can find another position. You should go to a hotel for the next couple of weeks."

She laughed. "You don't have any idea how much an assistant curator makes, do you?"

He could see her personality coming through her discomfort. Her eyes were sparkling with humor.

"We'll pay. I've made a reservation at the Waldorf Towers in my name. If you want, I'll go over with you and get you settled."

"You want me to stay in your room. No way." She was almost laughing.

"No way is right. My wife wouldn't appreciate it. I just didn't want to use your name. So think of some name you want to use and we'll change it."

"Let me get this straight. I get paid for doing nothing and have a two-week vacation in a luxury hotel?"

"Yup. Not too bad, is it?"

"I'll do it." Her voice was firm. She seemed glad to break away.

"I'm sorry this has been so hard on you," he said. He wanted to reach out to her.

"Hey, you're nice guy. I'll be lonely. Maybe you could come for lunch. You know, come up and see me sometime." She laughed and vamped.

"Sure. I'd like that," he said, ignoring the urgent signals in his head.

Chapter 34

The item about the HST Heartcare merger appeared in column right on page one of the Wall Street Journal three days after Victor Rollins' telephone call to his London broker, ordering the puts on the Witten's stock. The reporter didn't trade in the stock of HST Heartcare before the item appeared. That was strictly forbidden by the rules of the Journal. Besides, the reporter knew that the S.E.C. would follow its usual procedure and review all recent trades in HST Heartcare to turn up anything suspicious.

He liked his job. In addition, he was Jewish and operated under the theory that no matter what anybody else could get away with, he would go to jail. The HST Heartcare stock jumped nearly 50 percent the same day.

Alex Kinsky retraced his steps to the Internet café near Simon Aaron's office the morning after the Wall Street Journal article appeared. He had been rousted out of bed at 6:30. He hated that. His instructions had been terse and specific. No questions to be asked.

He logged in and ordered the sale of the HST Heartcare options. The proceeds came to $1.2 million. He wished he could figure out a way to get his hands on some of it. It was frustrating having that kind of money pass through his hands without even getting a taste.

Following the rest of his instructions, he pulled up a new application form at the Cayman Islands' brokerage firm and filled it out. The name he typed on the application form was the same as on the second postal box he had rented at the UPS store.

He then ordered 50 percent of the profits, almost $500,000 exactly, be transferred into the new account. He instructed that the statement be sent to the second UPS box he had opened previously. He signed off, paid in cash at the register, and left.

Alex Kinsky didn't understand what was going on. He had assumed William Atkins would want him to transfer the $1.2 million to another account in the Caymans. Then they would send it out of the Caymans. Just in case anybody came looking.

That's what they'd always done before. It was a lot of money. He had no idea why he had been told to establish a second account. Not at the same broker. He thought that was stupid. Maybe Atkins was getting sloppy. He'd have to watch that. After all, it was his ass, too. But he wasn't being paid to ask questions.

For that matter, he wasn't being paid enough for the risks he was taking, even with what he could skim. He and Atkins would have to have a talk about that one of these days soon, he decided.

Chapter 35

"Professor Franklin! I'm surprised to see you here." It was 10 past 10 in the morning. The wind had kicked up and was banging at the windows. A sound you could barely hear over the hum of the forced air heating. Jonathan had answered the knock on the door to Ailene Brown's suite at the Waldorf.

Jonathan smiled and extended his hand. "I'm pleased you remembered me, Detective Tritter. It's been a long time."

"You're a hard one to forget. Lieutenant Wayne still goes on about you, you know."

"Yes, I'm sure he's not my biggest fan."

"Well, actually, you're both right and wrong."

"You don't say." Jonathan's curiosity was piqued.

They had made their way into the sitting room. Jonathan was still limping a little.

"You okay?" Tritter inquired.

"Oh, yeah. Just a run in with a pizza box."

Tritter gave him a funny look.

"I tripped over it. Or rather slid."

"Ouch," Tritter said as they entered the living room of the suite.

"Make yourself comfortable, Detective." Jonathan motioned to a chair. Tritter instead chose the green striped settee. Jonathan took the matching chair.

"I'm surprised Lt. Wayne didn't come himself." Strangely, the remark seemed to make Tritter uncomfortable.

"He was busy," he said. He was looking around as he spoke. "This is a pretty nice suite. How can Ms. Brown afford it?"

"She can't. The museum is paying for it. We wanted to give her some peace from the press. She'll be right out. Powdering her nose, I think the phrase is."

"We?" Tritter said, picking up on the "peace" remark.

"I'm helping the museum out."

"Really?" He sounded skeptical. "I thought you taught law."

"I do, but I'm on a leave of absence. I just got married."

"Well, congratulations."

"Thanks, but tell me about Lt. Wayne. I'm pleased he speaks about me. I always thought he hated my guts." Jonathan was always interested in how people perceived him. Particularly if it was favorable.

"He does."

"Oh," Jonathan said, a little deflated.

"But he also thinks you're real smart."

It was a trait Jonathan had cultivated since his teenage years. Hold back. Don't venture out except to parry someone's idea. People think you're smart. It made him smile.

"He really does," Tritter emphasized, seeing Jonathan's smile as doubt. "You know, he's real bright, too. You wouldn't think it, not the way he talks, but he's got a good mind. Kind of self-educated. Always reading something. I went to college and have a master's degree, but let me tell you, he's hard to keep up with. He really is analytical. But I think he's insecure."

Join the club, Jonathan thought.

Tritter continued. For some reason, he seemed to like Jonathan. "That's why I think he's so grumpy. It's a theory I have. Insecurity. You know, kind of like an actor's ego tantrums."

"It's an interesting theory."

"Yes it is," said Ailene Brown, entering the room. "What are you talking about?"

"Ms. Brown," Tritter said. Both Tritter and Jonathan started to stand. She motioned for them to remain seated. "I'm Detective Tritter of the NYPD." He pulled out his wallet showed his badge. "I assume Professor Franklin is acting as your lawyer." She nodded, looking at Jonathan with uncertainty in her eyes.

He nodded back imperceptibly. He admired her poise. She'd been frightened this morning when she called him after receiving an unexpected call from Tritter. Peter Willson must have given Tritter the number. Even the

NYPD wasn't that good. He would have to speak to Willson about better coordination.

"Can I get you something to drink, Detective Tritter?" she asked, gesturing towards the hotel minibar. He shook his head. She settled onto the chair across from Jonathan and placed her hands in her lap. She looked up inquisitively at Tritter and tilted her head. It gave a feeling of close attention to what was to be said.

He fumbled in his jacket pocket and withdrew a note pad. "Ms. Brown, what is your position at the museum?"

"I'm an assistant curator."

Tritter opened the pad and made a note with a Cross mechanical pencil that appeared in his hand.

"How long have you been with the museum?"

Jonathan thought he knew the drill. A bunch of softball questions to get the person comfortable. He brought himself up with a mental jerk. Dammit, I know way too much about this stuff for a law school professor.

"Almost three years," she responded.

"And before that?"

"I was an assistant at the Museum of Modern Art. That's where I was working when I met Mr. Grahm. He hired me as an assistant curator."

"How well did you know Mr. Grahm?"

It was an innocuous question. Could the police have heard something of the rumored affair?

Something in Ailene Brown seemed to snap. "Mr. Tritter, what are you getting at?" Her voice was angry and a bit strained. Her face darkened. Jonathan was sure she was blushing.

Tritter straightened. He was suddenly very interested.

Jonathan interrupted. "Detective Tritter, this isn't easy for Ms. Brown. The circumstances of Andrew Grahm's death were unfortunate, to say the least. I'm sure you don't suspect Ms. Brown, so could you just ask her what you want to know."

Tritter seemed to be unsettled again. He shifted nervously in his chair. "We have no reason to suspect anyone. I'm only trying to tie up some loose ends."

Good Lord, he sounds like Columbo, Jonathan thought, shaking his head.

"Ask me anything." Ailene Brown's voice was normal again. She seemed to have regained her poise with Jonathan's interruption. "I'll be happy to tell you whatever you want, Detective. Please excuse me. I'm just a little stressed out. Nothing like this has ever happened to me, but I've got nothing to hide."

"Thank you, Ms. Brown," Tritter said, seemingly satisfied. "Can you just tell me what happened?"

"I'll try. Let me see." She paused and she closed her eyes as she thought back. Then she refocused. "I came to Andrew's office around 8:30 in the morning. That's after the time he usually gets in and he always pokes his head into my office to say hello. I noticed the time and was curious why he didn't come by. I thought perhaps he didn't know I was back from vacation."

Tritter nodded, as he continued making notes in tiny letters. He looked up at Ailene Brown inviting her to continue.

"So I went to his office. I found Andrew on the floor. He looked pasty white. I've never seen a dead person before."

She stopped and gave a little shiver at the recollection.

"I'm sorry to put you through this, Ms. Brown," Tritter said, "but please go on."

"Yes. I guess I ran over and kneeled beside Andrew. I don't remember doing it. I tried to shake him, but he wouldn't stir. Then I noticed he wasn't breathing. I must have screamed because a secretary came running in. She called Peter Willson, I guess."

"Do you remember anything about the room? I mean anything that was unusual or out of place?"

"Well, my slacks were wet at the knees where I was knelling by Andrew. They were soaked completely through. I had to throw them away."

"The port," said Jonathan.

"Port?" Tritter said.

"Yes, a bottle spilled on the floor."

"How do you know it was port?"

"My dog was licking at the carpet, so I smelled it."

Tritter made a note and turned back to Ailene Brown.

"What happened then, Ms. Brown?"

"Mr. Willson sent me home. I don't even remember how I got to his office. I guess I was in some kind of shock or something."

Tritter stirred and focused more closely on her. "Ms. Brown, did you have a relationship with Andrew Grahm?"

Jonathan expected her to hit the ceiling. He instinctively tightened his grip on the arm of his chair.

All she said was "Yes."

Well there you are, Jonathan thought. A perfect lawsuit. It was a good thing he was involved. And a better thing that Ailene Brown said she wasn't going to sue. He'd have to stay very close to Ailene Brown until this whole thing was resolved.

"You did know Andrew Grahm was married, didn't you, Ms. Brown?" Tritter said.

"Yes, but he wasn't happy." She stopped and broke eye contact with Tritter and looked down at her hands. "Never," she said, shaking her head, her eyes starting to tear up. "Detective Tritter," she said without raising her eyes, "I'm not some husband-stealing bitch. What Andrew and I had was special. I never intended to become involved with him. We were in love. We were going to get married."

She stopped again and looked up at Tritter. "I know he had a reputation as a womanizer. Everyone knew."

Certainly not Jonathan. He'd have to make a note to follow up with Willson.

"But, it was . . . Look I know this sounds corny, but it was magical. He was such a brilliant and exciting man."

"Ms. Brown, do you know a Barbara Nadine?"

"Of course, Detective. Everyone in the world of Contemporary Art does. She is one of our most outstanding young artists. As a matter of fact, Andrew and I discussed her not more than three weeks ago. Andrew was putting together an exhibit called 'Artists for the New Millennium.' He was not going to include her work. It made me quite angry. But he refused. He was quite curt with me. I couldn't understand it."

"What was Mr. Grahm's relationship with Ms. Nadine?"

That's a peculiar question, Jonathan thought. He made a mental note to find out why Tritter asked that question.

"He knew her, of course. But there was no relationship," Ailene Brown responded, oblivious to the peculiar nature of the question. Or at least seemingly so.

"Did anyone know about your relationship?" Tritter asked.

She shook her head. "No. He was very careful about our relationship. Very secretive. He didn't want to harm my reputation at the museum."

Or his own, Jonathan mused more cynically.

Tritter glanced down at his notes. "Did you know he had a heart problem?"

"I think we all did. About two years ago, he had a heart attack in the middle of a major reception for the opening of a new exhibit. Everyone was there. The directors, the collectors, the big donors, everyone. It was the talk of the museum for days. Even Mr. Seeling asked me about him. But Andrew came back to work four weeks later and said he was fine."

"Did Mr. Grahm smoke?"

"He was trying very hard to give it up. It was very difficult for him. His job was very stressful."

"Well, thank you for your time, Ms. Brown," Tritter concluded, shutting his notebook. "If you remember anything else, please call me." He handed Ailene Brown his card.

Her resolve crumpled like a paper cup when Tritter left. She ran up to Jonathan and started crying into his best tweed jacket. He put his arms around her to try to comfort her. She pressed herself in to him as a child would. He felt himself start to respond. Yikes.

"You did great," he said, pushing her away and patting her on the back. "I know how hard it must have been."

"It was so awful," she said through her tears. She looked up and sniffled. It was a charming gesture. "Would you mind taking me to lunch? I don't want to be alone right now."

How could he refuse? Besides, he liked her, and he wasn't so sure Tritter was as harmless as he seemed.

They were at a small table at Oscar's, down the escalator at the Waldorf, in the corner away from the windows. Ailene Brown picked at a small salad. Jonathan had always marveled at how little women ate.

"This will be over soon, Ailene," Jonathan said. "A few weeks at most. And Peter told me he's had some good leads for you. Some real opportunities for a full curatorial position at some great little museums."

Jonathan took a bite of his cheeseburger and observed Ailene Brown as he chewed. She seemed receptive. He put down the sandwich. "I think he mentioned the Santa Barbara Museum of Art. Have you ever been there?"

She shook her head.

"I was in Santa Barbara last year." Actually this year too, on his honeymoon, but he didn't mention that.

"It's really great. Small town, but wonderful culture. It looks like Andalusia or Tuscany or something like that. Everyone walks around with a smile." He was laying it on a bit thick.

"You make it sound like paradise." She seemed to be recovering her spirits.

"I don't know. It may be. Great wines too. Did I tell you I own a piece of a winery out there?"

"Really," she said tipping her head to the side and looking straight into his eyes.

The waiter came over with the bill. He hovered close by.

"I guess they want us to leave," Ailene Brown said, smiling at Jonathan.

Jonathan looked around the room. They were the only two people left. He had been totally oblivious.

"I'd like to hear about the Santa Barbara Art Museum," she said brightly, "and your winery." She stood up and he followed. She took his arm.

"Oh shit," was the thought that coursed through his mind.

Jonathan had been attracted to women all his life. Some people at the law school thought he was a womanizer. He thought they were jealous.

And this woman was attractive and intelligent. He was certainly attracted. But it was time to grow up. He loved his wife. For goodness sake, he was newly wed. He almost shook with the effort, but he said, "Gosh, I'd love to," he glanced at his watch, "but I've got another appointment."

She squeezed his arm. "Thank you for everything you've done. You've helped." She stood on her tiptoes and kissed him on the cheek.

Jonathan fled like the hero and coward he was, his mind caressing the idea of what might have happened. He felt good about himself, and he felt he just had to tell someone. Rufus seemed like the ideal choice.

He never knew that Ailene Brown had majored in theater as well as art at Princeton.

Chapter 36

"I have no idea." Simon Aaron made a palms-up gesture that went with his turned-down mouth. "It's never happened before. I got a call from the Securities and Exchange Commission."

"They must have said something," Jonathan said. "I mean, they just didn't say 'How about coming down to Washington for a little chat?' did they?"

Simon tilted his head to the side and pursed his lips. He looked up the ceiling, trying to recollect the conversation. "No. This guy was on the phone. He identified himself as a lawyer with the Enforcement Division. He said the S.E.C. wanted to have an informal conference with me. Could I come to Washington next week. They were extending me a courtesy. "

"So?"

"Well, I asked him what it was about."

"And?"

"He said it was a regulatory matter and perhaps I'd like to be represented by counsel, although it wasn't required. He wouldn't tell me what was up. He said they wanted to discuss it face to face."

"Strange. Any idea what they can be interested in?"

"Not a clue. We've never had a problem at Witten's. At least nothing serious. Our filings are up to date. We filed our last 10-Q two days early. Things are going well. Nothing unusual in that filing."

"Could it have anything to do with Sanford's?" Sanford's was the UK confections company that Simon also controlled. "I know you don't file in the United States, but is there anything?"

"Not that I know of. We don't even do much business here."

"Could they be concerned about the accounting at Witten's? Sarbane-Oxley is still a pretty big deal down there. Any issues with how you report revenues? That's one of their bugaboos."

"We're basically on a cash basis at Witten's. I don't see how there could be an issue with how we report sales. And we've put all the controls in place so I can certify the financials. No, I don't think so. I'll be damned if I know. That's why I called you."

"Maybe it has to do with someone Witten's does business with. Maybe they want information on some of your customers. That would make more sense."

"Yeah, it would. Maybe that's it." Simon sounded relieved. "You don't think it could have anything to do with the tender offer for Quintiles?"

Jonathan shook his head. "Nope. Too soon. They wouldn't have processed our answers to their comments yet."

"Want to come down with me? We'll take the plane."

"Sure. I haven't been to D.C. in a couple of years. It could be interesting."

"Okay. So where are we on the Quintiles deal?" Simon said, changing the subject. That was Simon's persona. Once he had satisfied himself on a matter, he could focus immediately on something new. "Have we gotten the shareholders list?" The shareholders list was crucial to starting the tender. You can't mail an offer to people you don't know.

"Champlin thinks we'll have it next week. They fought us tooth and nail, but Whiting & Pierce pushed them hard. We'll be able to circulate the tender offer in about two weeks."

"Why so long? Can't you control the damn lawyers?"

That made Jonathan laugh and wince simultaneously. He remembered his own experiences with Simon when he was his lawyer, and the scars he still had from those experiences.

"I can. And I have. This isn't their problem. Once we get the list, the proxy solicitors have to input it. There are around 20,000 shareholders and that includes all the shares held by the brokers in street name." Shares brokers hold in client accounts are listed on a company's books in the name of the broker. "We have to get those lists to, at least the ones that are available. It's a pain-in-the-ass process. You've been through it before."

"No," Simon said.

That surprised Jonathan. He looked hard at Simon. "You're kidding. I thought you'd done a tender offer before."

"No. Just mergers. No hostile takeovers. But this is kind of fun."

Simon said it as if he wanted to move on. Jonathan needed to make a point.

"You may not think so when we get further into it. I know that much. They're going to find a way to build defenses and hit back. They'll sue us for something. And they'll do everything they can to make us look unattractive to their shareholders."

"So what. We've got nothing to hide."

Jonathan gave him a pitying look. "Can I get a cup of coffee. I'm really dragging."

"No problem." Simon dialed someone and spoke softly. Then he looked back to Jonathan. "So, go on. I'm really clean. You know that."

"I've already had interesting discussions with some of the major shareholders of Quintiles," Jonathan started again. "I've been led to understand that you're not such a nice guy. Just let me tell you, Simon, when I was doing this, we never played defense. No lawyer would. We always tried to take the fight to the other guy. Rollins and his lawyers will pull out all the stops. They'll dig around and sling every mud ball they can lay their hands on. And there'll be rumors."

"Hey. No problem." Simon's voice was emphatic.

"No one's that clean. No one who's been in business as long as you have. Wait until you find out about your financial problems."

"What are you talking about?"

"Rollins will want people to have second thoughts about tendering. He's not above lying."

A young woman interrupted with a coffee carafe and two cups. She laid it on the edge of Simon's desk. Thank you, Denise," Simon said, nodding at her. When she had left he picked up his thought.

"But that's why we're paying cash for the shares."

"Not if our financing falls apart," Jonathan countered. "And Quintiles' board just passed a poison pill. A poison pill floods the buyer with newly issued shares if a buyer acquires more than 10 percent of the company without the board's approval. But you know that.

"We can't close the tender into it. The flood of shares would kill us. We'll have to go to court to ask a judge to strike it down. It's going to take a while."

"Damn lawyers." One of Simon's favorite phrases.

"I resemble that remark," Jonathan said, quoting a line from an old television show.

"Yeah, but you're in recovery," quipped Simon. "I like you better."

The thought brought a smile to Jonathan's lips. "Anyway, it'll give us time to meet with the rest of the large shareholders and review our offer. There's a lot of hands-on work to do. A lot more than in a friendly deal. It's going to require a lot of face time." Jonathan watched the steam curl out of his coffee cup and took a sip gingerly. "Hot," he gasped, using his free hand to wave at his open mouth.

Simon ignored him. He continued. "How about you handle the legal stuff and the public relations. I'll arrange the financing details and try to drum us up some analyst support. Rollins has been raping Quintile's shareholders for years."

Jonathan stopped waving. "Just remember, we need to get more than 50 percent of the Quintiles shares tendered to us. Actually, more like 90 percent if we can."

"Why?" Just then, Jonathan's cell phone rang. He looked at the caller ID. He clicked it and said "Hi, Frankee." Then he turned to Simon. "It's Frankee Perone," he said. Mind if I take it?"

"What's Frankee for?" Simon asked.

"Nothing to do with us. This is about the mess at the Nauton. You remember, Tae got me involved."

Simon nodded. He rotated his chair to face out the window.

Jonathan started to rise to go into the reception area, but he felt a sudden jolt of pain from his sprained ankle when he put weight on it. It still hurt sometimes. You heal slower with age. He winced. It sent him spilling back. "Sorry," he mouthed to Simon as he rubbed his ankle, the cell phone in the other hand. Simon waved away the apology and motioned for him to sit.

Jonathan turned aside and spoke into phone. "Hey, Frankee, what've you got?"

"I have the forensic report. You'll find this interesting," she said.

"Oh?"

"Those carpet clippings you sent me. You know, from where the guy smoked himself."

"He didn't shoot himself, Frankee."

"No, he smoked himself." Frankee's voice was bright. Her wicked sense of humor was showing.

"What in the heck are you talking about?"

"The carpet fibers show a concentration of nicotine."

"I don't get it."

"Jonathan, nicotine's a poison. It's deadly."

"What was nicotine doing in the carpet?"

"How should I know?"

"Right. Thanks, Frankee. Send over the report. See you soon." He certainly hoped not. When Frankee was involved, there was trouble.

"What's that all about?" Simon asked, rotating his desk chair around as Jonathan closed out the call.

"Some peculiar stuff happening over at the Nauton."

"Nothing to do with us?"

"No."

"Okay, let's get back to our deal. The last time I checked, the Nauton was in the expense category, not income."

"Yes, let's." Jonathan was a lot more comfortable in the world of finance, where the only poison was a poison pill defense.

Simon picked up where they had left off.

"Why do we need 90 percent of the stock? That's tough."

"It is, but we need 90 percent to do a legal cram-down merger and get all the other shareholders out," Jonathan said. So we can own 100 percent of Quintiles. That's what we need to refinance and restructure the company. Otherwise we'll have to keep all the debt on Sanford's books."

"I can do that."

"Sure, but we'll have a lot more flexibility if we own it lock, stock and barrel. And minority shareholders can be a real pain in the ass."

"Tell me about it."

"I just did."

"Don't be a wise ass. You see any problems you can't handle?"

Jonathan chuckled. "No. No way." He had even forgotten about his throbbing ankle.

Chapter 37

"Peter, Derek Lissome.

"Who?"

"Derek Lissome of the Sifford Gallery."

"What can I do for you, Mr Lissome?"

"I was sorry to hear about Andrew Grahm. He was a good friend. It's a real loss to the world of art."

Peter Willson's antenna rose and twitched like an ant in the sunlight. He knew Lissome casually from the art party circuit. He remembered a small man with a swarthy complexion. Eastern European, he would guess. With noticeably small hands. Lissome affected an Ivy League accent, as he recalled.

He was purported to be one of the most successful contemporary art dealers in town. Particularly with a certain type of client. Rumor had it that he had been involved in some nasty litigation in the past year or so. Why was he calling him? Willson looked down and flicked a piece of lint off his trousers.

"Yes, Mr. Lissome, Andrew's loss was a great one for all of us here. He will be sorely missed." Willson was not above gilding the lily a bit himself.

"Please call me Derek. You know, Peter, we really don't see enough of each other. Perhaps we could have lunch together soon."

Willson raised his eyes to the ceiling and yawned. He placed his hand over his mouth to stifle the sound. "I would enjoy that," he finally said, "but I'm afraid, with Andrew's death, and with the matters we have to attend to here, it could be quite a while before I come up for air. I'm really sorry, Derek." Like hell.

"A pity, really, you know. Business matters are always so much better discussed quietly over lunch," Lissome murmured.

"Business matters?" Now Willson was surprised.

"Yes. I was hoping to talk to you about the exhibit that Andrew was putting together. 'Artists for the New Millennium.' I'm quite concerned that Andrew's wishes, his vision if you would, be carried out. And I thought it wise that we discuss it as soon as possible."

"Exactly which of Andrew's," Willson paused a beat, "wishes were you concerned with, Derek?" Willson's voice contained the hint of a cocked eyebrow. He knew as well as anyone that having an artist in a museum show, particularly one entitled "Artists for the New Millennium," at a museum like the Nauton, would add thousands of dollars to an artist's sales price. Many thousands.

It was one of the more troubling things about the museum trend towards contemporary art. They were supposed to be reflecting great art. Not anointing it, for goodness sake. That's why he had opposed Grahm's idea in the first place. But he'd been insistent, and frankly, with all the other problems he was having with Grahm, it hadn't been worth the fight. Besides, he wasn't sure he could win, what with the board being so agitated about everything else that was going on.

Lissome's voice cut into his thinking. "Andrew was very committed to having Arthur DeRuk's work represented. He told me many times that DeRuk was a seminal force in today's art. And perhaps you would now consider Barbara Nadine. The only reason Andrew didn't choose her, of course, was to avoid any question of a conflict."

Willson almost laughed out loud. This man was beyond belief.

"He admired them, you know," Lissome smoothly went on. "Andrew even had several of their pictures in his personal collection."

So that was it. He was pushing his artists. And with Grahm dead, there was no further reason to exclude Barbara Nadine's work from the exhibit. If it went forward, that is. Interesting.

"Derek, I appreciate your calling this to my attention. We haven't yet turned to questions about the exhibit, or how to deal with it."

"You're not thinking of canceling it are you?" Lissome's voice was suddenly anxious.

"We're not sure."

"It would be a great blow to Andrew's memory. He was deeply committed to it, and his name will be associated with it."

"I appreciate your concern and we will certainly consider that when we make our decisions. I want to thank you for calling." Willson clearly wanted the call to end, but Lissome quickly started talking.

"Peter, I want to assure you that the Sifford Gallery would be pleased to extend the same considerations to you that we extended to Andrew."

"Oh?"

"Any art the museum wants to purchase from my gallery would have the same museum discount as before. 50 percent. And Peter, if there is anything you want for your personal collection, we would of course extend to you at least the same discount."

"I appreciate your generous offer, Derek. And I will pass it along. I must ring off. Someone is waiting." That was a lie.

Once again, Willson reflected on the inherent conflict between the museum and the dealers in town. He hadn't exactly been offered a bribe. At least he didn't think so. He wasn't entirely sure.

The museum discount was a standard way for galleries to get their artists into museums and enhance their sales. Museum representation was of prime concern to collectors.

Even discounts to curators were not that usual, though more on the edge. But this bothered him. Maybe it was Lissome's tone of voice. Or maybe it was "50 percent or more."

What was going on that he didn't know about? Whatever faults Grahm had, and God knows there were many, he was a first-class professional. And his reputation was beyond reproach.

But there was always that conflict. Besides the one arising from his relationship with Barbara Nadine. What the blazes was Lissome up to? What had Andrew been doing?

Chapter 38

"Mr. Aaron," the man said, rising from his chair, "I'm A. Winston Wirth and this is my investigator Sam Johansson." He motioned to another man sitting at the table. The man nodded. "Please have a seat." The trip to Washington had been uneventful, but the weather hovered between rain and snow and had made the drive from the airport slow.

The room was bare except for the standard issue Securities and Exchange Commission wooden conference table and chairs. The off-white walls were bare of decoration. The lighting seemed deliberately harsh. There were no windows.

The lawyers seemed to get younger every year. This one looked about 28. Trying to play grown-up in his father's suit. He had a baby face. But he had the eyes of someone who was used to being lied to. Maybe that's why he sounded so rigid.

"This is an informal meeting. We wanted to present you with information we've obtained concerning certain transactions in the stock of HST Heartcare, and allow you the opportunity to explain. You need not respond, but while you are not under oath, I should advise you that lying to a federal official may constitute obstruction of justice, which is a crime."

Jonathan didn't like this at all. This wasn't the way an informal inquiry was supposed to go. It was more like the interrogation of a potential target. He had a bad feeling about this. Simon could be in real trouble, and for the life of him, based on what Simon had said, he had no idea why. What the hell was going on?

"Is this your lawyer?" Wirth inquired, turning to Jonathan.

Jonathan made a quick decision. "Yes. I'm Jonathan Franklin, and I'm representing Mr. Aaron."

That seemed to catch them off guard.

Good, Jonathan thought. I still have something of a reputation around here after all these years. It pleased him that he still commanded respect after his years of practice before the Commission. Simon leaned over and spoke urgently into Jonathan's ear.

"What's this all about?" Simon whispered.

Jonathan ignored him. His attention was focused completely on Wirth. He continued with more confidence. "Mr. Aaron doesn't own any shares of HST Heartcare. We don't understand the reason, or for that matter, the purpose, of this meeting."

In Jonathan's experience with the S.E.C., you had to nip this kind of thing in the bud. Once a civil investigation got rolling, Simon would be in a world of pain, and it would be very difficult to extricate him from the morass. Jonathan wanted to make sure that didn't happen.

Simon looked as puzzled as he felt. It became even stranger when Winston Wirth got up suddenly and without a word, left the room, leaving Sam Johansson sitting there.

And Johansson just sat there.

"What was that all about?" Jonathan asked, an echo of Simon's confusion. Johansson just shrugged and remained silent. His face was impassive.

They all looked at each other for a full five minutes. Simon started to say something but Jonathan put his hand on his arm and gave him a small shake of the head. He didn't want to have any discussion in front of this S.E.C. investigator before he knew what was happening. This whole thing was becoming weird. The silence seemed almost tangible.

The door finally opened. Wirth's return broke the mood. He resumed his seat at the table. His face was fixed in a frown. "We'll have to postpone this meeting," he said. No explanation.

"Why?" Jonathan asked somewhat aggressively. He didn't want to let go at this point. Something was wrong, and this was the best time to press. Maybe he could stop it right here.

"I'm afraid you can't represent Mr. Aaron."

That was a shocker. Jonathan had never heard that one before. The S.E.C. dictating who could and who couldn't represent someone they were investigating? Were they still in America or had something slipped past him?

"You're kidding!" Jonathan said, leaning forward aggressively, his voice hardening. "I'm licensed to practice law in New York, Massachusetts and the

District of Columbia, and I'm qualified to practice before the S.E.C. There's no earthly reason why I can't represent Mr. Aaron."

"I'm sorry, Mr. Franklin." Wirth responded without emotion and started to rise.

"Wait a minute," Jonathan said, in an urgent voice. Now he was really pissed. He wasn't going to let this bureaucrat, this kid, walk out on him. They'd come all the way to Washington for this meeting. It was damned inconvenient for Mr. Aaron and he shouldn't just be shunted aside cavalierly.

"I want to see the Associate Director of Enforcement, and I want to see him now!" Jonathan's voice seethed with suppressed anger.

"That won't do any good, Mr. Franklin," Wirth said, shaking his head, his face set in an infuriatingly passive expression.

"Dammit, I want to know what's going on!" Now Jonathan was almost shouting. He'd experienced nothing like this in his entire career. Simon was looking bewildered.

"You see, Mr. Franklin," Wirth said with what appeared to be the trace of a thin smile, "you're also a potential target of this inquiry."

Chapter 39

"This is nuts!" Simon Aaron shouted, frustration suffusing his voice.

It was 2 a.m. in the morning, the day after the visit to the S.E.C.. That is, if 2 a.m. could be considered the next day. The atmosphere was morose and the three of them seemed to be too many people to occupy the room.

They had rousted Harvey Champlin, Jonathan's former protege, and now head of the Corporate Department at Whiting & Pierce, as soon as they left the S.E.C..

The trip back from Washington had been torturous. Jonathan and Simon buried themselves in their books. There was nothing they could say to each other.

The suite Simon maintained at the Carlyle was fully alight. Simon certainly didn't want to disturb his new wife. Not with this.

Cups of cold coffee sat on the table in front of them. Jonathan had shed his coat, pulled down his tie and rolled up his sleeves in preparation for another long night. He had never been the target of an S.E.C. inquiry. It scared the hell out of him. He didn't like it.

Apparently, neither did Simon. He stood by one of the dark windows, staring at his own reflection.

"Go over it again for me," Harvey Champlin said. Champlin had immediately contacted the S.E.C.. He had just gotten the basics of the matter from his discussions with people there he trusted. The basics were news to Simon and Jonathan.

"There's nothing to go over," Simon said wearily, turning towards Champlin. "They asked us down. They started in. It was almost like they expected me to confess. Then Jonathan introduced himself. And they called off the meeting."

Champlin looked towards Jonathan expectantly.

Jonathan shrugged and lifted one hand, palm up. "I told them I was acting for Simon. Then they said I was a target too. I've got no idea what's going on. None, except that this involves HST Heartcare."

"We represent them. That's the company that just disclosed merger discussions. There was a leak. "

"I know," Jonathan replied, his fatigue showing.

"Do you own any stock? Either of you? Simon," he turned to look at him, "do you?"

They both shook their heads and said "No," simultaneously.

He turned back to Jonathan.

"Do you have anything to do with the company?"

"Well, yes and no."

"Let's start with 'yes.'"

"I'm informally representing Sir Adrian Asheton in a matter involving some paintings he gave to the Nauton. But it has nothing to do with the company."

"Asheton's the chairman, right?"

Jonathan nodded to confirm.

"Did you know about the merger discussions?"

Jonathan paused, then spoke slowly. "Yes, actually. He told me in confidence when he was explaining the background on his issue with the gift."

"Gift?" said Champlin.

Jonathan waved it aside, "Irrelevant."

"I don't know what's relevant. In fact, I don't know anything. So tell me." Jonathan told him the whole story.

"Okay, so he told you about the merger discussions."

"Yes."

"That's not good. You were in possession of inside information."

"So what," Jonathan said rather testily. He was feeling the stress. "Ethically, it was confidential. I certainly didn't use it."

"You never mentioned it where someone might hear you? Never alluded to it in any way in anyone's presence? Say Simon for instance."

"Never. You know how tight we always were with that kind of information. It's second nature to all of us. Good lord, if I tipped anyone, I could lose my license and my professorship. My reputation. No way."

"You forgot 'Go to jail'," Champlin added with a grin.

"Funny," Jonathan responded, not amused.

"Look, I'll contact the S.E.C. and see if I can find out what they have. If I get to them in the morning, I'll call. Jonathan, you'll be on your cell phone?" Champlin paused. "No pun intended."

Jonathan nodded glumly.

"Now," Champlin yawned and stretched as he got up, "why don't we go home and get some sleep."

Simon couldn't leave it alone. Champlin's professional detachment annoyed him. "They can't think we're that stupid. To risk everything for a few dollars profit."

"Simon, it was $1 million in profits.

"That's small change."

"Well, maybe not to guys who make $80,000 a year," Champlin said.

Simon shrugged.

"And does the name Martha Stewart ring a bell?" Champlin carried on. "Remember, how pissed the S.E.C. was when Eliot Spitzer made them look like idiots? They've been on an insider trading vendetta ever since. And they'd like nothing better than to have another high profile case. Right now, you're it."

Chapter 40

Lt. Julian Wayne was having a good morning until he returned the call to Captain Rodriquez. Good days were rare.

His son had finally been accepted at City College. Maybe the kid would move out now. What was he, 23? What kind of man was he raising? Wayne had left home at 17 and good riddance.

And another small miracle. His wife had actually smiled at him this morning.

There was the usual snarl of traffic coming in over the bridge. There had been an accident, of course. Only one. Some kind of a record. But they were tearing up the road again. Always tearing up the road. Wayne believed the city only worked during rush hour. At least he had been some books on tape. He liked Jack Reacher. Reacher just killed the bad guys. Wayne envied him.

The message slip had been on his desk. "Call ASAP." Never good. Rodriquez was an okay guy. He had come up through Robbery-Homicide and knew his business. But he was what Wayne called a stove dancer. When the stove got hot he could really dance.

If there was one thing Wayne hated, it was being asked a question by a superior he couldn't answer. Hell, he even had been surprised by the question this time.

Julian Wayne was not a man to suppress his emotions. He liked to share.

Detective Robert Tritter was shifting from foot to foot in front of Wayne's desk. Wayne was smiling. There was nothing more frightening than Julian Wayne smiling at you.

"I'm impressed by your efficiency, Detective Tritter."

"Thank you, sir." What the hell was this about? He looked around the cramped office to see if anything was different. Nothing. Tritter tried to smile back but lost it in mid-effort.

"I want to thank you for easing our case load around here."

"I'm sorry, sir, I don't understand."

"Of course you do."

"But I haven't cleared any of the cases I'm working on."

"Don't be so modest," said Wayne. The smile returned.

This was bad. Sharks had better smiles than Julian Wayne.

"I know you wouldn't want to disappoint me, Robert."

Robert? "Absolutely not, Lt. Wayne. No." He spoke quickly. There was a little catch in Tritter's voice.

"So tell me how you resolved the Vincent case. I haven't seen your report yet. I thought it was going to be a lot of work. You must have been brilliant."

"But I haven't."

"You haven't what?"

"Closed the Vincent case."

Wayne's face adopted a confused expression. "No? Well, what was the result of Rostioff? The husband did it, right? When did you make the arrest?"

"We're making progress. I think it will be another week or so." Tritter was starting to fell a dampness in his armpits.

"Really?"

"Yes, sir. And all my other investigations are going well. Where we hoped they would be now. I'm very busy." He had to do something to stop this.

"Golly, I'm sorry to hear that. I wanted to assign you the three new cases that just came in."

"I couldn't possibly handle another case, sir."

"Then what the hell have you been doing at the Nauton?" Wayne thundered. His fist hit the desk so hard the paper cup of cold coffee tipped over. Tritter jumped. He watched as the contents dribbled over the corner of Wayne's desk and onto the floor. It made little dark puddles on the linoleum. Next to other dark spots.

Wayne's face was suffused with blood. "I just got a fucking call from the Captain who had just heard from the Mayor. Somebody at the Nauton complained about how we were making all kinds of problems." He paused. "No, how you," he paused again and raised his voice, "you were causing all kinds of problems. The Captain wasn't happy. I'm not happy. And believe me, you're not happy."

Oh shit! "But, I thought. . ."

"We went through this before, Tritter. The New York Police Department doesn't pay you to think. I think for you. It wastes less time."

Tritter nodded bleakly.

"And I thought. . ." Wayne let that sink in. "I was responsible for assigning cases around here and making important decisions like when you can go to the crapper and what our priorities are."

"Yes, Lt. Wayne." Surrender was the best course. Retreat wasn't an alternative. Resistance was futile.

"I told you I didn't want to pursue the Grahm case, didn't I?"

"Yes, but. . ."

"Didn't I?" Wayne's face had gotten a deeper red, if that was possible. This was not a good sign.

"And did you listen to me?"

"No, sir, I just. . . "

"There you go again. Do I seem to be asking for an explanation?"

"No, sir."

"Shut up."

"Yes, sir."

"You know I do your performance report."

Tritter nodded.

"And you do understand that you would have more fucking time to think if you were walking a beat. Queens is always short of smart cops."

"Yes, sir." Tritter's answer was more of a whisper.

"So stop doing it, God damn it. And don't you ever do this to me again."

"No, sir."

"It's a good thing I like you, Tritter." There was that awful smile again. "Get out."

Julian Wayne felt a little better.

Chapter 41

Why do they always get greedy? Vincent Rollins wondered, his lips a straight line, his pale blue eyes hard, as he stared at the dead telephone receiver in his right hand. "He must be an idiot, if he thinks I'll let him do that."

He laughed aloud, a barking sound. "You can't get good help these days." He was amused at the cliché. A cold smile. He replaced the receiver in its cradle.

What was this, the second problem he'd had in six years? Well, you had to expect it. His face turned serious and his mouth threaded into a thin smile. He leaned back in his chair to consider his choices. He never liked to act impetuously.

He closed his eyes and sat silently for several minutes with his hands folded together on his desk, his index fingers peaked. He reviewed the telephone conversation with Alexander Kinsky in his head and considered what he had to do.

After a few additional moments, he sat upright and opened the cigar box on his desk. He lit one of the cigars he had custom-made at Davidoff's. His fifth of the day. He again reminded himself that he needed to cut down. Then he tipped his chair back, letting the smoke he slowly exhaled drift towards the ceiling.

He remained totally still except for an occasional puff on the cigar, rolling it in his fingers. Those who knew him well were fascinated by his ability to concentrate, no matter what was going on around him.

Kinsky thought he was a tough guy. He had to consider that. He had worked for him, for what now, four years. They had never met, of course, but he was bright enough and he knew enough to be dangerous.

The telephone number Kinsky used to call him wasn't a problem. That had been arranged long ago. And he certainly didn't know his real name. But there were details in the transactions that could be traced if someone were determined enough and had the resources. At least they would be able to make some guesses. Rollins didn't like anyone making guesses.

He wondered whether he could buy Kinsky off. He dismissed the thought with a shrug. Kinsky would still have too much information. He was too greedy. It would just be a matter of time until he had his hand out again.

Oh, he knew Kinsky well. The investigation he had done on Kinsky before he hired the man had been thorough. The file, including Kinsky's photograph, was now open on his desk.

He sighed. There was really only one way to go. He had known it from the moment he'd been threatened him in that crude fashion that Kinsky thought was so subtle.

It was too bad. He never liked to do this. It was a tool to be used, but he never liked it. It wasn't that he was squeamish. He just didn't like taking chances. And sometimes, it could get messy. Sometimes you have to take a risk, he consoled himself. He still didn't like it.

Two risks, really, he acknowledged. He would need to sterilize Kinsky's office. That was a loose end he couldn't ignore. He brightened at the thought that he would be using Kinsky's money, the money he still owed him, to clean up the problem he had created. But he'd have to find someone else soon. Not for this transaction. That was all set. Self executing. But soon. That was never easy.

He got slowly to his feet and slipped on his jacket. He groaned. He couldn't sit too long in one position anymore without getting stiff. The thought flitted through his mind that he was really a grown up. Every time he got up, he groaned. He barked a sterile laugh.

He wanted to make this call from a payphone, one of the few still existing in New York. It was like some kind of movie.

He stepped back to his desk and picked up Kinsky's photograph. He slipped it into his pocket. He also picked up the cell phone he used to call Kinsky. He dropped it to the floor and crushed it with his heel and put it in his other pocket. He wouldn't need it again. It would go into a trash bin along with Kinsky's file.

This would probably happen as it did before. His contact would want the photo and his fee left in a locker. He'd have to call again with the name, the locker number and arrange for a key to be delivered.

He also had to arrange for the cash he needed to put together with the photograph in the locker. Then he'd call a messenger. Just in case someone was watching.

"No sense in jumping out of the frying pan," he mused. "No fingerprints, either, he reminded himself," laughing at his sense of intrigue. He took out the photograph and wiped it with his handkerchief. He opened the door to his office.

His assistant started to call for his car before he shook his head. He hailed a taxi a block down from his building and gave the driver an address in midtown. He liked having lunch at the Four Seasons. They were very accommodating. And there was a telephone, two blocks away, which was private in a public sort of way. He could make sure no one was listening.

He dialed the number he'd memorized some years ago. He didn't use it often, but it stuck with him. He lowered his voice and covered the receiver, holding his face close to the phone. A familiar voice answered.

"I need a favor," he said.

Chapter 42

"This isn't good, Jonathan." Harv Champlin sounded upset. That, in itself, was disturbing. Besides, it was 10 in the morning. Jonathan had been at Harv Champlin's office for 15 minutes. The pleasantries were long past.

"The S.E.C. sounds confident. They're already working with the prosecutors. Damn close to smug. This is criminal, not civil. They made it real clear. They won't even consider a plea bargain."

"Plea bargain?" Jonathan practically shouted. Talk about disturbing. "Harv, this doesn't make any sense. We didn't do anything. What the hell do they have? Why are they doing this?"

"Look, I don't want to cause you more grief, but I think they've got information that would support an indictment."

Jonathan felt his stomach turn over. My God, I could go to jail, he realized. He gritted his teeth to bring his emotions under control. "What's their evidence?"

"A lot. They've got a brokerage account in the Caymans. Two actually. Both in phony names. Confirmations go to P.O. boxes."

"That sounds like the way it would be done."

"Yeah, but it gets worse. They've traced the e-mail brokerage application back to Simon's office."

"Shit."

"The P.O. boxes are just a few blocks away. So they're real convenient. They got a subpoena on the boxes and found the trade confirmations."

"Why were there two accounts?"

"They think Simon got a tip on the HST Heartcare merger. From you."

He knew it was coming, but it still was hard to hear it said out loud.

"They have a record of dozens of calls between you and Simon at the time. Cell phone and land line."

"But, dammit, Simon and I are business partners and friends. We call each other all the time."

"I know. They know it too. It doesn't matter. We have to expect that when they put Asheton under oath, he's going to tell them he told you about the merger. From their standpoint, it's just frosting on the cake."

"What does that mean?"

"Come on, Jonathan. You were a partner here. We represent HST. You have lots of contacts."

"But I still don't understand why there were two brokerage accounts."

"The second one was established on the same day as the sale. The payoff for the tip. It all fits."

"They seem to have a lot of information," Jonathan said. The discouragement showed in his voice.

"I thought about that. Their review process would have turned up the option trades. But it would've taken them a long time. They moved way too quickly here. They seemed to know where to look. I think they got a call from someone."

"Any chance we can find out from whom?"

"Come on."

"But it's all circumstantial evidence," Jonathan said hopefully. "You think they can make a case?" Even asking the question challenged Jonathan's composure.

"I think they can. I don't like to say it, but yes, I think so." They looked at each other in silence.

Finally. "Why?" Jonathan was getting more and more upset. His face was a stiff mask.

"You want to know the real reason."

"Sure." Actually, he didn't want to hear it.

"Because there's $1.2 million in those accounts. Someone's going to ask themselves who would spend that kind of money to frame you."

"But don't they think we would've been a little smarter, dammit. It's all so obvious."

"You want to make that argument to them?"

Jonathan sighed. "No."

"I didn't think so. I don't either."

"Harv, I don't know what to do. We've been framed, big time." Jonathan made gesture with his hands that seemed to take in the office and all of New York.

"I suggest you call Frankee Pereire. We need some facts. Anything. I'll try to slow down the indictment. The holidays may help. Christ, even an indictment would be a disaster for you."

"Tell me," Jonathan said, almost to himself.

Chapter 43

"It's Jonathan Franklin."

"You sound like hell. What's up?" He must have sounded really bad. Frankee Pereire wasn't even making a joke. It had to be a first.

"Simon and I are in trouble. Really big trouble, Frankee. We need your best people. Money isn't an object this time. We need help quickly."

"Come in. I'll cancel my appointment."

"Thanks." He paused. "I mean it."

Pereire, Brill's offices reflected its status. Glass and chrome. High-tech. Efficient. Frankee Pereire had wrested respect from an industry dominated by tough men.

She got up from behind her desk and greeted Jonathan. Her look was serious. Over the years, Frankee and Jonathan had had a bantering relationship. It was an innate part of both of them. Not this time.

"Good to see you, she said. "Sorry about your troubles. Let's get right down to it and see what we can do." She didn't even mention money. Or his tweed jacket. Another first.

At 5 ft. 3 in., with a square build and a motherly face, no one would describe her as pretty, but she was a top-notch investigator, ex-FBI, still fit and solid, in her mid-50s. Tough as nails.

But first she was a businesswoman. After all, she ran the most important private security firm in the country. Not the biggest, but she had hand selected her people, ex-FBI, CIA, Interpol and other security services.

There were few police and security agencies in the world in which Pereire, Brill didn't have friends. And she selected her clients as carefully. She got the difficult problems. Perone, Brill was good, and she knew it.

She motioned Jonathan towards the armchairs around a low chrome and glass coffee table. There was a carafe of coffee and cups already set up.

"Can I get you anything?" she asked.

Jonathan shook his head as he sat down. He launched immediately into an explanation of everything that had happened. Every nasty detail.

"Frankee, they're going to indict me and Simon unless we can get some evidence. It's incredible. Somebody went to a lot of trouble to frame us."

"It sure sounds like it. You said they've traced the original brokerage application back to Simon's e-mail?"

"Yeah."

"That's the place to start. I want to get some hotshot computer people into Simon's systems and see what we can turn up. Maybe it'll help us to know where to go."

"No problem. I'll call Simon as soon as we finish."

"I'll also get some people over to the mailbox place to see if they can tell us who set up the boxes. Probably not. And I doubt it'll do any good to send someone to the Caymans. It's unlikely they had contact with any living human being."

"Makes sense."

"We'll treat this as a top priority. I'll have people on it today. You on your cell if I need you?"

"Sure."

"Tell Simon to give us access. I'll give you a report daily."

"Frankee. I really don't know how to thank you enough."

"We've worked on things together for a long time, Jonathan. I don't like people screwing around with my friends." She paused and smiled for the first time. Her eyes twinkled.

"Besides, it's not good for business," she said.

Chapter 44

He woke up sweating. His head hurt. It was going to be a lousy day. Some days, nothing goes right. Today, that would count as good.

How the hell was he supposed to tell his wife, sleeping there so peacefully, that he could be indicted for insider trading. Jonathan wasn't even sure how to broach the subject. He hadn't been able to find a way last night. He had a silly thought. Stupid humor, she would call it.

Nicole, dear, I may be late for dinner. About two years late. It didn't sound funny, even to him. As he lay there fretting, he felt her hand caressing his arm.

"Cheri, you seem so concerned. Tell me what it is."

The telling wasn't as hard as he expected. She sat up in bed, holding the covers over her small breasts with one hand and listened attentively. Her gray eyes were quiet.

"But how could they think that you could do such a thing? Or Simon? It is not possible."

"I don't know, darling. All I know is someone spent a lot of money and went to a lot of trouble to set up a trail of circumstantial evidence. The damnable thing is that it's so clever. We would say and do exactly the same thing, whether we were guilty or innocent. I can't figure out how to attack this. My mind seems to be frozen."

"It will be all right, Cheri." What else could she say?

He reached out and took her hand. "To tell you the truth, Nicole, I'm scared." It took a lot for him to admit it.

She reached over, letting the cover slip, and took him in her arms, drawing him to her. For once, even Rufus lay quietly at the foot of the bed, licking his own toes.

"Do not fear, Cheri, I am here for you. It angers me that someone would attack my husband and my friend."

Nicole still amazed him. She exuded a determined energy that was lmost boundless. Jonathan found that she rarely sat still. It left him a little breathless.

And yet she could melt into a kind of enveloping warmth with him. It was like a secret between them.

He thought she was beautiful, but he never seemed to be able to convince her of it. It seemed to him as if she spent a fortune getting her hair cut, but it never seemed to change. She always looked terrific. At least to a guy who had given up getting his nails manicured.

And sometimes she had the ability to be frighteningly direct when she confronted a problem. As she was now.

"We must look very high. Someone powerful wants something very much to attempt this. They spent a great deal of money. Have you considered why?" Anger crackled in her voice.

He found her anger more productive than the self-pity he had been wallowing in. His mind was starting to tear itself loose from the muck of his fear. "I agree. And it must be something that involves both Simon and me."

She nodded, glad to see him respond. She didn't know whether she was right or wrong. She didn't care. She just couldn't stand to see him helpless.

"That really narrows it down," Jonathan mused aloud. "We have the investment in Zager Vineyard's together." Jonathan had acquired his interest a few years ago as payment for helping Mimi, Simon's ex-wife, out of a jam involving a dead artist, Arthur DeRuk. He always drank Zager Chardonnay.

"But that's unlikely. It wouldn't be worth it," he continued to muse. Although he was talking to himself, he was speaking aloud. Jonathan also realized that the people involved in the DeRuk affair probably weren't sophisticated enough, at least in the securities world, to pull this off. That was an art dealer crowd. Someone might have hired a person knowledgeable in securities, but that seemed unlikely. Particularly with $1.2 million in play. There would have been questions.

Nicole simply sat beside him, watched and listened. Occasionally she nodded.

"It's much more likely to involve this bid we're making for the Quintiles Group," Jonathan continued. "Maybe Frankee can find a loose thread we can start pulling on." His thoughts turned to the investigation. He wondered how it was going. Maybe Frankee would call soon. At least he sure hoped so.

He felt a lot better now. Nicole leaned close to him and caressed his cheek with the back of her hand. She put her arms around his neck. He felt her breath on his cheek and the lingering scent of her perfume. He could feel her warm naked breasts against his arm. She whispered in his ear.

"Make love to me."

Chapter 45

"Professor Franklin," she said in a too sweet voice. "How nice of you to visit."

Autumn had wandered into winter and today was overcast and cold. It matched Jonathan's mood. He shrugged off his overcoat and removed his gloves. He reached into his pocket to assure himself that his silver snuff box was still there.

"Dressed so debonairly too, in your nice tweed jacket. And golly, what a pretty tie."

Jonathan was wearing a red Challis. It made him feel better.

"It makes such a nice target."

Frankee Pereire had been kidding Jonathan about his tweed jackets for years. It usually amused him. Today it didn't.

"Cool it, Frankee. Why'd you want to see me so urgently? You've had a whole week. Did you come up with anything?"

"If you're not going to be nice to me, maybe I won't share." It was amazing that a 50-year-old plus woman could do a pretend pout so well. Notwithstanding all of his anxiety, he found himself laughing.

"Dammit," he said between chuckles. "You're going to kill me one of these days. Would you please tell me some good news?"

"Okay, Mr. Cranky, but first, can I get you a nice cup of coffee?"

"I could use one, to tell you the truth. I haven't been sleeping well."

"I don't doubt it," Frankee said, as she rose and went to a panel in the wall. She touched it and it opened into a mini-kitchen. She went in and Jonathan heard the coffee grinder and then some other sounds. The scent of freshly brewing coffee reached out to him. It was wonderful. Frankee was a coffee nut and only used the best Kona. She came out with two thick white mugs and put one down in front of Jonathan.

Frankee turned back into the pure professional she was. Now it was all business.

"Okay. First we had our computer people track back on the computer records from the brokerage firm to Simon's computers. There was only one e-mail. We had to check the computers one at a time. It was on Lauren's." Lauren Lucier was Simon's Director of Administration. "We had to dig down into the hard drive. Someone did a pretty good job of covering up."

"But that's exactly what the Feds would expect, isn't it? I mean, if we were guilty."

"Sure, but we weren't looking for the e-mail. We wanted to see when it was sent."

"How does that help?"

"Well, we weren't sure it would, but, in fact, we found something interesting."

Jonathan leaned forward in his chair.

"The e-mail was sent in the very early morning. Around 2:15. What does that suggest to you?" She paused for effect. "Assuming of course, you're not guilty," she chuckled.

"Someone broke in?"

"Maybe. But probably not. Too dangerous at that time of night. The janitorial crew is still around. You'd do it later if you wanted to break in. We checked the locks. There were scratch marks. But it just didn't make sense."

"Then you figure it must've been someone in the building."

"Right. Of course it was just a guess. That narrowed it down, but there were still a lot of possibilities. It might have been one of Simon's employees. No one would question an employee being in the suite, working late.

"Of course."

"If so, why not use a key. Unless it was to throw off the police." She paused to shake her head, doing away with the possibility. "But I don't think they'd have figured anyone would look. So we thought it was probably maintenance or building personnel or maybe the janitors. Like most buildings, Simon's building uses an outside janitorial service."

Jonathan was fidgeting in his seat. This was the first hopeful glint of light in a very dark winter day.

"We began checking all the possibilities. But we prioritized. Simon has so many long-time employees, we put them off until last."

"I get that," Jonathan said, lifting his thick white mug and taking a sip of coffee. It was still too hot, but it tasted great. He didn't take his eyes off Frankee. She was concentrating on handwritten notes in front of her, skipping from page to page.

"We started checking the office building people and maintenance staff, one by one. Some were possibilities, but in my opinion, unlikely."

"And janitorial?"

"That's when it got interesting. We went to the cleaning company the building contracts with. They gave us access to the records of the janitorial staff that was in the building on the date the e-mail was sent."

"How did you get them to do that?"

"Don't ask. Anyway, we wanted to look at all their people in the building, not just those assigned to Simon's floor. We figured that once someone was in the building, it would be pretty easy to slip away and get into Simon's office during a break or something."

"Don't they screen their people?"

"Some, but it can be hit or miss. Pretty basic stuff and it would be easy to fake. It's not high-security work you know."

"Okay. Did you find anything?"

"Yep. There was one guy. He was hired a few days before the e-mail was sent. He quit the day after. Just didn't show up. Didn't call or anything. That's not unusual."

"So?"

"What was strange was that he didn't try to pick up his paycheck. For people like that, they live from check to check. That really got our attention. The cleaning company tried to mail him his check. It came back. Wrong address. We checked the address. It was a phony. My guy figured he was on to something. He asked for a photograph, and we lucked out. The company photographs each of its employees. So he brought it back."

She slid a snapshot sized photo across to Jonathan. He picked it up and looked at it carefully. He handed it back to her and shook his head.

"I've never seen this guy before."

"I have," Frankee said.

Chapter 46

"That's incredible," Jonathan said into his cell phone more loudly than he intended. He was excited. His voice startled Rufus awake. Rufus had been having such a pleasant dream. He looked at Jonathan with a peeved expression. He didn't like his nap interrupted. He gave a small bark of displeasure. Jonathan looked over. "Sorry."

Jonathan's feet danced a little jig and his smile threatened to tear a hole in his face. Maybe this was a good omen. By god, one of his crazy ideas had actually worked.

"I understand. That's terrific. When do you intend to make the announcement?"

He listened.

"Would you mind if I told him."

Jonathan hung up. Rufus put his head down but cocked an ear when Jonathan started dialing another number. Was this going to go on forever?

The phone in Jonathan's hand seemed to ring endlessly.

Finally, a subdued "Hello."

"Sir Adrian, it's Jonathan Franklin."

"Oh, Jonathan. It's good of you to call."

"I have great news."

"I could certainly use some. Been a bit of a downer around here, I'm afraid."

"You remember the forensic analysis I recommended for the Nichlosons.

"Yes, of course."

"You paid Frankee Pereire to arrange it," Jonathan continued.

"Yes."

"Well I just got a call from Peter Willson. The results just came in."

There was silence on the other end of the phone.

Jonathan bulled ahead. "There was a partial fingerprint on the back edge of one canvas. It was covered by the frame."

"Ah," said Asheton. He sounded uninterested. Not at all the reaction Jonathan had anticipated.

"They matched it to a set of Nicholson's prints. There were some from the war. There's absolutely no question that the paintings are genuine. The Nauton intends to re-announce the gift and recognize your generosity."

"How grand." His voice was flat.

"Sir Adrian, I thought you'd be chuffed." Jonathan deliberately used the English term.

"Quite right. But I'm afraid it is all too late. Bit of a shame."

"But why?"

"I thought Tae had told you. That you called for that reason. I'm afraid I've gotten a notice from your Inland Revenue Service that they intend to pursue an audit of my tax records."

"So it's likely to turn up the tax scheme."

"Alas, I'm afraid so."

"Is there any way you can put them off? Delay the audit?"

"We are doing everything that we can. My accountants do not feel it can be delayed for long."

"What are you going to do?"

"Well, my boy, keep a stiff upper lip and hope for the best. Very British, you know. Perhaps it will turn out right."

"How is the sale of HST Heartcare coming? Is there any chance it will close soon?"

"The negotiation of the draft agreements is going very slowly. I don't know. But we can only wait, I suppose."

Nothing was turning out right, it seemed to Jonathan. Nothing for anyone at all.

Chapter 47

The small hairs on the back of Alex Kinsky's neck did not stand on end when Frankee Pereire spoke his name. Nor did his ears burn when Frankee bluntly described his ethics, not to mention his business practices.

No, it had been a really good day for Alex Kinsky in the detective business, and he was looking forward to his reward. William Atkins had been receptive when they had had a serious discussion about what Kinsky was worth. He thought he had handled it quite well. Atkins was just a Wall Street pussy.

Alex Kinsky liked to party. Tonight he was feeling especially good. Champagne was flowing, and there was a fine, bare-breasted young woman hanging on his arm. He had a table at the back.

The meatpacking district was becoming prime New York real estate, but there were still places that the developers hadn't reached, places where the bars still catered to a working class clientele.

His favorite bar was just across from a large parking lot where a meat cutting plant once stood. Great parking was a luxury in New York. The bar was known for its topless waitresses. The policy of the bar was no implants. Only naturals need apply. He liked doing the interviews.

The bar also had a policy about watering the drinks. It did.

Not Alex Kinsky's. He owned 25 percent of the place. He got it for nothing. Sweat equity, although he wasn't the one to sweat. There were some embarrassing facts the landlord hadn't wanted to make public. He was very accommodating on the lease terms.

Kinsky was the one who came up with the name. "The Meat Market." Catchy.

It was almost 3 a.m. Kinsky had partied hard.

"You want some more champagne?" he asked the statuesque young woman sitting next to him. She shook her head drowsily.

He didn't have any desire to take her home with him. That desire had been dissipated a couple of hours ago in a small room upstairs. It was one of the reasons he liked owning the bar.

"Let's call it a night." His tone was brusque. He got up slowly and left a wad of bills on the table. He tucked a 20 into the waistband of the girl's panties. "That's for you," he said in a flat voice. The girl didn't seem to notice.

Just outside the door he stopped and patted down his jacket. He found his cigarettes. He extracted one and tapped it on his watch. He pulled out a pack of matches the club provided and struck one. The flair of the match ended whatever night vision he had.

He could hold his liquor, but it was late and he was a little tired. His hat was pulled down over his ears. Otherwise he might have heard the car start up as he left the bar. It was a peculiar because no headlights appeared. It was cold, but the car window was down.

As he started across the street to the parking lot, the middle-aged, balding man in the car rolled forward. He'd never seen Alex Kinsky alive. He wouldn't again. All he had was a picture.

Kinsky's reactions were slower than normal. He turned towards the sound and started to move to his left. That required the driver to make a small correction.

It was nothing personal. Just business. He'd gotten a call yesterday, and the balding man had been following Kinsky since morning, waiting for an opportunity. He didn't know why. He wasn't curious.

The two muffled pops were hardly noticeable. Kinsky felt a peculiar sensation, almost like a punch. The alcohol had dulled more than his reflexes. He slowly collapsed to his knees, then to his face.

The car rolled to a halt and the door swung open. The man leaned out and shot Kinsky one more time, in the head. It wasn't necessary.

The balding man took pride in his skill. He drove slowly away from the still form lying face down in the street. He would dispose of the car soon. It was stolen this morning.

He knew he didn't have to check the body. It was easy money.

Chapter 48

It was a beautiful early winter's day. The temperature hovered around 30 degrees. The sunlight was brilliant, dancing off the stray patches of snow harbored in the nooks and wells of trees set along the sidewalk. Women hurried past clutching their holiday parcels. Smiling people seemed to have a peppier step.

Nicole passed several Santas on the street, each ringing his bell enthusiastically. It was a little disconcerting. The first had ear phones sticking out from under his beard. One actually went "Ho, ho, ho." She put $5 into his pot. Ah, it is Christmas, she said to herself.

She had chosen to walk. Nicole pulled her coat tighter around her. The doctor had been quite certain. They had another appointment in two weeks.

Nicole was deeply worried. Not about herself, but about Jonathan. He was so stressed. More than she had ever seen. This would only add to his concern. It might be perhaps too much. Her jaw tightened.

The lines of people stretched around the block, moving slowly in front of the cleverly decorated holiday windows. Trains ran up and down. Ballerinas twirled. Hot air balloons filled with gifts drifted across snow-laden hills.

She looked across the street at Atlas, who bore the weight of the world on his shoulders. He appeared as burdened as Jonathan. No, she would have to keep this secret as long as she could. It would be best.

She turned into Saks. The store was a festival of colors. Her spirits lifted. She had never been much of a shopper. Art was the only material thing she ever loved. It was the only thing that kept giving her joy, even after it was weeks old. No, years old.

That was why she had the perfect job, running Witten's. And that perfect job, and her husband, and her partner were all now threatened.

But this was Christmas. She smiled to herself remembering when her father had taken her shopping. He had tried so to be both the mother and father to her.

Yet he had been so formal. The way he carried himself, straight-backed, as he held on to her hand to be sure she didn't get lost. He felt so bony when she hugged him. She felt safe.

How he had hovered over her life after they were alone together in the apartment on Central Park West. Her mother's death had devastated her father. She knew, even though he never showed it. Sometimes at night, when he thought she was asleep, she heard him weeping softly.

It was the apartment she now shared with Jonathan. How much longer would they be able to share it? It brought a tear to her eye. She wiped it away with the back of her finger.

She and Jonathan would never have been together but for her father's death. She missed her father, but she silently thanked him. She and Jonathan were so happy. What a terrible price to pay for her happiness. How strange it was that awful things can lead to good things and how random it all seemed. And how swift an end.

She thought back to that other time, when her life almost had been destroyed. She felt the muscles in her jaw start to bunch up. Jonathan had been there for her. Indeed, it was he who finally had found her father's killer and resolved the disposition of her father's fortune. Now he was in trouble and she couldn't save him.

Mon Dieu, how did this happen. This helplessness. It was unfair. She was startled by the voice.

"May I help you?" The girl behind the counter was young and bright. A student perhaps, making some money during the Christmas holidays. She had never been allowed to do that. How little this young girl knew of what to expect. It was all so very complicated.

"I am looking for a pair of gold, antique cuff-links," Nicole said. "Do you carry them or must I go to a specialty store?"

"Golly, I've never seen anything like that here, but I'm new. Let me go ask." She scurried away returning after a few minutes with an older man, graying at the temples, his hair thinning on top.

"Good morning. I'm the manager of the jewelry department. How can I be of service?"

192

"As I told the young lady, I am looking for antique cuff links. My husband is fond of antiques. Something he can wear with his tuxedo."

"I'm afraid we don't carry antiques in this store. But we do have some beautiful custom-made pieces. There is a wonderful set of bulldogs in 18K gold. May I show them to you?"

"No, no. They would not be appropriate," she said. Rufus would not appreciate the competition. Goodness, no.

"Ah, I'm sorry."

"I just thought I would try. I was on my way to the jewelry district and I love your windows."

"Please come back. We would look forward to serving you." He made a half bow. "And Merry Christmas."

"Thank you." It made Nicole think of her father again. Why was it so difficult. The two most important men in her life were in desperate straits. And far from helping, she could only add to their troubles. She started to cry again.

Chapter 49

The call startled Rafael Del Gado. The day was going so well. The sun was shining. The lawyers had called to confirm the closing date on the electric company. The world was good.

His secretary had buzzed. "Mr. Del Gado, Peter Willson is on the line."

"I don't know him. What does he want?" Del Gado's voice was gruff. He didn't like new people. New people could be a problem.

"He says he's the director of the Nauton Museum."

Damn, Del Gado thought. "I'll take it," he said, somewhat reluctantly. He raised his hand and motioned for his driver, Alejandro, to leave. As the door closed, he picked up the telephone.

"Yes, this is Rafael Del Gado. How may I be of help?"

"Mr. Del Gado, I am calling to personally express our thanks to you. You have helped us tremendously with your gift of the Purland oil. A magnificent addition to our collection."

Del Gado worked to keep his voice calm. He picked up a pen and worried it nervously. "Yes, it was my pleasure, Mr. Willson." He had been assured by Derek Lissome that there would be no disclosure. That the gift would have no publicity.

"I'm also calling to invite you to our unveiling of this contemporary masterwork and to let us properly show our gratitude for your generosity. We do not often get a painting worth a $1 million, if I may say so, out of the blue. It will be a pleasure to introduce you to our community of people, who love the Nauton Museum, as you do."

Willson paused, then continued. "The event will also honor Andrew Grahm, our late head curator, who convinced you to entrust your munificent gift to us."

Del Gado ignored the reference to Andrew Grahm. He'd never heard of him. Something else this pompous ass said had caught his attention .

"A million?"

"Well, yes, there are questions about the value of this series of Purland's work. And there are questions about condition, of course. But, yes, I would say a million. What I don't need to say is how pleased we are." He had just said it for the third time.

Del Gado snapped the pen he had been playing with in two. Ink stained the desktop and spattered his crisp white shirt.

"Son-of-a-bitch," he muttered.

"I'm sorry, what was that?" Willson asked.

"Nothing," said Del Gado. "Just a little issue here."

"Oh, fine. I know how busy you are. Let me just tell you that the reception will be next Wednesday at 8. Of course, you will receive a written invitation, but I wanted to speak to you personally. We at the Nauton want to celebrate you."

"It is not necessary," he said, a little too curtly. "I mean, I am pleased, but really, it is not necessary. In fact, I would not want any publicity."

"Oh, Mr. Del Gado, we insist. A gift to the community like yours must be celebrated. Please come. The art press will be here and there will be some of our most prominent members. The mayor has confirmed that he will attend. I know they would all welcome meeting you."

"I'll need to check my calendar. I may be traveling." That was quick thinking. "Let me get back to you."

"Of course, if you can't be with us, we hope that you'll send a representative whom we can properly thank on your behalf."

Del Gado restrained himself from banging down the phone. The entire tax scheme turned on the $8 million valuation of the Purland that Derek Lissome was to provide. It would mean over $1.8 million in his pocket after he paid Lissome for the painting and another $1 million as his fee. He most certainly couldn't have this ass announcing a $1-million gift. He picked up the phone and dialed.

"I can understand your concern, Mr. Del Gado," Derek Lissome said. Lissome had some concern himself. "Leave it with me. I assure you everything will be exactly as we discussed."

"It had better be. I do not like people who do not do what they promise. I do not like them at all."

196

"I know how to deal with this." Lissome certainly wished he did, but he needed time to think. Maybe he could persuade Peter Willson this wasn't a good idea. Not likely. He shook his head angrily.

"Should I go?"

Del Gado's voice jolted him out of his thoughts.

"Go?"

"To the reception, of course." Del Gado was getting more upset.

"Yes, yes. I think it will help resolve everything."

It had occurred to Lissome in a flash of insight. Actually, the only thing he had to do was to keep any mention of value out of the presentation. That was something he thought he could do rather easily.

"Well, Mr. Del Gado. I'll see you there. It will be a splendid evening."

Lissome immediately called Peter Willson. He used Willson's private number.

"Peter, it's Derek."

Silence.

"Derek Lissome."

"Derek, I didn't know you had this number." Willson certainly hadn't given it to him.

Lissome ignored the comment.

"What can I do for you," Willson said, finally.

"I just spoke to Rafael Del Gado, Peter. You know, of course, I was the one who arranged his gift to the Nauton. I hope he mentioned it was out of my respect for you."

Willson murmured his thanks. He didn't believe a word of it.

He buzzed his secretary to freshen his coffee and made a note to change his private number.

"But there is one thing, Peter."

"Oh?"

"Yes. You see, Mr. Del Gado is sensitive about discussions of money connected with his name. He's quite modest."

That sounded unlike the person to whom he had just spoken, but Willson made no objection.

"He's very generous," Lissome continued, "but he would appreciate it if there is no discussion of value connected with his gift."

"I don't think that will be a problem, Derek. After all, it is the thought we want to honor here at the Nauton." There was no sense in angering a big donor.

"Thank you, Peter. Thank you for understanding."

Lissome put down the phone and smiled. He was good, wasn't he.

Chapter 50

The sun had finally come out, but there was no warmth in it. How could it seem so gloomy? Jonathan raised his hand to shield his eyes from the glare where the sun hit the polished surface of the kitchen table. He turned aside.

He was listening to the phone scrunched between his shoulder and his chin. His tie hung loose. His feet were up on a kitchen chair. He had just picked up the call from Frankee Perone and he was hoping for good news. It wasn't to be.

"Oh, shit," Jonathan said, swinging his feet down flat on the floor and grabbing the phone as it fell away from his shoulder. "Frankee, that's terrible."

"Yeah, ain't it the truth," she said. "A real loss to our profession."

"How did he die?" He reached into his pocket with his free hand and started compulsively rubbing his snuff box.

"He was shot. A week ago. We just found out. Couldn't track him down at his office or his apartment. We started checking.

"Kinsky was our only lead."

"That's a downside all right."

"Was it murder? Was there anything suspicious?"

"Look, this creep was into a lot of shifty stuff. He wasn't known for having a lot of friends. Seems like he was coming out of a bar, late, and someone popped him in the parking lot. Small caliber. Two shots narrowly grouped in the chest, one to the head. Very professional. No witnesses. At least the police say there were none. It's not the kind of place where the patrons seek out the cops to confess their sins."

"Are the police looking into it?"

"As a matter of fact, your old buddy Julian Wayne has the file."

"Would it do any good for me to talk to him?"

"Not unless you don't have enough trouble."

Jonathan was stuck.

"What do the analysts say? Has anyone changed their ratings of the stock?"

"Yeah. One guy raised his rating yesterday."

"Rumors?"

"Not that I've heard."

"Maybe there are short-sellers."

Short sellers borrow stock to sell in anticipation of a decline in the stock's price. When the price finally drops, they buy up the stock at the lower price and return the shares to their lender. And keep the profit.

"Why should there be short-sellers?" Simon asked.

"I don't have any idea."

"There's no way. You'd have to be an idiot to short Witten's now," Simon said.

"It's weird. Have you checked with the transfer agents?"

"Of course, but the selling is coming from all over the place."

"You think we should get Frankee to look into this too?"

"I guess so," he said in a deadened voice. "She's sure got nothing else to do," he added, bitterly.

"Simon, I really don't like what's going on. We've got all these problems, with the S.E.C. and everything. Now strange things are happening. What's up?"

Chapter 51

The traffic was thunderous on Central Park West. A pulsing vein in the heart of New York. There was a distinct smell of exhaust emissions floating in the crisp winter air. It would ordinarily have annoyed Jonathan, but more urgent issues were distracting him this morning.

He held up his hand to hail a cab and told the cabbie to take him to the Carlyle. His mind was turning over the S.E.C. issues. He was feeling haggard.

This had been the third night in a row he'd awakened and not been able to get back to sleep, his mind running over and over his problems. He awoke, without recalling when he fell asleep, exhausted. He would stand in front of the bathroom mirror, making funny faces at himself. A sure sign of insanity, he reckoned.

Sometimes he found himself imagining what might happen, worst-case scenario. The perp walk, with his hands handcuffed behind his back, a man from the Justice Department holding his elbow. Cameras flashing in his face. People standing and pointing. A hand on the top of his head as he went through the back door of a big, black Crown Victoria. It was a horror. Unimaginable, except that he did imagine it.

He would get up and use the bathroom and sneak out to the living room, quietly closing the doors so as not to awaken Nicole. He'd pick up a magazine at random and look for something to read and then find himself reading the same paragraph over and over again. Last night, he'd finally tried a sleeping pill before he crawled in again beside Nicole. Even so, his sleep was disturbed. He wondered if Simon was doing any better.

He wasn't.

"Dammit. Where have you been?" Simon had answered the door. "I called an hour ago. Champlin's been here for 15 minutes."

Jonathan's head came up and he looked hard at Simon. He opened his mouth, then closed it. He took a deep breath.

"Look, I'm feeling really ragged. Please cut out the bullshit." Jonathan's voice was calm but emphatic. He'd never spoken to Simon in that tone.

Simon stopped, startled. Jonathan wasn't sure if he would blow up. To tell the truth, he didn't really care at the moment. The response was a surprise.

"Sorry," Simon apologized. "My nerves are on edge. I haven't been sleeping too good."

"Join the club," Jonathan said tersely. "This is really getting to me. Let's hope Harv has some good news."

"He doesn't look like it."

They walked from the hall into the living room of Simon's suite. Harv Champlin put down his coffee cup and stood up to shake Jonathan's hand. "Hey, man. You look like shit."

"Thanks for the pep talk. What's up, Harv? When Simon called, I hoped there might be some good news."

Champlin looked down and shook his head. His mouth was rigid. Jonathan didn't like the look.

"I'm getting a bad feeling," Champlin said. "Real bad. I think the Attorney General is going to present an indictment to the grand jury soon. We may have to bite the bullet here." He spoke in a dry, professional voice that was uncharacteristic of him.

"If we have to bite the bullet, let's just be sure it's pointing out," Jonathan interrupted with a grim smile. "What's happened?"

"I'm glad you've retained your sense of humor. Such as it is," Champlin riposted. "It's their tone, more than anything else. Look, I know you're not going to like this, but I think we should be considering making arrangements for a release bond. We should also talk about what we can do to arrange for you both to surrender to the Feds if an indictment comes down. I sure don't want to have a media circus. I hope those guys will be reasonable. But they like to put on a show with high profile defendants."

"Shit!" Simon struck the coffee table. "I don't want to hear this. I'm not paying Whiting & Pierce's rates so I can be indicted. I want you to do something," Simon raged. "Dammit. We're innocent. Doesn't that mean anything?"

"Simon, I know," Champlin said. He made a small palms up gesture with his hands. "But as your lawyer, I at least have to face up to this thing. And I don't want you guys disgraced in the press, if worse comes to worst. Don't kill the messenger. I forgot to wear my bulletproof vest today."

"He's right," Jonathan said morosely. "We've got to deal with it."

It was late afternoon when he returned to his apartment building. He was glad Nicole had a dinner meeting. He thought about asking the cabbie to drop him off across from his building, at the entrance to the park.

A walk in the park would do him good. There was a small path by the lake he had found years ago where he could usually be alone.

The cabbie turned around to him and smiled. "Great Christmas weather, isn't it?"

Jonathan's mood soured. He let the cabbie drop him off in front of his apartment building.

"What about the guy's office?" he asked.

"Well, you know, I had exactly the same question. As it turns out, our man was either very secretive, with a really great memory, or someone helped themselves to all his files. The file cabinets were empty."

"It sounds like someone didn't want to be connected up to Kinsky."

"Sure does. But that doesn't do us much good. Right now we have exactly zilch to go on. Sorry, Jonathan."

"Simon, bad news." He had called as soon a she hung up with Frankee.

"It's that kind of day. Come over, can you?"

When Jonathan told him, he took the news more calmly than he had expected. Simon did look worried. But he had looked worried when Jonathan entered his office.

"Tell me about it." He apparently didn't mean Jonathan's news. Jonathan didn't understand.

"No, really. Kinsky's dead. We've got no leads. We're up a creek."

"Yeah. I hear you. That's bad. Damn." He paused, then went on in the discouraged tone. "Jonathan, we've got a problem here too. On top of everything else, Witten's stock price is going to hell and I have no idea why. It's killing me. I've had half a dozen margin calls this morning."

"Witten's stock?"

"Yeah. It's been going on for a while now. A lot of selling. It's been building for a few weeks. The stock dropped another half-point yesterday. I'm worried it's going to accelerate."

"How much has it dropped?"

"About eight and a quarter points in all. I've been so wrapped up in this S.E.C. thing, I haven't been paying much attention."

"That's more than 24 percent. Is anything wrong? Besides our problem, I mean."

"No way. It's the one good thing. Fees at Witten's are up. Profits are terrific. With the economy improving the outlook is strong. We got our share of the art collections for the fall sale. This is the best business has looked in the last couple of years."

Chapter 52

Museum receptions are boring. They follow a hallowed progress of bad wine and pastry bits that look good but are actually made of cardboard. A deeply trodden rut. Once in a great while, there is an exception.

The reception to honor Rafael Del Gado was it. Peter Willson had pulled out all the stops. This was his chance to set a new course for the Nauton.

The room was pulsing politely. The clink of flutes, full of pretty good French champagne, added a musical note to the chit chat. A pleasant bottle of babble.

The Mayor was in his element, attended by those who adored him and those who did not, but liked the aura. Or those who wanted something. He smiled and chatted, turning from admirer to admirer. A handshake here, a beefy arm around a shoulder there. He was in his element.

Rafael Del Gado was enjoying himself too, much to his surprise. These people were important people in New York. And they seemed to like him. Exactly what he had hoped. Doing well by doing good. The slum boy from Brazil. He had even been introduced to the Mayor.

He was speaking to a couple. A roly-poly investment banker and his trophy wife. The investment banker had already suggested that Del Gado consider a public offering for his business. Del Gado wasn't sure what a public offering was, but he wanted no part of anything public.

Derek Lissome crossed the room and approached him from behind. He touched his arm. Del Gado turned slightly from the waist and Lissome leaned in to speak into his ear.

"It's all taken care of. Enjoy yourself."

Del Gado grunted. As he started to turn back to his conversation, Lissome said, "I've got to run to a meeting." He said it to Del Gado's back, shrugged and made for the door. He had better things to do.

A small dais was set up in front of the room. At 8:45, Peter Willson mounted the platform and held up his hands. An easel covered by a cloth stood to one side. The room quieted slowly and unevenly.

Willson waited patiently.

"Ladies and Gentlemen," he finally said. "Thank you for turning out on such a cold evening. And we thank you for giving us part of your precious holiday season. Particularly, thank you, Mr. Mayor. We are honored by your presence here at the Nauton."

The Mayor nodded happily at the polite applause and held up his hand in a modest gesture.

Willson continued. "It may be cold, but ours is a purpose that warms us all. Our honored guest, Rafael Del Gado is new to our city. But he has the depth of appreciation to understand the importance of a great museum. What it means to our city and to our future." Willson was again interrupted by applause.

"And the importance of art to us and to our children. We need to preserve great art for them."

Peter Willson paused to reach into his pocket for his handkerchief. He dabbed at his forehead. He needed to speak to the custodians about always over-heating this room. But he felt that his remarks were really hitting home. He hoped the press would quote him. There were several reporters in the room. He thought they probably would. Certainly after his surprise.

"Whitman Purland is a major artist. He is recognized by his peers and the art world for his unique perspective and intellectually challenging canvases. His work evokes thought and introspection. Many say he is the most import-ant contemporary artist alive today. He does not pursue public recognition. He rarely appears in public." You can say that again, Willson thought. I don't think he's been out of his house in three years. He hates people.

I have a surprise for you this evening. As a special favor to the Nau-ton," and $200,000 plus expenses, Willson mused, "I am pleased to welcome Whitman Purland here from his home in Manchester, England." It had been hell to get the old man to come to the United States. He must have really needed the money.

This time the applause was enthusiastic. A door to the side of the dais opened and a small, emaciated old man dressed in black with a scrawny beard and red glasses entered the room. He had on red tennis shoes. Purland was bald and his lips were set in what might have been a sneer or a smile. It was hard to tell. He gave a limp hand gesture and retreated into a corner of the room.

"Welcome, Whitman," Willson said. Then he turned to the purpose of the show. "The acquisition of a Purland oil has been a profound desire of the Nauton for some time." Since immediately after the gift. "Unfortunately, recent economic times have made that impossible. But now, through the generosity of Rafael Del Gado, we have a wonderful Christmas present." Willson again paused. As the applause subsided, he continued. "A major Purland to further enhance our magnificent collection of Contemporary Art.

Applause again. It gave deeper scope to the meaning of the term "clap trap."

"We hope that Mr. Del Gado and all of you will join us in continuing to build a great museum. We welcome him to our community."

Good grief, Del Gado thought. Will this man never finish?

But just then, Peter Willson did.

He said, "Thank you, Mr. Del Gado," as he drew aside the sheet covering the painting and let it fall to the floor. Applause exploded.

It died abruptly when Whitman Purland suddenly thrust himself off the wall, red in the face and shouting.

"Bloody hell! That's not mine. It's a fuckin' forgery."

Del Gado stood rigid, his face in stone.

Rafael Del Gado slammed the car door. He was seething as he entered his apartment. Derek Lissome had defrauded him. He couldn't let that happen. He now had to deal with several issues. The Internal Revenue Service. He assumed that they would come as soon as the forgery became known. He also could not let others believe he could be taken advantage of. That would be most dangerous. And Derek Lissome certainly could not be allowed to testify, if it came to that.

"Alejandro," he said to the driver. "Come with me to the office. I have a problem. A business problem."

It was the morning of the day after the disaster at the Nauton. Del Gado had dark patches beneath his eyes. He hadn't slept. But now he was sure of the course he must take.

He closed the office door behind Alejandro and locked it.

"There is a man who threatens us. I am concerned he may create an embarrassment. We do not need such an embarrassment."

"Of course, Senor Del Gado."

"We need to remove this threat. Can you do this?"

"What is it you wish, Heje?"

"I will leave that to you, but he must be removed permanently. It is important this be done quickly, you understand. And it must appear to be an accident."

"Yes, Heje."

Chapter 53

The New York Times played the story on page six. Another unfortunate accident in the teeming city. Careless drivers. Hit and run of the mill.

They sat over a hurried deli lunch. Jonathan had a copy of the Times open in front of him. He was paging through the paper to show Simon an article relating to the HST merger. Something else caught his eye.

"Simon." Simon wiped the grease from his corned beef sandwich off the corner of his lips with a paper napkin. Jonathan waited. He pointed at Simon's face. "You still have a spot of mustard at the side of your mouth."

Simon swiped at his lip again.

"Other side."

Simon swiped.

"Got it."

"What?" said Simon gesturing to Jonathan's other hand holding the Times.

"Didn't you speak to me about the guy who was arranging to get that Klimt painting out of Russia for you? What was his name?"

"Lissome. Derek Lissome."

"That's what I thought. I don't think he's going to do the job."

"What?" Simon cupped his ear. The sound level in the deli at lunch-time was awe inspiring.

Jonathan raised his voice. "I said I don't think Derek Lissome is going to get your deal done."

"Why?" Simon frowned.

Jonathan pushed the folded Times across the table. "Page six."

Simon fingered through the pages, opened the paper and scanned page six."

"Near the bottom," Jonathan said.

Simon's eyes moved down the page.

"Shit," he said slamming the paper shut.

"Don't speak unkindly of the dead," Jonathan teased. "I'm sure his cat liked him."

"I gave him $250,000."

"Oops. Do you have any idea what he did with the money?"

"Absolutely none."

"So what do you do?"

"I talk to my lawyer."

"Harv's a little busy right now, in case you forgot."

"I meant you."

"Simon, I'm a bit distracted."

"It will do you good to take your mind off our S.E.C. problem. You can't do anything about it, can you?"

"Actually," Jonathan paused, "no. Unfortunately."

"I have no intention of walking away from $250,000. Besides, I still want the Klimt. Maybe I can get someone to take over if I can find out who Lissome's contacts were."

"Simon, we may be going to jail. How can you worry about a painting?"

"Because I do."

"Right." Jonathan shrugged. That was the way Simon had always been. Unpredictable. He gave up. "Do you think you can get into Lissome's gallery files? There should be some records. At least some notes. It's the way to start. Maybe Peter Willson can help you."

Simon lifted his cream soda and took a long sip. He lowered the bottle and smiled at Jonathan. His predator smile.

"That's a good idea. You do it."

Sometimes I talk too much, mused Jonathan.

Chapter 54

"Jonathan." It was Frankee Perone. "Can you come over. I think I may have something."

"On my way." He needed no encouragement. He desperately wanted some good news.

"I got a look at Kinsky's bank account," Frankee said.

They were sitting in Frankee's office. The lights were on. The clouds looked downright ominous. Jonathan could hardly sit still.

"My God, how?"

"Will you quit asking that question."

"Sorry."

Frankee looked over a page of paper in a thin file. "Anyway, three days before Kinsky took that janitorial job, he made a $10,000 deposit into his bank account."

"A retainer?"

"Kinsky? No way. He was small time. The other deposits into his account were less than $2,000. No, I think it was something else."

"Maybe the payoff for planting the e-mail?"

"Too much, I think. But what it could be is a skim. This guy was a real weasel."

"What do you mean, 'a skim'?"

"He probably paid for the information. They always do."

"Yeah."

"And Kinsky isn't big enough to play that game. Besides, someone went to a lot of trouble to clean out his files."

"So?"

"I think he had a client who put up the money. And he kept part of it for himself. It would be the way he thinks. Or thought."

"Maybe. It's certainly possible."

"Where do you think these people got the inside information?" Frankee asked.

"I don't know. The company, the law firms, the acquirer. Maybe even the printer. It could be any of them. Everyone has tightened up their security, but, you know, people get access. They still give in to temptation. They think they'll never be caught. I guess they're not Jewish."

"Huh?"

"Frankee, you know I'm half Jewish."

"I forgot, if I ever knew it. You don't look Jewish."

"Thanks." Jonathan paused. "I guess."

"Yeah, I always thought Jews dressed better."

"Come on, Frankee, spare me." He continued with his thought. "Jews always have the feeling that if anything can go wrong, it will. I think half of my ethics is based on fear."

"That sounds healthy. You got enough trouble with Harris Tweed."

"Okay, Frankee, back to work. What do you suggest?"

"We got a loose thread. We have a date for the deposit and an amount. We pull on it. See if anything comes out, maybe it starts things unraveling. Can you get me a list of everyone with access to the discussions?"

"I can get you a list of people who worked directly on the deal, but who can say who they talked to or who was looking over their shoulder. I'll ask Sir Adrian and Harv Champlin, but we may have to cast a wider net."

"I know, but we've gotta start somewhere. Get me the list. We'll use a two week time frame on each side of the date of the $10,000 deposit. Ask about any quirky behavior. Anything at all out of the ordinary of anyone who might have had access to deal information. Even if they didn't work on the deal. We might get lucky. These guys are likely amateurs."

"Will do. It's the holidays and I don't know who's working. But, I'll get back to you in a couple of days."

Jonathan went down in the elevator humming.

Chapter 55

"How's the newlywed?" The voice was full of bounce. Upbeat, as Benjamin J. Cohen, the dean of the Harvard Law School, always sounded. It was part of his management style. And it was effective.

"Ben. Good to hear your voice. Things are great." Jonathan lied. He certainly couldn't begin to detail his problems to Cohen. He didn't even want to think about them.

"And Merry Christmas."

"Thanks, Ben. And Happy Holidays to you, too." Jonathan was working hard to keep his tone light.

"I know it's still early, but I wanted to talk to about next year," Cohen said.

"Oh?" Was the ax about to fall?

"I want to be sure you'll be with us. Your Business Transactions course is one of the most popular classes with the kids, and you do it better than anyone. You left a big hole in my schedule."

"Why? Bob Temkin's a good man." Temkin had taken over his Business Transactions class when Jonathan went on leave of absence. "He's doing okay, isn't he?"

It was good to be wanted, even valued. Even Bob Temkin couldn't fill his shoes. He was reminded of Oscar Wilde's line, "It's not enough to succeed, it's also necessary that your best friend should fail." Talk about schadenfreude. He chuckled at his own joke, but he felt better.

"Bob really doesn't like teaching the course," Cohen said. "He spoke to me a little while ago. He doesn't want to do it next year. I thought I'd better call and make sure you were on board. It's hard to get someone to teach Business Transactions."

"I see," Jonathan said, his voice suggesting the leak in his deflating ego. Cohen could almost hear the wind whistle through the pinprick. It wasn't what he had intended.

"Come on, Jonathan. You're a great teacher. We're anxious to have you back." Cohen was an expert in morale building. It was a great skill. "You are coming back, aren't you?" he added with a touch of anxiety.

"I think so, Ben."

"What do you mean, you think so?"

Well, I may be in jail," is what he didn't say. What he did say was, "I love teaching. The kids are great. But I miss doing deals. And I don't want to be away from Nicole so much. She can't leave New York. I just feel conflicted."

No point in mentioning all the petty academic politics that drove him nuts. Ben wouldn't understand. He was a master of the game. Otherwise he wouldn't be the longest tenured dean in the history of the Law School.

"How can I help you figure this out? I really want you here," Cohen said. The "I" was significant. "If we could work something out, so you can do both, maybe live in New York, would that do it?"

Jonathan straightened a little in his chair. His voice perked up. "That sounds really interesting. What are you thinking?" Jonathan was excited. He had never considered the possibility. He might be able to have his Zager Chardonnay and drink it too. He even almost forgot his problems.

"I don't know," Ben Cohen pondered. Cohen was good at pondering and he was intensely practical.

"Maybe we could make you an adjunct professor, limit you to teaching Business Transactions and group your classes so you can teach three days a week," he continued. "Maybe you could come up Tuesday morning and leave Thursday night. That way you'd only be away two nights a week."

"That sounds great, Ben. Is it possible?"

"I think I can make it work. Let me see what I can do." He sounded chipper. "If I can, will you do it?"

"I have to talk to Nicole, but yes, it sounds good."

"There's one thing."

Uh oh, he thought to himself, here comes the zinger.

"As an adjunct professor, you wouldn't be able to be on committees, participate in academic decisions or hold academic posts at the Law School."

Jonathan was listening closely to see if Ben Cohen was being ironic. He sounded dead serious.

"It'll be a sacrifice, Ben. But I guess it's okay, if that's the way it has to be."

He was working hard to keep the broad smile out of his voice.

Chapter 56

"Mr. Franklin." The lady was middle-aged, maybe around 45, but handsome and well-coiffed. A little on the plump side. She had a nice smile. Her hair was dark brown with a gray slash in front. She had soft hazel eyes.

"I'm Sylvia Kris, Mr. Lissome's associate," she said extending her hand. "Mr. Willson spoke to me. We do so admire Mr. Aaron."

He had been delayed in getting the names he had promised Frankee. Everyone was still closed down for the holidays. He had reached Harv Champlin on vacation and set up a meeting, but that was about it. So, there was nothing else to do. It had surprised him that the gallery was open.

The space was white, accented in deeply stained cherry wood trim. The room lighting was soft and subdued. Each art work on the wall had its own light. An elegant but understated space on the second floor of a building on Madison near 74th Street.

"I'm sorry about Mr. Lissome. It must have been a shock."

"It was terrible. I was crushed."

"Thank you for coming in over the holidays."

"It's no problem really," Sylvia Kris said. "We always stay open between Christmas and New Year's. You would be surprised at how much business we do. But it feels lonely this year."

"Well, thank you anyway." Jonathan hesitated. How could he best get this woman to help him?

"Have you been with Mr. Lissome a long time?"

"More than 20 years. I came just after I graduated."

"What will happen to the gallery?"

"We don't know. We don't even know if there are any heirs. Or even a will. It was all so sudden. It's very upsetting." She searched in the pocket of her dress and brought out a lace handkerchief. She dabbed at the corner of her eye. "I'm sorry."

"Please. I understand."

"Let me show you Mr. Lissome's office." She sniffled a little as she led the way up a short set of stairs into another gallery space. She pointed to her left and they went through a second door into an office flooded with light from two large windows overlooking Madison Avenue.

The office was spartan, but the furniture was modern and expensive. Chrome and leather. Jonathan thought the furniture was probably the work of a famous designer or architect, but he had no idea who. He could see racks, showing the edges of many paintings in a storeroom that opened off the office, as well as several sculptures in bubble wrap. Every surface was covered with stacks of art magazines and catalogs from museums and auction houses. Books from gallery shows were in piles, some of the spines fading with age.

"Mr. Lissome's files are here," Sylvia Kris said, pointing to a wooden credenza, "and in the storeroom. He was a very meticulous man."

"There are no files off site? I know galleries often have off site storage."

"We do have storage space, but only for art. Mr. Lissome has . . .," she faltered, "I mean had a very extensive inventory. It was the envy of the gallery world."

"Thank you," said Jonathan, "I won't take too much of your time." Not with everything else I have to do, he thought. I don't know why Simon has me doing this. It's a waste of time.

His thoughts were interrupted by Sylvia Kris. He was surprised she was still standing there.

"May I bring you tea of coffee?"

"Oh. No. Thank you." The sooner he got done the better, as far as he was concerned.

"If there is anything I can do for you, I'll be in the gallery. We don't like to leave it unattended. And please, don't smoke."

"It's a bad habit I never adopted. One of the few, I'm afraid."

He smiled. She didn't.

"Mr. Lissome was always so concerned with his health. He watched what he ate and never smoked or took drugs. He was quite strict that way. It created problems with clients on occasion. Funny?"

"What?"

"He was so careful and yet he died so young. Oh, my."

She started to sob and turned away.

"Just one thing," Jonathan said.

She turned back. "Yes?" She sounded a little startled. She swallowed a sob.

"Are the files locked?"

"They normally are, but I opened them this morning to prepare for your visit. I hope that was all right."

"Yes, of course. Thank you."

Sylvia Kris retreated, wiping her eyes with her handkerchief, leaving Jonathan alone in the office.

Jonathan sat down behind Derek Lissome's desk and took a deep breath. He looked around slowly, taking in the paintings and the stacks of catalogs. He hadn't spent a lot of time in galleries, and what little he had spent was almost always in exhibition rooms.

He was curious about the business of art dealing. He wanted to know how every business ran. How it earned money. The pitfalls. It was what had made him a successful Mergers and Acquisitions lawyer. Jonathan's powers of concentration were such that, when he was interested in something, he was fully focused. He had forgotten his misgivings. In that, Simon had been right.

Jonathan suspected that the art gallery business was different from any business he had ever explored. It occurred to him that finding out the answer might help frame his search.

Not a bad place to start, he thought, as he got up and went back into the gallery. Sylvia Kris was sitting at a small desk to the side with a chair on the right.

"Can I help you, Mr. Franklin?"

"It would be better if you called me Jonathan. But actually, you can." He pulled the chair towards the front of the desk so he was facing Sylvia Kris. "I don't know much about the gallery business. Perhaps you can tell me how it operates."

"Of course. But I never actually ran the gallery, you understand."

Jonathan nodded. "Was Mr. Lissome an active dealer?"

"We prefer the term 'galleriest'. 'Dealer' sounds so common."

"Sorry. Did Mr. Lissome just buy and sell paintings?"

Sylvia Kris gave a small laugh. She covered her mouth with her hand in a demure gesture. It was sort of charming. "Oh, no. But we did have one of the finest inventories of Contemporary Art. It was very important. We mostly represent living artists. Generally, when one of their painting is sold, we would give them 50 percent of the sale price, less, of course, anything they owe us."

"You mean you took the paintings on consignment."

"It's not really consignment with the artists we represent. But, now that I think of it, I guess it's about the same thing. We do take collector's paintings on consignment sometimes, if they want to sell them."

"50 percent's a great margin. And you don't even have to buy the painting."

"Mr. Franklin. . ."

"Jonathan," he interrupted.

"We only get that with the paintings of the artists we represent. And not even that with the most important ones. And a gallery has a lot of expenses. Of course, we have rent on our space and storage. And insurance and security are costly.

"Sure." He smiled. Jonathan gave her his nice smile. It was warm and inviting. His eyes crinkled. He wanted her to keep talking.

"We have to mount shows for our artists and publish a catalog. And we buy the art of some of our artists. Mr. Lissome also bought and sold contemporary art at auction. He had a wonderful eye."

Jonathan re-crossed his legs and nodded as Sylvia Kris continued. He crooked his head to the side.

"Sometimes, we would advance money to a young artist so he could live. Making art isn't a very good living if you're an emerging artist. Of course, most of our artists were already well known, but Mr. Lissome liked to have a few artists he thought had potential. It is important in our business to cultivate emerging talent."

"How much capital does it require to run a gallery like this?"

"Oh, millions of dollars, I believe."

Jonathan whistled.

"Was Mr. Lissome a wealthy man?" he asked.

"Certainly not wealthy enough to run a major gallery such as ours. He did make money from commissions and consulting. But ultimately, we were dependent on our sales."

"The last few years must have been a rough patch, with the recovery that never quite recovered."

"My goodness, yes. So many galleries closed. Even the wonderful old ones. Mr. Lissome never spoke of it, though I could sense the strain he was under. But Mr. Lissome was resourceful. Our business has been getting better slowly."

"Where did Mr. Lissome get the money to support the business? I know the banks withdrew almost all lending to the art market."

"I really have no idea. But I do know it was very distressing for him. We cut back on staff. And we did almost no advertising."

"I had no idea galleries advertised, except maybe for new exhibits."

"Marketing is very important to us. We advertise in all the major art magazines and we often curate exhibitions where little or nothing is for sale, almost like a museum. It raised our stature in the community."

"Did you know anything about Mr. Lissome's dealings with Simon Aaron?"

"No, I wasn't aware of them."

"Do you know anything about his brokering a Gustav Klimt that was in Russia?"

"No."

"Well, thank you, Ms. Kris. I learned a lot. I'll spend some time with the files and get out of your hair as quickly as possible."

Actually, Jonathan was beginning to enjoy himself. He hummed a little on his was back to Derek Lissome's office. He was a man with a curious mind.

Chapter 57

Jonathan started by opening the credenza in Derek Lissome's office. There on top was a file marked "Simon Aaron." Sure there was. It was never that easy.

He spent an hour going through the "Current Correspondence" file. There was no relevant correspondence. The only things of note were several demanding letters from creditors, some quite strident.

Jonathan had no context to determine what that meant except that the gallery was behind in its bills. He didn't know whether that was business as usual or whether the gallery was in trouble. He made a note on his note pad to check further if necessary.

There were a series of client files and Jonathan went through each of them carefully, but without success. The latest file seemed to be for a Rafael Del Gado. That name was familiar, but he couldn't place it. He jotted down the name, address and a telephone number. He might need to contact him to get some more information on Lissome. He also wrote down a few other recent client names for possible follow-up.

He got up from the desk and groaned. He reached over his head and stretched his arms. That's the problem with getting old, he thought. You get stiff in all the wrong places. He chuckled at his little joke as he swung his arms to limber up his back.

He went into the storage room off the office. There were file drawers that seemed to contain inventory cards. Each piece was designated with a number and a letter.

Jonathan assumed that the letters designated location since some of the numbers were duplicates. Each card gave size in centimeters and inches, as well as the artist's name, medium, certain reference information and notations on condition.

Jonathan pulled a painting from the rack to verify the inventory records, then replaced it carefully. There was no mention of the Klimt. Not very productive, Jonathan thought, as he went back into Lissome's office.

He sat down behind Lissome's desk and placed his hands on his knees as he turned slowly in Lissome's chair and looked around. The only thing left were the drawers in Lissome's desk. Jonathan drew out the middle drawer. Pens, pencils, the usual things. An unopened e-cigarette package. That was odd. Sylvia Kris said Lissome didn't smoke. Maybe he wasn't as pure as he seemed.

Lissome wouldn't be the first. Then he remembered what Sylvia Kris had said about the clients. Maybe that was it. They were for clients who wanted to smoke and made a fuss. Possible.

The front side drawer was empty. But the bottom one was locked. That was hopeful. He looked around for a key. He looked under the leather desk pad. He hoped Lissome didn't carry it on his key chain.

He reopened the top middle drawer and moved the objects around, but there was no key. He looked in a box of paper clips and poked at them.

"'Genie'," he congratulated himself aloud as he withdrew a small key and held it up between two fingers. He fitted in the key and unlocked the bottom drawer.

His disappointment was palpable. There were two books of gay pornography and a series of unfortunate pictures. There was also an envelope with 10 $100 bills.

This visit had been a waste of time. Maybe he should follow up on his idea to call some recent clients. Perhaps they could shed some light on Lissome and his recent activities.

If he was going to do this silly errand, at least he was going to do it thoroughly. No time like the present. He picked up the phone and dialed the number for Rafael Del Gado.

Jonathan was pleased. At least something was going right. He had some trouble getting through to Del Gado until he told the secretary that he wanted to talk to Mr. Del Gado about his recent transaction with Derek Lissome. Then Del Gado picked up immediately.

"Mr. Franklin? What may I do to help you?"

"It's very nice of you to speak to me, Mr. Del Gado."

"You said you wanted to ask me about my dealings with Derek Lissome?" Jonathan sensed that Del Gado was wary. He wondered why.

"Yes. You see I'm representing Simon Aaron. I'm trying to understand a transaction that Mr. Lissome undertook for him."

"And you are calling me, why?"

"Well, I noticed the transaction you had with Mr. Lissome when I was reviewing his files."

"I see."

"And I thought that understanding your transaction might help me."

"Mr. Franklin, I am a very private man. I do not believe I can be of any help."

Jonathan was used to reluctant witnesses. He'd been there before.

"Mr. Del Gado, I won't take very much of your time. And I appreciate your desire for privacy. In fact, I'm trying to protect it. If we can talk, I won't have to discuss this with anyone else."

Del Gado paused. Was this man threatening him? If so, why? What did he know?

"Mr. Franklin, can you explain more of what you are seeking?"

Headway. Now was the time to push hard. Jonathan decided to exaggerate.

"Mr. Del Gado, let me be frank with you. I have some concerns about the legitimacy of Mr. Lissome's dealings with Mr. Simon. It may even be a matter for the police. I hope you can help me resolve my concerns."

Del Gado struggled to keep his voice in check. Was he being blackmailed? It appeared so. He couldn't let that happen. And he certainly didn't want the police examining his dealings with Derek Lissome. He needed time.

"Mr. Franklin, I would be happy to meet with you. But I need time to review my files and gather the relevant documents. Can we meet next week?

"Of course, I'll come to your office."

"No, no. I think it would be better to meet outside the office. Then we will not be interrupted." Yes, that was best. Then he would not be seen with this person.

"Certainly, wherever you like."

"Possibly my accounting firm. They have a private conference room."

"Sure."

Del Gado gave him a name and address and set the date and time. He put down the phone carefully. This was a new and complicated problem. He had to think.

Jonathan was pleased. He'd done well. Now maybe Simon would get off his back and let him deal with things that were really important.

Chapter 58

The snow had cleared and the stars squeezed down between the buildings. It almost seemed as if everyone in New York had come out on the street to celebrate.

The play had been good, but not great. Great plays were even harder to find than great wines. Maybe, Jonathan reflected, that's why he liked wine better.

The evening was cold, but not unpleasant, and he and Nicole had decided to walk back to their apartment. Jonathan had on his cashmere overcoat and a fur hat. It gave him a feeling of security. He needed all the security he could come by these days.

Sixth Avenue was busy. Yet it was somehow more laid-back than in the daytime. Nicole had her arm through his. She dropped it and took his gloved hand instead.

"Perhaps a penny for your thoughts, Cheri. More even, if you will talk to me."

Jonathan let out a sigh. "Darling, I'm sorry. I don't know how you put up with me. I've been rotten company since this insider trading thing came up. It seems to eat me up inside. I find myself consumed with thinking about it."

He paused reflectively. The fear was almost a physical pain. When he went on, it was as if he was extracting something from deep inside himself.

"I wish we could go back to laughing a lot. Just be with each other. I miss it. And I'm scared I won't be able to make this right. I'm scared of being indicted."

Nicole squeezed his hand and looked sideways into his face as he continued.

"Do you remember Kevin Krispinson, the investment banker? I think I introduced you once. He was tried for securities fraud. They acquitted him. But he never came back. Everyone was a just little bit leery of him. He finally left town." Jonathan's voice showed the stress. He bit his lower lip.

"I do understand. It is a terrible thing. I see Simon with the same look in his eyes. He does not even seem to hear me on occasion."

Nicole was wearing a long, sleek fur coat. Jonathan slipped off his glove and stroked her arm absently. The fur was very soft, almost erotic.

"I just hope somehow it gets better soon. We've got to find a thread. Something to unravel this with. Frankee hasn't come up with anything since that detective, Kinsky, was killed. The whole thing's so damned clever. Whoever's behind this doesn't seem to have made any mistakes."

"Simon is afraid of the impact on Witten's if he is indicted," Nicole said. "He is concerned that he will have to step down. And the impact it will have on the stock. At Sanford's also. Sacre bleu. So many people will be hurt. And the lawsuits."

"He's right. It's not fair. Particularly to you. You get it from both ends. Witten's will be in a tailspin, and our life will be in complete turmoil."

"Give me 30 days," he continued, trying to crawl out of his mood with a joke, "and if this doesn't go away, I give you permission to shoot me." He let out a small, hollow laugh.

"Oh, Cheri," Nicole said. Her tone was serious. "I would not shoot you." Now a smile spread on her lips. "I am still French, of course." She emphasized the word "French" in her slightly accented English. "I would poison you. We French women are very passionate. It would be a crime of passion, because I love you so, and you are such an idiot to think I would shoot you."

He burst into laughter. One of those deep, gut-busting laughs that brought tears to his eyes. Nicole joined in. Perhaps it was the tension they had been under, but when one of them stopped laughing, they'd look at each other and start all over again.

As Jonathan gasped for breath, he changed the subject. "Ben Cohen called. He wants me back."

"Of course he does. You are a wonderful teacher."

"It's only because he couldn't get anyone else to teach my courses."

"Cheri, that is not true."

"Well, he really bent over backwards. I'll give you that." Jonathan told her what Cohen had proposed.

They made their way home laughing. People stared at them on the street, but they were oblivious to everyone, absorbed in each other for the first time in weeks.

He reached over and pulled her close. Her hair smelled of good shampoo and faintly of perfume. He felt himself stirring. That was a sensation he hadn't had in a while. He looked down at her and put his hand under her chin, turning as he raised her head towards him. He kissed her as they walked.

"Lady," he said, "we better hurry. We've got a lot to get straight between us."

"Ooh la la," was all she said, returning his smile and placing her hand on his chest.

Jonathan didn't know he had another problem. One even more serious than a securities fraud indictment. He had scared Rafael Del Gado. And Rafael Del Gado had a lot to lose. If Jonathan was poking around, what might he come across and how long before others did also. No, the problem had to be stopped here. Alejandro had made another call.

Jonathan and Nicole didn't notice the white Chevrolet Malibu with the young black man at the wheel, patiently dogging their steps. As luck would have it, it didn't make any difference.

Chapter 59

The dancing had stopped. Couples looked towards the front of the ballroom expectantly. Jonathan held Nicole's hand.

"Three. Two. One. Happy New Year!"

Jonathan turned into Nicole and took her gently in his arms. He put his hand under her chin and raised her mouth to his. God, she looked beautiful to him. He kissed her and felt the warmth of her surge through his body.

Auld Lang Syne broke out. Jonathan sang from his heart, as he always sang Auld Lang Syne. An uninvited tear ran down his cheek. He had a lump in his throat when he sang the song. Its minor key touched him, as did the weight of the passing days.

He wished he knew what the words to the song meant. Once again he made a mental note to research it.

They were in the ballroom of the Lotos Club, just off 5th Avenue at 66th. The old brownstone mansion was stately. A wedding gift to a Vanderbilt scion at the turn of the 20th century. They did things right in those days.

The club was one of the oldest literary clubs in the country. The strange spelling of "Lotos" came from a Tennyson poem. Mark Twain had been a member. It was formed as an "inclusive" club. In 1870, that meant actors, artists, writers and musicians. Not blacks or women.

Some serious history had been made in its elegant rooms. How Simon had become a member was a mystery to Jonathan. He wasn't exactly the literary type. It must be his connection with art.

The club was astir with people blowing horns and popping noisemakers. Jonathan was feeling down. He wished they hadn't come. But Tae and Nicole insisted it would be good for them to get out. Christmas had been so solemn.

Who knew what this New Year would bring. Disgrace. Prison was definitely in play. He hoped not.

Maybe Frankee could pull off a miracle. And soon. The indictment would be imminent now that the holidays were over.

It had been so simple a few months ago. He would gladly go back to being bored. If he had only known. A thought struck him and he gave a little mirthless chuckle.

"What, Cheri?" She wiped away the wetness on his cheek with her fingers.

"I think I've invented a new diet. Fear. I've lost 10 pounds in the last month. Don't I look swell."

"You are too thin, Cheri. I like you a little more plump." She gave him a poke with her finger. "We must feed you more." Jonathan laughed in spite of himself. "Do not worry. It will be a good year. I feel it inside of me."

Tae and Simon came up. Jonathan and Nicole turned to greet them.

"Happy New Year." She gave Simon a hug.

"And to you."

Tae Simon was elegant in a long, red, sequined gown that showed her back and was slit on one side to her knee. Her hair was up in a chignon, pinned with something that glittered. Diamonds sparkled at her neck.

Simon. Well, Simon looked like Simon. But the big teddy bear was extremely well dressed in a beautifully cut tuxedo. He took two flutes of champagne from a passing waiter. The waiter turned to allow Jonathan also to take champagne.

Jonathan couldn't resist asking. "What are they pouring tonight?"

"Pierre Peters 2002, sir," the waiter said.

Jonathan was impressed.

Simon lifted the glass of golden liquid. "To the New Year. May it sparkle like this champagne and improve with age." Then he broke. "Oy."

Tae elbowed Simon playfully in the ribs. "I'll give you 'oy'."

"Here, here," Jonathan responded in a fervent voice, lifting his glass as well. It actually was good to get out. He felt better. He hoped the feeling wouldn't pass.

Chapter 60

It was New Year's Day. They were sitting on their bed, watching the Rose Bowl and dreaming of warmer weather. A comforter covered their feet. UCLA was leading by seven.

Jonathan was in his pajamas, unshaven. Nicole was leaning into him. He had his arm around her. It was snowing hard outside and the temperature had plummeted overnight. Jonathan felt as if he were in a little cave and the world was asleep.

Then the phone rang.

"Jonathan, my dear chap." It was Adrian Asheton. Thank goodness it was halftime.

"Sir Adrian. Good morning to you. And I hope the New Year treats you well." All of us, please God.

"And a happy New Year to you too. I'm calling to say goodbye and to thank you for everything you have done for me. Quite sterling."

Jonathan was suddenly alert. He hoped Sir Adrian was not running. That would be silly. He made his voice light. "Where are you going?"

"Flying to Brazil, actually."

"But why Brazil?" Jonathan knew the answer to that. Brazil does not have an extradition treaty with the United States on tax matters.

"I rather like it there."

Nicole made a quizzical face at Jonathan. He mouthed, "I'll tell you about it," and then made a hand motion to indicate that he would do so when he was finished with the call.

"Sir Adrian, have you really thought this through?" Jonathan readjusted his position on the bed. "You know, there must be another way."

"I really don't see it, old boy." He sounded resolute.

"But. . ."

"Why should I not take an airplane? It seems foolish to go any other way. Rio is on the coast. But still."

"Huh?"

The phone went silent for a moment, then Asheton chuckled.

"Forgive me, my boy." Jonathan thought he could hear the smile.

"Why?"

"I'm afraid I'm having rather a good pull at your leg." He sounded gleeful.

"Sir Adrian, I'm glad." At least someone felt like joking.

"Yes, I wanted you to know promptly. The leak we had."

"Oh, I recall it very well. That was a disaster." For me too, he thought.

"Not quite."

"Really?"

Nicole poked Jonathan in the ribs and made an opened handed gesture. There was a pouting turn to her lips. She wanted to know what was going on. He shook her off.

"Yes, it brought a bid from a private equity group. Rather first class people, I think."

"Was it a good offer?"

"Quite good. An 18-percent increase in the price, all cash and no conditions."

"Gosh, that's terrific. What has the board decided."

"We met yesterday. We are recommending it to our shareholders. There are no antitrust issues so the lawyers feel it will proceed quickly."

"That's great. Does this take you off the hook with the IRS?"

"Yes, I believe it does. I shall be able to pay your IRS people and perhaps still have a little."

Jonathan could do the math in his head. He was good at it. It came from years of deal making. 'A little' in this case was $117 million give or take a few million.

"Actually Jonathan, I called to invite you and your lovely wife to a small dinner party I am having in a fortnight. A small celebration, you know. I really do have to go to Rio on business for several days."

"Sir Adrian, I would love to come. But this decision is beyond my rank and pay grade."

"I'm afraid I don't understand."

"A little joke of my own," he said, ducking the pillow Nicole threw at him. "I need to speak to Nicole. May I get back to you in the next day or so?"

"Of course."

Actually Jonathan hoped he would be able to attend at all. Horizontal stripes just wouldn't look good with a black bow tie.

Chapter 61

"Good Lord, what was he thinking?" Jonathan said aloud to a stranger who ignored him. He was staring at a crushed black Lincoln Town Car, awash under the geyser from a broken fire hydrant. Its airbag pinned a young black man to his seat.

Two policemen were busy trying to extract the driver, but the door was jammed, leading to a good deal of vociferous cursing from the officers. The water had soaked through their uniforms, making their hair look like limp worms clinging to their heads. A squalling squad car screeched to a stop. Jonathan could see a police officer on his radio verifying the car's license information.

That's the second time in a week one of these crazy drivers almost hit me. His eyes passed over the driver. Funny, he thought idly, it doesn't look like his kind of car.

Then he remembered how close a call it had been. It's getting worse here by the day, dammit. If that other guy coming through the intersection hadn't creamed him, I could have been killed.

Close enough for Jonathan to get his feet wet in the gushing water. He glanced at his watch and realized the accident was making him late. He didn't want to be late for his meeting with Rafael Del Gado.

The problem with Derek Lissome somehow piqued his interest. Why was there no record at all of Lissome's Russian contacts, or his efforts to secure the Klimt?

There probably were some illicit payments involved but you would think Lissome would have kept some kind of records. Even vague notes or something encrypted. After all, he needed to know dates and follow up. He also had to know how much he had spent. But there was nothing. At least nothing he could find.

And now Lissome's connection with the forged Purland was suspicious. You would think an art dealer would have a better eye. Of course, it might be coincidence, but it made Jonathan wonder. It tickled a memory he had forgotten. He was thinking about an incident that occurred when he was trying to purchase his Porsche 356 some years ago. Then he looked at his watch and his thoughts reverted.

Del Gado's secretary had called to confirm the place and time of the meeting yesterday. It was an easy walk from Central Park South. But Jonathan hadn't allowed time for the accident.

He started to walk in his squishy shoes towards the high-rise office building two block further on, leaving wet footprints behind him on the sidewalk. No time to change. This was not the way to meet someone you didn't know, he reflected. It detracted from your gravitas.

The sun went behind a cloud and brought a shiver. It reminded him that Frankee Pereire still hadn't found that loose end they needed. She was interviewing people from the lists Jonathan had finally supplied, but without success. And Harv Champlin was getting really nervous about being able to hold off an indictment.

He'd have to call Frankee again. He'd also set her working on the Witten's problem. Maybe she'd been able to find out why the stock had taken a nosedive. "When it rains it pours," he sighed aloud, to the accompaniment of his squishy footsteps illustrating the phrase. His feet were getting cold. He walked faster. There wasn't a taxi in sight.

The elevator doors opened into a large, luxurious reception area, done professionally in shades of brown. The burnished wood on the small reception desk was deeply grained birds eye maple, and the young lady sitting behind it was a knockout. An etched steel replica of the accounting firm's international logo filled the wall behind her. Things had changed in the accounting business. The receptionist looked up as Jonathan entered and smiled. She had the whitest teeth he had ever seen.

Then she looked down at the wet indentations trailing Jonathan in her deep brown carpet. Her voice went frosty.

"May help you?" she asked. What she meant was, what could a man in a tweed jacket and wet shoes possibly want here. Her tone made the subtext painfully obvious.

It gave Jonathan some small pleasure to say in an authoritative tone, "I'm here to see Rafael Del Gado. He's reserved a conference room for us."

She looked down at her appointment book. Then she picked up the telephone and dialed an extension. She spoke briefly to whoever was on the other end of the line. She carefully replaced the receiver and looked up at Jonathan, her face set in a neutral expression.

"I'm sorry, sir" she replied, tersely. "We have no conference room reserved. I've spoken to the audit manager who deals with Mr. Del Gado. He said Mr. Del Gado had reserved a conference room, but canceled it this morning."

Jonathan was thrown off. "Are you absolutely certain? Mr. Del Gado specifically asked to see me here today. I've got the message slip confirming the meeting," he said, fumbling for it in his side pocket.

"Sir," she said, the exasperation beginning to show through in her voice, "I keep the schedule for all of our conference rooms. As you can see," she said, turning the computer screen towards him, "there are no conference rooms reserved at this time."

He turned to leave.

"Excuse me," she called out. He turned his head.

"Would you mind taking off your shoes. You're all wet."

Chapter 62

Jonathan had called the meeting. It was 9:30 in the morning. They were walking in Central Park. Their breath came out in white clouds before being blown away in the cold breeze. Simon shrugged deeper into his vicuna overcoat.

"It's cold."

"Simon, you need the exercise," Jonathan said.

"No I don't. I pay a guy to exercise for me. He's really good."

"It's beautiful in the park at this time of year. Quit complaining."

The sun was out and the temperature hovered just above freezing. Almost no one else was on the path. As Simon was about to retort, they were overtaken by a jogger in shorts and a down vest. Simon looked at the retreating figure, shut his mouth and just shook his head.

"So, what's so important that you bring me out in this," Simon finally asked. He made a gesture with his hand that seemed to indicate they were exploring an undiscovered land where the natives were decidedly unfriendly.

"I don't have a good feeling about your deal with Derek Lissome. I think you were scammed."

"That's ridiculous."

"Simon, let me tell you a little story. I had completely forgotten it."

"Oh, goody. Is it a bedtime story?" Simon reached inside his overcoat and pulled out a cigar.

"Maybe. Just listen." This was new for Jonathan. Maybe for Simon too. "I thought of it the other day."

"So?"

"You know I have a Porsche 356."

Simon shrugged and made a 'get to it' gesture with his hands.

"Be patient. When I was looking for the car, I saw an ad. It was in Cars. com, I think."

"I know you'll get to the point. I just don't want to freeze to death first."

Jonathan ignored him. "It offered a great car, fully restored, low mileage. Must sell."

Simon cut the end off his cigar with the cutter he extracted from his pocket and lite it. He rolled it in his fingers as he looked at Jonathan through the rising smoke.

"Only an e-mail address," Jonathan continued. "No telephone number. So I e-mailed the guy. He apologized and said he had just arrived in Greece and hadn't had time to get a phone. That's why he had to sell the car."

"So he could buy a phone?"

"No. He'd accepted a five year consulting assignment in Greece and he couldn't take his car."

"I'll bet you got a deal."

"We negotiated a price. It was on the low side. I said it was conditioned on my seeing the car."

"Of course. Even you wouldn't buy a car without looking at it."

"Not this time."

Simon looked at Jonathan sharply. Jonathan waggled his eyebrows. Simon tapped the ash off his cigar onto the ground.

"Well, the seller said he had dropped the car at a shipper in Boston so it could be shipped when he sold it. It would also be safe."

"That makes sense."

"I thought so too. I said I would go to Boston to see the car but he said it was wrapped up in preparation for shipping."

"You passed on the deal, of course."

"No, not then. The seller offered to let me put the purchase price into an escrow, and if the car wasn't as he had advertised, I could get my money back. I just had to deliver the car and the keys to the escrow holder. I could choose the bank for the escrow."

"Just as I did with Lissome. It's the only smart way. Will you get to the point?"

"That's when I figured it out."

"I can't wait." Simon said it with some exasperation. He pulled the vicuna coat closer around him.

"It was a scam. I would pay the shipper. You have to pay them in advance. No car. I'm out the shipping fees."

"That's peanuts."

"About $3,000. And however much more they could get out of me when the delivery truck broke down somewhere in upstate New York. Multiply that by the number of people who fall for the scam. It's a lot of money. And I'll bet you there was a Porsche 356 in Massachusetts registered in the name of the guy."

"You think Lissome was defrauding me." Simon's mouth sagged. He looked dour.

"Yep, and there's no telling how many times he pulled the scam. There are a lot of rich men who would want that Klimt. No one would talk about it."

"But what about his contacts? I was going to pay him a lot of money."

"Not unless he could deliver the painting. I'll bet he never had any contacts in Russia. How would you know? Besides, he could make a lot more money this way if he found other takers. And he didn't have a whole lot of expenses."

Simon grunted.

"And before you ask me about what this would do to his reputation, let me ask you. What if he came to you and said he'd made the payments, but the Russians found out and arrested everyone. It was practically foolproof. He just had to have the guts to pull it off."

"Shit."

"Oh, there's one other thing Lissome knew."

"You're going to tell me, if I want you to or not."

"Even if you suspected something, you never would have gone to the police."

Simon pulled the cigar from his mouth. Ash sprayed into the breeze. Jonathan raised his hand to flick ash away from his face. "That's crap," Simon said.

"Not the Simon I know. Not when someone might get the silly idea that he was conspiring to bribe officials of a foreign government."

"You got me." Simon looked deflated.

"No, Lissome did. But, don't feel so bad. You were dealing with some-one you knew, or at least knew of. It made you less suspicious."

Simon's cigar burned in his hand untouched. "I'd kill the son a of a bitch, if he weren't already dead," Simon growled.

It made Jonathan think of something.

Chapter 63

"You know," Harvey Champlin said, rubbing his chin, "there was something peculiar that happened around here about that time." He emphasized the word 'was.' "Just a small thing."

Harv Champlin was sitting with Jonathan and Frankee Pereire in one of the small conference rooms at Whiting & Pierce. There were bagels and cream cheese in the middle of the table. Jonathan had a cinnamon-raisin bagel in front of him. He had broken off a piece and was spreading it with cream cheese. A cup of coffee was steaming next to his plate.

Champlin had just returned from a short vacation. They had asked him about the time frame Frankee was exploring concerning Alex Kinsky's movements. She had already spoken to the printers and the lawyers for the buyer without success. Whiting & Pierce was representing HST Heartcare, Sir Adrian Asheton's company. They had talked to the lawyers assigned to the deal. Harv was the last person they were to see because he had been away.

"It's probably nothing. It doesn't even concern the team working on the HST Heartcare deal. It stuck with me because it just doesn't happen here."

"I'd like to hear it anyway," said Frankee, making a note in her small precise handwriting on a leather-bound pad she was holding in her lap. She looked up at Harv and smiled. "You know how we work. God knows, we've been through it enough."

Frankee was the investigator of choice for Whiting & Pierce as well as for Simon Aaron. She and Harv had worked together a dozen times over the years.

Champlin was always shocked at the amount of money W&P paid her every year. He was glad it didn't come out of the firm's pocket. It would have made a sizable dent in their profits.

"I want to know anything that seems out of place," Frankee said. "No exceptions. You never know where stray facts lead. Usually nowhere. But. . ."

"That's why I brought it up. You know that part of my job, in heading the corporate group, is to deal with issues that come up with the professionals."

Jonathan nodded, chewing happily on his bagel. Been there, done that. Trying to forget.

"We handle a lot of big deals that involve a lot of people on each team, both lawyers and paralegals. When you're doing a deal, the pressure is relentless."

"Why?" asked Frankee, curious. "There's no deadline really."

Jonathan jumped in, swallowing and putting his bagel aside. "That's true, and not true Frankee."

Frankee chortled. "Thank you, counselor. Now I'm clear."

"Well, the clients press hard, of course."

"Sure."

"And they're paying W&P a king's ransom."

She turned back to Champlin. "How much are you charging now?"

"$1,200 an hour."

Frankee whistled. Jonathan winced.

"That's the base rate we expect, but our clients agree to pay us a reasonable fee for the work we undertake," Champlin said. "It usually comes out to be more."

"So, they own you," Frankee said. It was a statement.

"Yeah, I guess that's true. But that's not the real pressure, as Jonathan can tell you. When you've been in this business as long as we have, you've seen deals crater because something off-the-wall happens. You're always running up against an unknown deadline."

Frankee raised an eyebrow.

"For instance, the Greek debt crisis that suddenly erupted. Bank lending snapped shut like a bear trap. Deals cratered right and left. That's what makes it so stressful. It's harder than working against a deadline."

Jonathan cut in. "Harv's right." He took a sip of his coffee. "You'd rather have a deadline. Then, at least, if something happens, it's not your fault."

"Amen, brother," said Champlin.

"And if a deal tanks, it's a disaster for everyone," he continued.

"Except the lawyers. They get paid anyway," Frankee said.

"I wish. We usually have to eat a major portion of the fees we haven't collected. And the clients are pissed. Besides, I have to answer to the firm's executive committee because of the write-offs. Those guys are worse than the clients."

"Okay, got it. So, what was peculiar?"

Frankee's question pulled Champlin back into the moment. He had been praying at the altar of the Deal God.

"Oh. Well, when a team is put together to work a deal, it's understood that no one goes on vacation. Even sick leave is frowned upon. Absence disrupts the critical paths."

"You're kidding me. Critical paths?"

"No, really, Frankee. Everything is layered. People review stacks of documents given to us by the other side and prepare summaries. We need legal research to negotiate deal terms. And we need to draft documents to do a deal.

"Each step relies on someone else. Everyone on the team has a job. It's like a manufacturing process. Or maybe a staircase. You can't climb unless the lower stair is in place. And we don't pad the bill with extra people. Everyone is necessary."

"That's not what I heard."

"Come on, Frankee."

"Just kidding."

"Well, anyway, this paralegal who was assigned to the team working on one of our big deals. . ."

Jonathan interrupted. "Not the HST Heartcare deal."

Harv shook his head. "No. Another one. I can't tell you the name. It hasn't been announced."

"What about the paralegal," Frankee asked.

"Well, he takes off. I never approved the time off. He never asked. It really screwed things up. The partner in charge of the deal was pissed beyond belief. Came screaming into my office. Wanted him fired. He refused to take the guy back on his team."

"The paralegal returned?" Jonathan asked.

"Yeah, about four or five days later. I had him in my office within 15 minutes. I read him the riot act. He squeaked and squealed about being sick, but I didn't buy it. He looked great. Had a nice tan. And he never called in."

"Did you fire him?"

"No, I gave him a warning. I scared the pants off him. But experienced deal paralegals are hard to find. And the guy had never been in trouble before."

"Can I talk to him?" Frankee asked.

"Sure."

"What's his name?"

"Justin Winnett." He spelled it. "Do you want to see him now?"

"No," said Frankee. "I want to do my homework first. Can you have H.R. give me his information and a copy of his file?"

"I'll get you what I can, but they're ogres about giving out information."

"Let me remind you, we're talking about the internal investigation of a possible criminal act that could involve an employee of your firm."

"I know. I'll push."

"Then get me what you can. After all, I am a detective."

Chapter 64

The rental car tended to over-steer and the ride was mushy. It made Jonathan think fondly of his restored yellow, 1963 model 356 Cabriolet Porsche. The one he had told Simon about. It had been his gift to himself when he quit Whiting & Pierce to teach at Harvard. Now he'd have to decide what to do with it.

"As if that were the worst of my problems," he recalled with a suppressed shudder. He was driving through the farmland stretching alongside New York Highway 22, the north-south, two-lane road that parallels the Taconic Parkway. The back way up to Boston.

He had chosen to drive instead of fly because he wanted time to think. Besides, it was a glorious winter's day, the cold, moist air filling the car. The trees were singing their winter song, their bare branches festooned with bits of ice.

He told Nicole he needed to sort out what to do with his house in Concord now that he was going to live in New York for most of the week. And he did have to figure it out.

But that was assuming he had a job in the fall. The Law School didn't have too many professors who were under felony indictment, at least as far as he could recall.

Which brought him back to his central problem. What the hell was going on? So far, Harv Champlin had successfully held off the indictment, but how much longer did they have?

Would this gamble Frankee was pursuing pay off, somehow? How soon would she question that paralegal, Winnett? They would be incredibly lucky to hit the nail on the head. But to drive it home one blow? Boy, that was a long-shot. Jonathan just knew he wasn't that lucky.

Did they have enough time even if she did? And what did they know? Who had the kind of money to let $1.2 million slip away in order to pull off this kind of frame-up? And why? Someone must be looking for a really big score somewhere. "Or hate Simon and me most fervently," he acknowledged.

Okay, he thought, let's parse this. His hands were steering independently of his mind. Someone went to a lot of trouble to set us up. So who has that kind of money and the desire to do it? He stared unseeing at the fleeing landscape. He snapped back when the car shuddered as the tires hit the dirt shoulder.

There were only two possible reasons, he figured. One was revenge. The other involved something current. And it had to include both Simon and me. That narrowed it down. Was it possible that this was related to Andrew Grahm's death? Maybe, but he didn't see how. How about Derek Lissome? Kinsky?

What did he and Simon have to do with the museum? He was certainly working for the Nauton, trying to keep a lid on all of their problems. Tae was a director. But why would anyone care?

His mind flashed on the embrace between Rebecca Grahm and Peter Willson the day when Rebecca had come to clean out Andrew Grahm's office. The strange look Peter had given him. He thought it was odd at the time. Something between embarrassment and guilt.

And Ailene Brown had told Detective Tritter that Grahm was going to divorce Rebecca. That was interesting. If, of course, it was true. It wouldn't be the first time a woman killed her husband, certainly not with another man around.

"Could Peter Willson somehow be responsible?" But Willson was Tae's friend. And he was such a mouse. Jonathan shook his head and laughed aloud, but cut himself off abruptly.

It didn't seem so funny suddenly. Could they be concerned about what he might stumble onto. Maybe? Was the SEC inquiry meant to distract them? Well, it certainly had. But did they have the resources?

Rebecca Grahm was obviously rich, at least he thought so, based on what he knew about her lifestyle. But what about the skills? Did she or Peter Willson have the skills and knowledge?

It wouldn't be too hard, he thought. All they'd have to do was hire Kinsky. Maybe that's just what they did. Who knew what kind of experience

Peter Willson or Rebecca Grahm might have in the stock market, or, for that matter, what relationships they had in the Caymans.

"Okay, it's possible," he said aloud.

But why Simon? he asked himself. Was it the only way to get to me? Did Willson or Rebecca Grahm have something to gain by destroying Simon? By hurting Witten's?

Was Witten's competing with the museum in some way? Tae Simon was on the museum board. Did they want to hurt her? Through her husband? It didn't make much sense. His mind was going round and round with questions and connections without answers. He decided to put it all aside. He needed more facts. He mentally shifted gears.

Who had he and Simon angered? At least angered enough that they'd go to such lengths to retaliate? He sighed and let his mind run through a catalog of the deals he and Simon had done together. Simon was single minded in his deal making, and as ruthless as any corporate raider. He had infuriated a lot of people over the years.

But who would also feel that way about me? he asked himself. Who would hate a lawyer. He stopped himself short. Don't go there. Could I only be collateral road kill here?

He didn't think so. The separate brokerage account. The post office box. The money transfer. No. It was quite deliberate.

They had been in some pretty fierce takeover battles, sure. But one name kept beating its way forward into his brain. Just one seemed personal. Vincent Rollins.

It made sense, he thought. Not only did we have that bloody fight when Rollins tried to take Witten's away from Simon. Just after I started teaching at Harvard. . . He stopped and his mind detoured.

That's when I met Nicole. Four years ago. Isn't it strange how coincidental life is? He shoved his mind back onto its track.

And we're now going after Rollins' company, he thought. He must hate Simon's guts. It's certainly mutual. We've personally embarrassed him with this takeover offer. Who knows what else might come out if we take over his company? Civil lawsuits? Criminal? It makes a lot of sense.

He also doesn't like me very much, Jonathan acknowledged. Their encounters had never been pleasant and he had made the call to Rollins before they announced the takeover bid.

He mentally counted on his fingers the reasons for Rollins to attack him and Simon. First, it's a great defense. He's distracting us. It also will make it impossible for us to pursue a tender offer. I can see Quintile's proxy now:

"Fellow shareholders, do you want to sell your shares to an unscrupulous company whose principal is under Federal indictment? Will they preserve shareholder value? Enhance it. Can you trust them to even close a transaction? Of course not."

Jonathan paused again.

Actually, it's better than that. I wonder if Rollins realized that we're going to have to pull the plug on the tender offer because of the financing problems this potential indictment creates. Simon and I just came to that conclusion yesterday. Could he be smarter than we are? He paused in thought at the idea. $1.2 million dollars was cheap to save his company. Was he that ruthless? Absolutely.

"Okay, big point there," he said on aloud, hitting his hand on the steering wheel.

Second, Rollins would cripple Witten's. He'd like that. Maybe even make it vulnerable to a takeover. Talk about turning the tables.

He nodded his agreement with himself.

Third, Rollins has the resources and the skills. He knew the drill. He understood the S.E.C. He had the contacts in the Caymans. The money would be no problem. And he'd do whatever was necessary.

His mind emphasized the word "whatever."

It all ties together, he concluded, rapping his fist again on the steering wheel.

"Now all I have to is figure out some way to save my . . . our ass." He said it to the interior of the car. "How do I get the proof?"

Chapter 65

"Mr. Morales. This is Alejandro. I am in New York."

Alejandro made the call to Bogata from a pay phone in Grand Central Station while Rafael Del Gado was at lunch. He knew of no other pay phone in the city.

He had a number written on a scrap of paper. He had copied it awkwardly last night and had gotten change from the jar he kept. It was quite a lot of change and it weighed in his pocket. He was concerned Del Gado might notice, but he did not.

Alejandro was not comfortable speaking to Mr. Morales. Morales was a powerful man. But he had been sent to New York by Mr. Morales to make sure all went well. He had never called him before.

"Yes, Heje, thank you. I do not want to disturb you, but if you have a moment, I wish to speak with you." He paused and listened.

"Yes, Heje, perhaps there is a problem. It is about Mr. Del Gado." Again he listened.

"No, Heje, it is not about the business. I think Mr. Del Gado do things I do not understand. Perhaps you understand better."

They talked for 10 minutes. Alejandro opened his coat and wiped his hands on his shirt. It was warm inside the station, out of the wind.

It was a week before Alejandro received the text message and returned to the pay phone. "I understand," he said into the phone. Yes, immediately, Heje." He hung up.

Morales had not explained. He had only instructed. Mr. Morales was a wise man, as Alejandro knew.

Tuesday afternoon was the time when Alejandro drove Rafael Del Gado to see his mistress. Alejandro was to wait three hours in the car. This was as always.

Del Gado returned to the car, a little drunk. He often fell asleep in the back seat on his way to his house in Westchester. The drive took an hour and a half.

The car made a detour onto a small gravel road, into a copse of woods and down to a lake. Del Gado stirred, but turned his head and resumed snoring. The road was lighted only by a pale sliver of moon. The few small houses beside the lake were dark. Weekend homes.

Rafael Del Gado slept peacefully in the back seat, aware that he had solved all of his problems. Except one.

"It is done, Heje," Alejandro said into the pay phone. Then he got onto the express shuttle bus to La Guardia and took a seat in back.

Mrs. Sophia Del Gado lived in a large gated house in an upscale neighborhood of Rio de Janiero. She had a splendid view of Sugar Loaf and Corcovado. Life was pleasant.

A package with a substantial amount of cash arrived one day in the next week. There was also a note. She read it and a tear came to her eye. She was a widow again. Then she shrugged.

No item ever appeared in the New York Times or elsewhere. Rafael Del Gado had disappeared. It wasn't news.

The Director of Development at the Nauton was disappointed.

Chapter 66

The FBI agents were holding him under the elbows. They came out of the revolving door. His hands were handcuffed behind his back. One of the agents placed his hand on top of the man's head as he bent him into the back of a large black, nondescript car.

A group of pedestrians had stopped and gathered to watch a few steps away. Only two of them knew the name of the man.

"Great work, Frankee," Jonathan said. "Where do we go from here?"

"Winnett deposited a $20,000 check in his bank account just before Harv said he went missing. And $20,000 about a week later. Not bad for a paralegal. The deposits was made around a week after Kinsky used Simon's computers to send those e-mails to the Caymans to establish the brokerage account."

"How did you find out?"

"The same way I found out about Kinsky's bank account. About which I would not tell you."

Jonathan raised his hands, palms forward in a gesture of surrender. "Sorry."

"Anyway," Frankee continued, "we had the bank records before I talked to young Mr. Winnett. And we had tracked his trip to the Caymans through his credit cards. His girl friend became very cooperative when I properly explained the situation to her. It seemed the prospect of jail was not appealing."

"I'll bet. And I know how she felt."

"It took about an hour with Winnett. When he was convinced I knew what had happened, he broke down. He cried like a kid. He was scared. You know, he knew he was never going to be caught. It was easy money. I asked him how he got the information. He had access to a partner's files. I'd say W&P has some work to do on their security."

"And you volunteered."

"A girl's got to make a living." A cold wind gusted. Frankee pulled her coat closer together. The weather people were predicting a major snowstorm.

"Why'd he talk to you?"

"I told him I wouldn't go to the police if he told me the truth."

"You lied."

"There you go again. I did not lie. I didn't go to the police. I went to the FBI."

"Ah." Jonathan stifled a smile. "So Winnett sold the information to Alex Kinsky."

"Yep. He identified Kinsky's picture."

"And Kinsky framed us."

"Sure looks like it."

"But with Kinsky dead, how do we find out who he was working for?"

"Well, I don't think we can. We've hit one dead end after another; you should forgive the pun. I tried the Wall Street Journal reporter who broke the story on the HST merger. She won't give up her sources. Even if she did, there's no guarantee that it's not a second or third-hand piece of information."

"Damn."

"I'm surprised we got this far. It was just luck, you know. This frame-up was pretty clever."

"I know, Frankee. We owe you."

"Don't worry. I'll give you a bill."

"That's not what I meant."

"I did." She smiled and reached into her coat and took out an envelope. She handed it to Jonathan.

"What's this?"

"My bill."

Jonathan grimaced and put it into the pocket of his overcoat. He'd dealt with Frankee before. And besides, he had more pressing concerns.

"What about the S.E.C.? And the U.S. Attorney?"

"Oh, I think you're okay there. We have the source of the inside information. We have Kinsky's role nailed down. And we have the conduit for the funds. Even the government isn't dumb enough to think Simon hired someone to break into his office to set up an incriminating bank account."

"Are you sure?"

"Pretty sure. Harv Champlin broke the news to them this afternoon. I understand the deputy U.S. Attorney said some unprintable stuff. Harv said he tried to write it all down, but the guy was swearing too fast."

"That's always a good sign," said Jonathan, his face breaking into an expansive grin that crinkled the corners of his eyes.

"But really," Frankee continued, "I don't see how they can bring an indictment. Even though we can't prove who did it, we certainly can make a strong case that you and Simon didn't."

"What about the money?" Jonathan said.

"What money?"

"The $1.2 million in the accounts in the Caymans."

"Oh, that. The Feds will impound it. There's a $1 million of profits from insider trading. But then, you weren't the ones doing the trading."

"So maybe we can get our hands on the money to cover our expenses and all the crap we've been through."

"Maybe, but it's a very long row to hoe."

"But perhaps a fertile one. And we might have a better shot at the $200,000. Unless, of course, the owner wants to claim it."

He put his hands in his pockets and was about to say goodbye when he felt Frankee's envelope stick him above the edge of his glove. He pulled it out and opened it. He whistled.

"Frankee, you should have been a lawyer."

"Why, and take a pay cut?"

"Worth every nickel. You saved our ass."

"Well shucks," Frankee said, "if you went to jail they wouldn't let you wear that tweed jacket. I might not recognize you when I came to visit."

Some things never change.

Chapter 67

"Simon, you did it again."

Jonathan, Simon and Harv Champlin were sitting in a Whiting & Pierce conference room, all at one end of the long polished table. It was crisp mid-winter day worthy of a celebration. There was a magnificent view out the floor to ceiling windows. The trees in Central Park stood as the bare sentinels of a distant spring.

"That's not fair," Simon said. "It wasn't my fault." Simon had adopted his innocent and hurt tone. He was really good at it.

"Of course you were. You got me into this."

"Gee, you try to do a favor for a friend and see what happens. You give him a job and all he does is complain. Oy."

Harv Champlin was leaning back in his black leather chair,one foot on the table, sipping his Diet Coke and grinning. He had known these two for a long time and he enjoyed their badinage. Particularly the sense of relief that suffused the room beneath the playfulness.

Jonathan was laughing, while Simon was wearing his patented kicked, but loving dog look. Seeing it, you would never guess how big and sharp his teeth were.

"A job?" Jonathan said. "I didn't make a cent. A slam dunk I believe you called it."

"I don't think I said that. And if I did, you can't be stupid enough to believe it." Simon made a dramatic pause. "Well, then again, you may have a point."

"Would that it were so," said Jonathan.

Simon was on a roll. "So you were one of those entrepreneurs. Sometimes we win and sometimes we lose. And I'm not even going to charge you for the experience, which I might add, is invaluable." Simon stopped and restarted. "And, you weren't bored."

"That, Simon, is an understatement. Let me see, we almost got indicted for insider trading. Derek Lissome took you for $250,000 and got himself killed, and the Quintiles tender offer was crushed by the S.E.C. investigation. Is that about all?"

"You know," Simon said, "you never look on the good side. Sure, we had a few small problems. But take it another way. Witten's stock has recovered and the short squeeze must have cost Rollins a bundle. A really big bundle." Simon rubbed his hands together in glee. A short squeeze occurs when the price of the shorted stock rapidly increases and the short seller can't buy the stock back.

"We don't know for sure it was Vincent Rollins who framed us or shorted the Witten's stock."

"You want to bet it wasn't Rollins?"

"No."

"So, it may cost us a little money, but it cost him a whole lot more. He's more vulnerable now than ever."

"Yeah, but other than that, Rollins came out smelling like a rose. He killed the tender offer. He still has his company. You know, it was some defensive strategy. He was going to save his own company and destroy Witten's at the same time. He may have even planned to take it over. In some vague way, you have to admire the man's genius."

"You admire him. Not me."

"Do you think the police can pin Kinsky's murder on Rollins?" Harv asked, taking his leg down and leaning forward in his chair. He put his Diet Coke carefully on the coaster. "My God, do you think he's really capable of that?"

"Well, Rollins is a very nasty guy," Simon said. "I wouldn't say no."

"Frankee doesn't think there's a chance the police can get him," Jonathan said.

"A shame. Hey, you know, we could make another run at Quintiles." Simon said it out of the blue.

"Simon, you have a great mind." Jonathan paused. "But perhaps we won't." Jonathan was thinking about what Harv just had said about Vincent Rollins.

"But another tender offer would be a slam dunk." The look of open innocence on Simon's face made Jonathan think Simon had chosen the wrong career. The stage had lost a great talent.

"Right," Jonathan said with all the irony he could muster. "Look, I'm glad we saved Witten's."

"And your asses," Harv added. "Maybe we should just call it a day."

They raised their glasses of soda and clinked a happy toast.

Chapter 68

It was a bright room. Quite a contrast with the lowering clouds outside, shouldering each other around, like bullies in a school-ground. Latex colored flowers bloomed around him in colors no garden had ever seen. Female laughter fluttered like butterflies among small round wooden tables.

Jonathan stood in the doorway, shifting self-conciously from one foot to the other. He was clearly out of place in his tweed jacket and knitted tie. There was a slight tang of human sweat. Not unpleasant.

Through a large interior window at the end of the room, he could see people, mostly women, climbing endlessly on StairMasters and running on treadmills. He looked around the large snack bar.

Detective Robert Tritter, in black sweats with red piping, detached himself from a table with two attractive women and waived. Tritter was one of only two men in the snack bar. The rest were shapely, nubile women. Jonathan wondered at what he had missed in his sheltered life.

"Professor Franklin," Tritter called. He motion towards an empty table in the corner of the room. Jonathan made his way across the snack bar, feeling the eyes of everyone on him. He shook hands with Tritter and sat down.

"Would you like some juice?" Tritter asked. "They really have a sensational spinich-guava. I know it sounds terrible, but it's really good."

Jonathan shook his head vigorously. "Could I get a Diet Coke?"

Tritter looked chagrined. "Gosh, I'm afraid not. The club has a thing about synthetic drinks. They're pretty firm."

Jonathan has never thought of Diet Coke as synthetic. "No problem," he said. "It was good of you to see me." His voice had a trace of hesitation as he took in the snack bar. "I felt I needed to talk to the police."

"You said it was about the Andrew Grahm case."

"I'm a little surprised you wanted to meet here."

"Oh. It's my day off."

"Still, I thought you'd want to talk about this in a place that's a little more private."

"Believe me, Professor Franklin, you won't find a more private place than this. No one listens to anyone, even when you're speaking to them."

A blonde in a form fitting leotard, with contrasting leggings, came up behind Tritter and put her hand on his shoulder. "Bobbie, hi."

Tritter looked up and a trace of panic fled briefly across his eyes. "Uh, hello, Sandy. Nice to see you."

"I guess not nice enough to call me after last week." She said it with a smile, but Jonathan thought she was kidding on the square. "I thought we had a good time."

"We did, Sandy. A great time. Really great." Jonathan thought Tritter would break into a sweat at any moment. He suppressed a smile. In some ways it was nice to be older. A lot quieter. "It's just that I've been swamped with work. He glanced at Jonathan. "Let me introduce you," he said looking up. "This is Jonathan Franklin. Professor Franklin, this is, uh, Sandy." Jonathan could see Tritter's mind working. "I'm really sorry, Sandy, but we're talking about some important business."

She looked at Jonathan. "Nice to meet you," she said turning away, a pout on her lips.

"Pretty girl," Jonathan said. "Seems to like you."

Tritter looked over at Jonathan. "Maybe you want to take off your tie. And jacket. It's kind of warm in here." It certainly was for Tritter.

Jonathan shrugged out of his jacket and hung it over the back of his chair. He pulled off his tie and folded it into the inner pocket of his jacket. Then he rolled up his sleeves and settled down. He looked at Tritter carefully for really the first time. Bobbie Tritter looked to be in his mid-thirties and starting to go bald. But he seemed to be in good shape. Probably spent a lot of time here. It had been a very long while since Jonathan had been in a health club. It showed.

"You said you wanted to talk to me about Andrew Grahm," Tritter said, interrupting his thoughts.

"To tell you the truth, I don't know exactly what to do. I had hoped to meet with Lt. Wayne too. I think it's clearly a matter for the police, but I don't know."

"I'm sorry, that doesn't make a lot of sense."

"Yeah, it doesn't." Jonathan paused to reflect on exactly what he was trying to accomplish. He really wasn't all that clear.

"So?" Tritter said.

"Well, you see, I'm convinced Andrew Grahn was murdered."

"I knew it!" Tritter slapped his hand on the table so hard Jonathan jumped and people turned to look.

Jonathan had never seen a police officer respond like that. It was puzzling. They paused as a slim brunette in lavender latex came towards the table. She was looking with concern at Tritter.

"Are you okay, Bobbie?"

Tritter pulled back from his thought. He looked sheepish. Then his face cleared. "I'm fine. Sorry Stephanie, it was just a business thing. I guess I got excited."

"Well, anyway," she said, "see you. Call me soon." Jonathan was starting to detect a pattern here. It cast Tritter in a new light.

"How do you know?" Tritter said.

"Huh?"

"That Grahm was murdered."

"It was my dog."

"You're dog killed him?"

"Of course not."

"You don't mean he told you."

"Well, not exactly. You see my dog was in Grahm's office."

"My God, Professor Franklin, you didn't destroy evidence." Tritter was aggitated. "I mean, you could go to jail."

Been there, done that, thought Jonathan. Everyone wants to put me in jail lately. "It wasn't a crime scene. At least no one believed it was. Anyway, Rufus, he's my dog, was licking at a wet spot in the rug. He got real sick, so I went aback to the museum and took a rug sample. I had it analyzed. It was Port wine that had been infused with nicotine. That's a deadly poison."

"Tell me about it," Tritter said.

An odd response, Jonathan thought.

"Do you have the bottle," asked Tritter.

"Sorry, its long gone. Even the glasses had been washed and put away."

"Damn. There's nothing we can do."

"But I think I know who did it. And I think I know why."

Then Jonathan told him.

Chapter 69

The pulse of the jet engines gave a rhythm to the silence. The Gulfstream 550 had been in the air for 2 hours. At over 500 knots per hour that put it more than 1000 miles East of Teterboro. Nothing but ocean could be seen between the breaks in the clouds. The sun was edging towards the Western horizon and light flashed on the waves 41,000 feet below, seemingly to invite the oncoming darkness.

The Gulfstream 550 executive jet is, in the vernacular of the trade, heavy metal. One of the biggest business jets, it can seat 16. Simon's was configured to seat 8. It flew over 7500 miles without refueling, easily enough to reach Paris, which was their destination.

Jonathan and Nicole sat in butter-soft, brown leather arm chairs, piped in dark blue, facing Simon and Tae. Lustrous tiger maple trim gave the cabin a warm elegance. A bottle of Cristal champagne was open and sweating in a silver ice bucket by Simon's elbow. Three crystal flutes stood on the table, filled with the pale yellow liquid.

Jonathan raised the fourth flute to his lips, moving slowly so as not to disturb Nicole. She sat with her legs tucked under her, her head rested against Jonathan's shoulder, her arms through his, sleeping softly. She was dressed in the old, comfortable black cashmere turtle-neck sweater and black cashmere pants that she called here traveling clothes.

February had tipped over and spilled into March. It had been a little over a month since the SEC investigation had collapsed. A very short and intense month. There were financial press releases explaining what had happened to Witten's stock and angry shareholders to deal with. But Witten's had avoided the avalanche of lawsuits that normally follow sharp movements of a company's stock. It helped that the stock had rebounded. Things had finally returned to normal.

"What a terrific idea," Jonathan said, his voice in a whisper so as not to disturb Nicole. The champagne flute was arrested in half flight. "I never thought I would see the day. Simon Aaron paying for a trip to Paris."

"Yeah, it'll be a lot more fun than being in jail, even at one of those posh Federal country clubs. You meet a better class of people at the George V. At least, I think so."

Nicole stirred, but resettled. She murmured something unintelligible in her sleep.

"Simon's really a minch," Tae said. "He just doesn't want anyone to know." Simon was shaking his head vigorously. "I think he feels a little guilty about all the trouble you had."

"Where did you learn the word 'minch', woman?" Simon spoke sternly but with a broad smile. "You'll ruin my reputation. Then where will we be?"

"Simon, we'll be in Paris. So you just hush up now and enjoy yourself. I haven't been there in five years. I'm going to."

"Oy," Simon said.

"Besides," continued Tae, " I want to hear all about what went on at the Nauton. Everyone is guessing. I think Jonathan knows."

"I don't care about the Nauton. That's your problem," Simon said. "I got enough problems of my own." Tae was on the board of the museum.

"First, Simon, as a board member, I think I should be concerned. Second, after we discuss the gift you are going to make, I can assure you, it will be your problem."

Simon bolted from his seat.

"Where are you going?" Tae asked.

"To turn the plane around. I can't afford this trip."

Tae gave Simon a look with a hint of a smile in it and pointed to his seat. Simon meekly sat down. It appeared that the vaunted Simon Aaron was now under new management.

"Jonathan," Tae said, pointing her finger at him, "sing for your supper."

Nicole said sleepily, "I also want to hear this." Jonathan jumped.

"We didn't mean to wake you up," he said.

"You did not."

Tae said, "Well, good, let's all hear it."

"Yes, let us do so," said Nicole, a small rust of sleep still in her voice. "You have, Cheri, how do you say it," she paused, "not come clean."

Jonathan ducked and weaved for 10 minutes. He would have done Sugar Ray Leonard proud. But finally, they had him on the ropes, winded and ready to comply.

"Okay, okay. I don't really know what happened. I suppose a real detective would. I can only make an educated guess. But I think I'm right." He took a deep breath, then plunged in.

"This whole experience has been such a bloody mess," Jonathan said. "And I mean that literally. I've never been around so much death. First, Andrew Grahm, and then Derek Lissome. Alex Kinsky. God knows what happened to Rafael Del Gado. He just disappeared. I had no idea art was so dangerous."

Simon shrugged. Then he chuckled with a look in his eyes. "It's passion and money. That's art. And that's what murder is all about. Some detective you are."

"Simon, don't call me a detective. I can hardly detect a change in the weather."

"But, Cheri," Nicole cut in, "you are too modest. Just yesterday, you told me it would snow."

"So?" said Simon. "Who already?"

"Derek Lissome killed Andrew Grahm."

"That's quite a jump," said Simon. "Would you mind explaining that to those of us less brilliant than you are. We're all ears."

"He poisoned him with a dose of nicotine in that bottle of port wine. The stuff Rufus got so sick on." Jonathan paused for a moment to organize his thoughts.

Simon made an impatient gesture.

"Sorry, Simon," Jonathan murmured.

Clouds drifted past the planes's windows, playing games with the light and creating an impending sense of closure.

"Do you understand any of this, Cheri?"

"Maybe. The port was sent anonymously to Grahm," Jonathan said. "No note. But it wasn't the first time, according to Grahm's secretary. I guess someone in his position got a lot of gifts."

"How do you know Lissome sent it?" Simon interrupted. "Why couldn't it have been one of the others? A lot of people didn't like Grahm."

"Simon, do you remember the guy at Sir Adrian's dinner party a couple of weeks ago? The one who made all the fuss about smoking."

"Yeah, that guy's was a real asshole. Went on and on about how his e-cigarette was harmless. Wouldn't hurt a fly."

"Right. I mean I don't know if the guy was right, but that's the guy. He started me thinking. I got to wondering how e-cigarettes worked. They contain nicotine. I knew that much. And nicotine is not something anyone uses to poison someone. At least I never heard of it."

"They usually poison themselves," Simon grunted.

"True, but much more slowly. So, I did some research on-line. E-cigarettes contain a small capsule of nicotine. A spark vaporizes a little of the nicotine when the smoker inhales and that gives him a nicotine hit to satisfy his addiction. So, I thought about whether you could buy a few, remove the capsules and then distill them into a deadly dose."

Simon sat forward in his chair. "So that's how it was done?"

"No."

"Huh?"

Chapter 70

"You see, e-cigarettes are expensive," Jonathan said. "They're made to last. So I started thinking about refills. It turns out, you can buy them in a lot of places, even drug stores. Can you believe it?"

"Cheri, you must have to sign for it."

"Nope. Just picked it up and paid at the cash register."

"How do you distill the poison?" Simon asked.

"Well, as it happens, you don't have to. You can actually buy pure nicotine online. As much as you want, no questions asked. People dilute it to refill their capsules instead of buying a new ones. Sort of like some people do with ink cartridges."

"Mon Dieu."

"Exactly."

"But why Derek Lissome?" Tae asked. She stirred in her seat and settled in a more comfortable position. "Why not others?"

"I thought about that." He started to go down the list. He absently put his hand in his pocket and began rubbing his silver box as he spoke. "There are at least three other possibilities. Peter Willson and Rupert Seeling hated Grahm for different reasons. Willson because Grahm was trying to undermine him. Seeling because Grahm was ruining the museum. His museum. Grahm's wife, Rebecca, is an obvious suspect."

"What about Ailene Brown?" Simon interrupted.

"Possibly," Jonathan added, reluctantly. Then he started up again. "Well, it had to be someone who dealt with Andrew Grahm a lot and knew his habits. Knew he liked port wine, for instance, which is kind of rare in this day and age. So, I figured that let out Rupert Seeling. Seeling knew Grahm, of course, but they weren't buddies. Seeling didn't have any buddies."

"He's not a nice man," Tae agreed.

"But Rupert Seeling loved the museum," Jonathan continued. "He knew Grahm was an asshole and how dangerous he was. He's also ruthless, as Tae implied. He could have done it. But the timing wasn't right."

"Why not?" Simon said.

"Grahm went to see Seeling just before he died. I saw it in Grahm's calendar. Probably to threaten that he was going to expose the Nicholson paintings Sir Adrian gave to the museum. It was Grahm's biggest threat. That might have driven Seeling nuts. It probably did. But Grahm died the same day. There wasn't time to set up an elaborate scheme. Besides, it would be more like Seeling to figure out a way to ruin Grahm, not kill him."

Nicole turned to face Jonathan. "But, what about the others, Cheri. Peter Willson must have known Mr. Grahm well. And certainly his wife did."

"True. But Peter Willson is a pussy. All he wanted was to have enough time to get out. I don't think his relationship with the museum was in such a critical state that he would kill Grahm to prevent him from taking his place. Besides, if he was going to get fired, what did it buy him? The museum would just bring in someone else to replace him."

Jonathan got up and started to stamp his foot.

"What are you doing?" asked Simon.

"Foot went to sleep," Jonathan said, continuing to press it on the floor.

"Forget that. I don't agree. What about time?" Simon said. "Wouldn't it buy him time? If they couldn't appoint Grahm, they'd have to conduct a search and that takes time."

Jonathan retook his seat with a sigh. "Yes, but the museum world is small. Once a search started, Willson would be damaged goods. He couldn't get one of the prime positions, and he knew it. But let me go on."

"And on and on," said Simon.

"Please. I want to hear this," Tae said.

"So, what about the wife? The wife is always the killer. And poison is a woman's weapon."

"Very good, Simon. I'm going to hire you. However, my dear Watson, you forget one thing. Peter Willson told me she didn't fight having Grahm autopsied. She might well have been able to. She could have gotten some doctor to certify to his heart condition or have gone to court. Even a delay in the autopsy might have satisfied her purpose. I don't know how long nicotine persists in the body. But Peter Willson told me she actually relished the idea of Grahm being cut into pieces."

Simon didn't look satisfied but he remained silent.

"Let me get to Ailene Brown. She's harder. Grahm was two-timing her. But I got the sense she didn't know it. When Detective Tritter asked her about Barbara Nadine, she didn't react. In fact, she spoke about trying to push Nadine on Grahm for the exhibit they were planning. She really admired Grahm. I don't think she's that good an actor, particularly in the state of agitation she was in when I first saw her." Even Jonathan could be wrong.

"And she'd been away for weeks before she found Grahm dead. On that point, why wouldn't she have let someone else find the body if she had done it? Why would she have come back then?"

"Do you think Kinsky's murder was related to Grahm's?" Simon asked, redirecting the discussion.

Jonathan shrugged.

"But why?" Nicole asked.

"Why Lissome?" Jonathan interpreted.

"Okay, it might not have been the others. How do you make the connection to Lissome?" Simon asked. He was now leaning back, relaxed and sipping his champagne.

Jonathan ran his fingers through his thinning hair. "It goes back to the e-cigarette I found in Lissome's desk when I was there trying to help you track down the Klimt. And for a man who never smoked, that didn't make a lot of sense. His secretary told me he had bad lungs. I thought he might have kept it for his clients, but the more I thought about it, the more I realized I was wrong. He would just more deeply offend a client who wanted to smoke."

"Cheri, I did not mean why was it Derek Lissome, I meant what could be the reason?"

"That's a very good question, darling." Jonathan paused dramatically. "I have no idea."

"I knew it," Simon said.

"But," Jonathan hesitated for effect, "Lissome was involved in a lot of weird things. I mean the Klimt thing he did to you," he said, nodding at Simon, "and the forgery of that painting Rafael Del Gado gave to the Nauton. I know he was in financial trouble and under a lot of pressure. I saw the papers."

"That's not much proof," Simon said. "Anyone could have sent the port. Why do you think Lissome was involved? I still don't see why he would want to murder Andrew Grahm."

"It's all circumstantial. It's really based on something Ailene Brown said that struck me as peculiar. Grahm asked that the Purland, the picture that turned out to be forged, be sent to a conservator for restoration. He never sought her advice. And when she looked at the painting, it didn't seem to need work. When she spoke to Grahm about it, he was brusque with her, which was unusual. He essentially told her to do as she was told."

"You seem to have spent a lot of time with Ailene Brown," Simon said.

Thank you for that, Simon. Jonathan hastily said, "Peter Willson asked me to see her. He was concerned about her."

"You mean about himself."

"Well, yeah. But she's a nice lady. I liked her."

Jonathan immediately wished he could learn to keep his mouth shut. He tugged at the foot he just had lodged in it. It must have been some quirk in his physical response or in his voice, because Nicole looked at him peculiarly. He changed the subject.

"Lissome clearly didn't want that picture looked at closely. I think it ties back in to the Nicholsons. Grahm would have scared him badly. Lissome didn't want people to start looking for forgeries at the Nauton. Recent gifts would be right there, up front. And he had a lot to lose."

Jonathan got up and stretched. Then he he turned back. "I wish I could have spoken to Rafael Del Gado. He canceled our meeting and just evaporated. It seemed to me like he had some idea what was going on with Lissome. Just bad luck, I guess."

The intercom crackled. "Mr. Aaron," a female voice said, "we are starting our decent into Charles de Gaulle. Please have everyone buckle up. We'll be on the ground in 20 minutes."

Chapter 71

Whoever said "too much of a good thing is a good thing" was absolutely wrong. Jonathan put his fork down on the half-finished plate of mille-feuille. It was a sin to waste that miracle on his plate, but he couldn't eat another bite. Or, for that matter, sip another sip of the luminous Le Montrachet, even if it was the finest white wine in the world.

They were in one of the many small rooms in the 18th century palace on the Quai de Conti that Guy Savoy had recently occupied. Even the modern paintings that decorated the walls were of the first tier. There were only 5 tables and, of course, all of them were occupied.

The meal had been indescribably good. The artichoke truffle soup was the best he had ever tasted and the zucchini flower and caviar salad, with egg foam had been a culinary wonder. But this was their third three-star restaurant in 2 days.

Lunch yesterday at L'Amboise in the Place des Vognes, near the Marais district, the old Jewish section that Nicole and Jonathan loved to wander. Dinner last night at Le Pre Catelan within the Bois de Boulogne, the wooded park in the middle of the Paris.

He burped quietly into his napkin. Why couldn't he be more like Nicole. She had picked at the food and only tasted the extraordinary wines. He felt like he was going to burst.

"Should you not have gone to the police?" Nicole asked out of nowhere.

Jonathan turned to look at her and smiled. "Oh, I don't think so. The meal was really quite satisfactory," said Jonathan.

She slapped his arm. "About Andrew Grahm."

"Good grief, where did that come from?"

"It has been concerning me."

"Well, okay. Rest your mind. Actually, I called Detective Tritter. I had the strangest meeting with him. He was interested, but with Lissome dead, he probably figured there wasn't any point." Jonathan paused a moment to reflect.

"There is one thing I don't get," Jonathan added. "I never told you. But it made me uncomfortable."

Tae, Simon and Nicole looked at him. Simon put down his fork.

"Two weeks ago, I got a typed note in an unmarked envelope."

"What did it say, Cheri?"

"It said, 'No longer fear. The contract has been canceled.' Weird. I have no idea what it meant."

"But, at least," Simon said, "it sounds like a good thing, right? Whatever it means."

"I guess that's true," Jonathan said, brightening.

They each seemed to have had enough. Simon and Tae picked up their wine glasses and sipped in silence for a few moments. The talk turned to more mundane matters.

"I understand that Peter Willson is becoming the director of the National Gallery in Washington," Tae finally said.

"I have also heard that spoken of," Nicole added.

"Well, Rebecca is moving there too," Jonathan said. "Peter Willson told me. I think she has high hopes. God help him."

Simon chortled. "Now there's a game that's more dangerous than art," he said, looking over at Nicole.

"What happened to Ailene Brown?" Simon asked, turning back towards Jonathan.

Big help. Jonathan really didn't want to go there again.

"I heard she got the curator's job at the Santa Barbara Museum of Art," he said. Actually Ailene Brown had called Jonathan and told him, when she had invited him to lunch again to celebrate. Jonathan had politely declined.

"Great, you can see her when you go out to Zagar," Simon added, to Jonathan's chagrin.

"Oh, I don't think so," Jonathan said casually, at least he hoped that's how it sounded. "She'll be very busy."

"I do not believe Jonathan will be going to Santa Barbara soon," Nicole said.

"Why not?" Jonathan asked.

"Yeah, why not?" echoed Simon.

"It would involve so much time. And I believe both of you will be most busy."

"I don't follow you, darling. Now that I'm teaching only three days a week, I'll have plenty of time."

She reached out and took Jonathan's hand and placed it on her stomach.

"I am pregnant. We are going to have a baby."

"Wow," was all Jonathan was capable of.

"Oy gavalt," Simon exclaimed.

"Are you not happy, Cheri?"

"Darling, I'm thrilled." Jonathan recovered admirably. "I'm just surprised." He pushed his chair back and knelt beside her. It caused some angry looks at the next table. He hugged her tightly to him. "Thrilled," he said again. He pulled his head back, still holding her. "Are you sure an old guy like me will be a good father?"

"You are not old. You are very active." She smiled and squeezed his hand. "And, yes, you will be a wonderful father."

"Whoa," Simon said. "What about me. I want to be an uncle."

"Of course, Simon. You will be the honorary uncle. And Tae will be the honorary aunt. We would have it no other way."

"When are you due, darling?" Tae asked, a dazzling smile on her face.

"We are due in seven months."

"But you didn't tell me," said Jonathan.

"Cheri, I could not tell you. You were in such distress. I did not want to burden you further."

"Well, now that we have that all settled . . ." Simon stopped cold. "What about Witten's?"

"Simon, I will continue my job. But you will need to do more."

"Darn, I was starting to like retirement."

"Pooh, Simon. You are incapable of retiring. I will be unavailable to you for only a few months."

"Of course. I can handle it," Simon said.

"No, I believe you will need help."

"I'll find someone."

"I believe you have someone. You will hire Jonathan. Then you can do it together."

"But . . ." said Jonathan.

"But . . ." said Simon.

"It will be fun," said Nicole.

"Fun?" they chorused.

THE END